THE
SECRET
DIARIES

of

JUAN LUIS VIVES

A Novel by

TIM DARCY ELLIS

388 4113

Tellwell Talent
www.tellwell.ca

ISBN
978-0-2288-3437-3 (Hardcover)
978-0-2288-3436-6 (Paperback)
978-0-2288-3438-0 (eBook)

TABLE OF CONTENTS

Dedicated in loving memory to
Nancy Rice Saunders (1921 -2020)

But who is there who surpasses Vives in the number and quality of his studies?

Sir Thomas More, 1523

He has an extraordinary philosophical mind.

Erasmus, 1524

He was the godfather of psychoanalysis.

Gregory Zilboorg, 1941

The only blemish on his character was his Judaism.

Lorenzo Biber, 1947

CAST OF CHARACTERS
IN ORDER OF APPEARANCE

All characters are historical, unless otherwise stated.

In Flanders

Juan Luis Vives (1493–1538) was a Spanish humanist philosopher born in Valencia to Jewish converso parents. He fled Spain at the age of seventeen and was educated in Paris. He taught in Bruges, Oxford, and London. He was a close friend to Erasmus and Thomas More. He was tutor to Princess Mary and counsellor to both Henry VIII and Catherine of Aragon.

Johannes Van der Poel (fictional character) was one of Vives's students from Bruges, Flanders.

Sir Thomas More (1478–1535) was an English lawyer, statesman, and confidante to both Vives and King Henry VIII and was Lord Chancellor (the king's chief advisor) from 1529–1532. He was the author of *Utopia* and was an opponent of the English Protestant Reformation.

Louis de Praet (1488–1555) was Grand Bailiff of Ghent and Bruges and later Ambassador of the Holy Roman Emperor, Charles V, to England.

Álvaro de Castro was a friend and confidante to Juan Luis Vives. He was from Burgos, Spain. Vives wrote of him, "I loved him like a brother."

Bernardo Valldaura was a Jewish cloth and diamond merchant from Toledo, Spain, who fled to Bruges.

Clara Valldaura was the wife of Bernardo and first cousin to Vives's mother, Blanquina March.

Marguerite Valldaura-Vives (1500–1548) was the eldest daughter of Bernardo and Clara. She married Juan Luis Vives in 1523.

Maria Valldaura was the second daughter and middle child of Bernardo and Clara.

Nicolas Valldaura was the only surviving son of Bernardo and Clara and became a physician in Bruges.

In England
Margaret Roper (1505–1544) was described by Erasmus as "the most intelligent woman in England." She was the eldest daughter of Sir Thomas More and his first wife, Jane Colt. She married William Roper.

Alice More was the second wife of Sir Thomas More and stepmother to Margaret Roper and four adopted children.

William Roper (1496–1578) was a lawyer and husband of Margaret. He was also a biographer of Sir Thomas More.

John Claymond (1468–1537) was a scholar and early naturalist, translator of Pliny the Elder's *Natural History*, and first president of Corpus Christi College, Oxford.

Thomas Linacre (1460–1524) was a humanist scholar and personal physician to Henry VII and Henry VIII, as well as tutor to Princess Mary before Vives.

Princess Mary Tudor (1516–1558) was the daughter of King Henry VIII and Catherine of Aragon. She was a pupil of Vives at Oxford and London.

King Henry VIII (1491–1547) was King of England from 1509 until 1547.

Queen Catherine of Aragon (1485–1536) was Queen of England from 1509 to 1533. She was the daughter of King Ferdinand and Queen Isabella of Spain, authors of the Alhambra Decree (1492), which ordered the expulsion of the Jews from Spain.

Cardinal Thomas Wolsey (1473–1530) was Cardinal and Archbishop of York and Lord Chancellor (1515–1529). He raised a subsidy tax on the nobility, which reduced taxes on the poor and helped pay for the establishment of Corpus Christi College. At one time, he was a strong supporter of Vives.

Reginald Pole (1500–1558) was one of the surviving members of the Plantagenet dynasty and later became the last Catholic Archbishop of Canterbury. He was a fierce opponent of Luther and of the re-admission of the Jews to England. He was the son of Margaret Pole, Countess of Salisbury.

Maria de Salinas, The Lady Willoughby (1490–1539), was a Spanish noblewoman and confidante/lady-in-waiting to Catherine of Aragon. She was married to Baron Willoughby of Eresby. Diana, Princess of Wales and the present Duke of Cambridge are among her descendants.

Anne Boleyn (c. 1501–1536) was lady-in-waiting to Catherine of Aragon and later the second wife of Henry VIII. She was educated in the court of Queen Claude in Paris, where she first met Vives. She was Queen of England from 1533–1536.

Mary Boleyn (c. 1499–1543), sister of Anne Boleyn, was at one time mistress to Henry VIII and lady-in-waiting to Catherine of Aragon. The Princess of Wales was one of her descendants.

Benjamin Elisha (fictional character) was a Portuguese Jewish émigré living in the street known as Houndsditch just outside the walls of the city of London.

Sarah Elisha (fictional character) was the daughter of Benjamin (above).

Antonius Moyses was an Italian (secretly Jewish) musician who played the viol at the court of Henry VIII.

Edward Scales was an English Jewish inmate from 1503 until 1527 of London's Domus Conversorum, a refuge for repentant Jews.

Iñigo López de Mendoza (1476–1535) was Spanish ambassador to England from 1526 to 1529. He was imprisoned alongside Vives on the orders of the king.

PROLOGUE

Jacques le Boeuf, electrician, was pushing his luck. He had a job to do and only an hour to do it.

It was one of those cold November nights when darkness fell quickly, like a stage curtain at an unexpected interval in a play. It seemed as if all the students and most of the lecturers had simply vanished as if, save for him, the whole College of Bruges was deserted. He'd been told to do whatever it took to finish the job in Professor Benitez's room, for there were funding interviews that had to go forward the following morning.

"Merde," he said as he got the brief. This was one of the college's medieval buildings, where the job was never simple.

"If only they could have told me earlier," he muttered, raking his deft fingers through curly black hair. And so, with faint tremors of frustration, he began moving a bookcase to the side. It was then that he saw the problem: crumbling, damp plasterwork and cloth-wrapped wires had almost rotted through. No wonder Benitez kept getting "blacked out." The wires must have been placed there long ago, probably before the Nazis came through Belgium in World War II. What stories of occupation and liberation, he wondered, would the room be able to tell?

"Sacre bleu," he said as he dropped the chisel down a cavity at the back of the plaster. "Stop rushing, you fool," he said to himself. The soccer match was starting in thirty minutes.

The tool room was locked, and he'd neglected to bring the key. Without the chisel, how was he going to get the job done at all?

He rushed around the room, knocking over piles of papers and books. "Slow down, Jacques," he told himself. He carefully picked up the books and papers and sat in Benitez's squeaking antique chair with its cracked leather arms and put his head in his hands. It was then that a thought arose like a cobra from a snake-charmer's basket. Could he possibly do what he'd promised not to? To retrieve the chisel, he'd have to use his blunt hammer and punch deeper into the ancient wall.

He leapt up from the chair, got the hammer, and punched out an extra piece of plaster. Droplets of sweat formed on his brow as he hammered. Cracks appeared, and then a chasm opened; a pile of plaster lay around his crusted brown leather boots.

He couldn't stop now.

The chisel had tumbled far back into the wall cavity. After some groping, he found it, but there was something else there, too. It felt like a wooden box, about the size of an encyclopaedia. It was wedged tightly into the cavity behind the plaster wall.

Jacques reached farther back, his breath coming in quick bursts. At last he got a grip on it and, inch by inch, breath by breath, he twisted it until it was free.

"Mon Dieu," he said as he brought it to the light.

It was a simple wooden box with an ill-formed star scratched on the surface. An old wasp's nest, gummed to the lid, disintegrated under his breath. Then, like a child not quite knowing what to do, he shook the box. Something inside rattled and rolled.

How long had the box been there? Was it hidden during World War II? He saw the star clearly now: the Star of David, ever so faintly. Jacques knew that there had been Jews in Bruges who perished during the war, so perhaps this box contained the lost treasures of a family that had been transported to Auschwitz or Dachau.

The professor's wood-framed clock, something that could have come from Dickens's London, ticked loudly and broke his train of thought. After all, every minute spent here was another minute of soccer that was wasted. Perhaps he would just throw the box in the skip with the plaster and be done with it.

He quickly fixed the wires with gaffer tape and swept up as best he could. He'd return the following day to re-plaster the wall, but at least the electrics would be working for the interviews. He dragged the bookcase back to hide the hole in the wall. Not knowing what to do with the box, he grabbed it and put it under his right arm. He slammed the heavy oak door shut, turned the key with a resounding *clunk*, and was gone.

* * *

The next day, Jacques, who usually avoided the academics, watched closely until the last interview was done. He then went back to the office of Professor Benitez and knocked lightly on the door. At Benitez's command, he opened it and, with his head down, approached the professor.

"Sir, I have something to give you," he said, stuttering as he held up the box. 'Truth is, I made a botch of that job last night, and I found this box stuck behind the wall."

"Made a botch of the job?" Benitez, the famous linguist, replied. He laughed like a beloved uncle. Jacques had assumed the professor would be furious with him or at least threaten him with disciplinary action. But he'd underestimated the kind-hearted Benitez, with his two-tone beard. When he saw what Jacques had in his hands, he jumped up like a man half his age. He pushed aside a sea of books that surrounded him and walked to Jacques.

"What on God's earth do we have here?" Benitez asked with a smile.

He gently took the box from Jacques's rough hands, and with his own soft white fingers, he drew it to his nose. Jacques watched as the professor put the box down and unhooked the brass pin, green with corrosion, and opened the lid. They both peered at the contents as if looking into an ancient tomb.

Inside lay a small book with a withered brown jacket. The professor lifted it and found a bundle of papers beneath it, as well as another book and tightly rolled parchment. In the corner of the box was a ring with a gold Star of David engraved on a blue enamel face.

"It's just that the plaster gave way behind that very wall, and the box was there," Jacques explained. "So, I took it."

Benitez leaned over and kissed Jacques le Boeuf on both cheeks like he was his own son. He then swore Jacques to secrecy.

*   *   *

Benitez abandoned his other work, even the funding interviews, while he spent the next two months in isolation at the Musea Brugge. It took him that long, with a team of conservators, to understand what Jacques had discovered. Much of the writing in the book was in code. It was tiny, as if it had been written under a magnifying glass. Some of it was in Spanish, some in Latin, some in Arabic. The latter part was written almost entirely in poor English. The small parchment was carefully unrolled and identified as a sketch by Hans Holbein of England's Sir Thomas More. The gold ring was unique, for it was in the English Tudor style, and yet it had the Star of David on its face.

It was at the end of the second month that Benitez realized that he was examining the secret writings of one of Bruges's great men. The books and parchment were indeed what he'd hoped they would be: the lost voice of one whose secrets were precious and beautiful. If revealed at the time, such secrets could have implicated hundreds or perhaps even led to civil war. These were the writings of a man truly ahead of his time, someone who had strived against insurmountable obstacles to make the world a better place. He had become the tutor of Princess Mary Tudor and was the confidante of both Catherine of Aragon and King Henry VIII, playing the impossible game of double agent.

It was a year before the writings were published. Benitez was torn as to how he should translate them, for the man who had written the ancient diaries hated lofty academic speech. He prized clarity, and Benitez was determined that the world would hear this man's authentic voice.

One year to the day Jacques le Boeuf discovered the box of secret writings, there was a press conference at the Musea Brugge.

"We have been blessed," Benitez broadcast at the press conference, "with a lost portrait of England's Sir Thomas More and a unique gold ring. But more importantly, we have the secret diaries of a great renaissance scholar, the friend of royals and the most secret of all Jews: Señor Juan Luis Vives."

PART ONE

THE EYES AND EARS OF THE KING OF SPAIN

Bruges, Flanders, is in the hands of the Catholic King of Spain, Charles V. Martin Luther would change all that, as would the peasant rebels determined to liberate themselves from the shackles of the Spanish overlords. It has been thirty years since the expulsion of the Jews and Moors from Spain. The armies of the Ottoman Sultan Suleiman are approaching Vienna.

Here lives the Spaniard, Juan Luis Vives. He is thirty years of age and engages with the greatest minds of his day: Erasmus of Rotterdam and Sir Thomas More of England. He is a humanist and humanitarian, a teacher who talks of the duty of all to "repair the world"; he lectures on the rights of animals and advocates literacy for all women.

But he has a secret that he must keep hidden at all costs.

Here are his diaries.

22 November 1522

With a slap on the table and a clap on my back, Johannes, the dazzling student, slams down this leather-bound book of nothing. It's full of blank vellum pages. It has a cover of filigree spirals, and the spirals form patterns like little eyes and ears that seem to follow me around the room. He, the lanky blond, says to me, the swarthy master, that I should write all my secrets here. As if I could do that! As if I could write my own death.

But those words—perhaps they've opened Pandora's box, for here I am, contemplating writing all my secrets. He must have seen the look in my eye, for when I looked up, I found him smiling with boyish dimples and a summer glint in his eye. He turned around and breezed out like a court harlot off to a better job.

So, diary, now that you're here, uninvited, what do I write? Maybe I should ask what do I not write? What secrets do I not tell? Perhaps I should ask you the questions, hoping that I'll get answers to the unfathomable. Let's start then. Why do they mean us harm when we mean no harm to them? Why do they hunt us to the very corners of the earth? And one more, please: Why, if we say we're good Christians and go to their churches, do they still try to root us out? But these questions, if they were found written here, would be enough to see me chained to the...

So, you force me, diary, to write in codes and ancient tongues on this cold November day with pine logs spitting and hissing in the grate. Here I am, the exile, sitting in the red leather-backed chair with its cracks and dimples moulded to my bent spine. What's here? I barely notice as a rule, but there's the smell of parchments and wines, of bits of spice and a lap-full of crumbs that I'm too lazy to brush away.

My gaze is drawn through the diamond-shaped windows into the cobbled street below. Pretty girls are running with hoops and sticks. The frayed ribbons in their hair go back and the hoops go forwards. I chuckle to think that the girls I stared at when I arrived here nine years ago are now teaching the game of hoops to their own daughters.

Could it really be nine years? Yes, that day I strode ocean-weary into the town of silted rivers and wooden bridges, of offal and butchers' carcasses. The carcasses float out to the ocean and then back in again on the next tide, and it's no wonder that the river is silting up and the town stinks like an abattoir. Nine years ago, I didn't have the flecks of grey that invade my dark brown hair like weeds in a poorly tilled field.

I beg your pardon, diary. Did you say something? It was my father's finances, generations in the wool trade, that allowed it to happen. But if the terrible thing hadn't happened when I was seventeen, I would not have left Spain. I made my way through university in Paris and Leuven, there a pupil of Erasmus the Great, promising always to go back one day to Valencia. But no, you're right. I could not overcome my fear of what I saw with my own eyes and heard with my own ears. To my own disgrace, I have not yet gone back.

And so I reached this town, just twenty years old, full of the Renaissance, but I quickly found I was human rather than humanist, for my heart and eyes were first drawn to the pretty girls with fair hair, plaited and constructed into lofty monuments. All I wanted to do was unfurl those lofty monuments and spend the hours reconstructing them.

All right, so you push me. Next, my searching eyes and keen nose hit upon a few of my own kind. They were living here silently as good Christian folk, but I could see the signs. We were unable to look one another in the eye in public, but at dawn and dusk, we gathered in warm places by candlelight, singing ever so quietly the old songs.

So, diary, the town of your birth has become my home, for though these lands are under the control of the Spanish king, there is, as yet, no Inquisition. There is no familiarity with the limpieza de sangre, the impurity of blood, that marks my family in Spain as Nuevos Cristianos, New Christians. The title means that we are always to be regarded with suspicion. Here, I am free to walk the cobbled streets and take deep breaths. Here, I have little fear of being pulled from my bed and taken to a destiny darker and colder than the mid-winter night.

What's that? Why do they call me the Striking Man? Well, I'm no giant, and I wouldn't pitch in for a wrestling match with a Flemish man. My spine is slightly twisted so that my hips go east while my shoulders go west. My teeth, though, are straight and shiny, beacons of my good fortune. My skin is sallow, olive, almost green in winter, but glows when a new girl saunters by.

Anna-Lise was a Dutch girl who sauntered by. I could pay her with a florin or, if I had one, a Valencian orange. She said, with one tooth missing, that my strike was the glint, the piercing eye. These were her words, not mine. Don't think me haughty, please, but she said there was a light that hovered about me, a countenance of loving kindness. I wasn't like the Dutchers, she explained, for I washed every day in the warm scent of lavender, and through vanity clipped my beard while looking in the shiny brass mirror. She left me for a merchant from Saxony with deeper pockets, bigger oranges. I have not been striking enough to capture the heart of the one I long for with every aching sinew, the one for whom my broken heart waits.

What strikes me is Señor Apoplexia, the alien within. He strikes with little warning and even less control. He will not be tamed and threatens to reveal me and devour liberty. Is that why I am striking? Will the apoplexies lead to the terror of the wrack and the screws, to a deportation in chains to the flames of the Plaza Major?

A glance around the room then. A quick sniff of the brewing infusion: rosehip for the body, nettle for the mind, camomile for the spirit. A tapestry of a solitary tree hangs high above the stone fireplace. It takes me to mystic places of buried truths in hidden corners. I look through the diamond panes again, and there are my pupil-boys, laughing and throwing soft punches as they rush to their warm homes in tall houses. They are strong now and almost as big as their fathers. And though their northern tongues sound to me like a hammer striking an anvil, their young lives remind me of the joy of waking to a new day. They bring back sweet memories and dreams.

I don't think I can write about my great dream for the future. It's too painful, and there is too much at stake. But how I long each moment for my family to be reunited in a new golden age, or to write about the past. Surely, that is just too hard, too tricky a horse to ride.

But you're here, beckoning me to write something. You were meant to be here, yes? And you have unleashed something, like fragments of a lost dream suddenly remembered. In my dream, my three sisters are in our family home in Valencia, my father strumming the guitar as they sing warm songs by candlelight. I look closer into the dream, and they huddle together in the cellar of the granary, not because it's cold, but because they never knew if it would be the last time. Eva, the eldest, would get up to sing and dance, stepping high and lighting up Father's face, taking the deeply etched lines off his worried brow.

Then there's the other dream: a memory of the fires, of a scream at midnight from a familiar voice—someone I was not able to save. I know I must go back there, and soon, and bring them safely here. But I also know that if I go back, the scream could very well become my own. These fragments of dreams are like leaves on this autumn day. Some are dazzling red and gold, while others are withered, grey, and brown. I must find the strength to weave them all together into a magical cloth. I must bring my fragmented family back together again.

But I can't do it yet.

No, now is for the now, and, sweet diary, you have found a man in the making. The now is for living! Come on, Juanito, *El*

Toro Bravo—The Brave Bull—live! I dare you, write it down—why you choose to live in this world of tyranny and injustice!

I am consumed with passion for a man, and though you might think that odd when my heart strikes so hard for women, it is because of him that I choose to live. His name is Aristotle, for to be conscious that I am thinking is to be conscious that I exist. And if do I exist, then I should fully exist, repairing the world rather than fearing it.

Today, thoughts of how I'd repair the world overwhelmed me as I rushed to lectures so fast that I stumbled on the uneven cobbles, tripping over my gown and dropping my manuscripts like a court fool in a comedy. At the lectern, though, I focussed intently on those young scholars. Those wide-eyed poor students in their black gowns and white shirts sat bolt upright. I laughed out loud and began my lecture.

"All of creation is equal, is it not?" I asked them. "Ha! Yes, we are equal and that must bring change, no?"

They looked at me as if I were crazy, but I wasn't frightened to challenge them, for I am the Brave Bull who always gets that matador. Off we went on slavery, heresy, how we treat the little ones, the animals, always quoting the Greeks, the Romans, the Hebrews. Afterwards, I retired to these four wood-panelled walls and slumped to my desk.

Hildegard, the maid, knocked so loudly that I thought it must be the officers of Louis de Praet, the Spanish king's man in this town. Had they come to take me back in chains? Hildegard, though, quelled that thought as she burst in muttering a clumsy, "Señor... señor."

I grabbed the white silk covering from my head and hid it in my trembling hand under the desk. She ushered me from my seat and pushed me out of her way with hips that have known no rest from childbirth. She brushed the crumbs from my breeches and pinched me on the cheek.

"Argh! Get off, woman!" I said. It was only then that I realised I was munching on the hardened bread she had left me the previous night, for I was too caught up in Aristotle to eat. She threw more food at me as she cleaned the grate and collected the bones of a chicken, a wine glass, and apple cores.

"Whatever you do, do not touch my papers and books," I told her. I prayed that if she did, I wouldn't murder her and throw her body into the stinky river Dijver. She put them in a neat pile while I watched, helpless. All I could do was laugh. I could challenge Aristotle but not Hildegard. So much for El Toro Bravo.

She slammed the door. How long had she been here? Was there an "Adios, señor"? I don't know, for I was sitting in the corner, ruminating on the success of my famous work, *In Pseudo-Dialecticos*, in which I wrote what I feel, that the poor should be in the care of the state, not the church. I wrote that academics— crusty old bastards—lack clear speech and common sense, and that a woman's voice must be heard at all costs. I need to bring what I was taught in secret places to the attention of the world. The poor were under the care of my father's family so they would not live in fear. Stop!

Ah, but I cannot stop, for we learned that we might all learn equally, one from the other. My middle sister, Beatriz, always a wild one, hair tied back but still flowing down to her waist, sang a song that Mother taught her. She changed the lyrics to reflect that she would get her revenge on the Spanish king. The song said that though the *kol ishah*, the woman's voice, is nothing now but a whisper, one day it will be changed into a roar. I must do them a service while I have the chance. As I think of Beatriz's song, I am reminded that what I need to hear most of all is a woman's voice. And though I am not yet permitted to hear it, I know to whom the woman's voice belongs.

Diary, you have found a revolutionary! Your writer is in conflict with the most famous thinker of our age, Erasmus of Rotterdam; for if God has not given man free will, then why has he created him at all? Does the alternative God-given justice mean that my aunt and my cousin deserved their fates in the fires of Valencia?

Will I face that now? Will it help to write about it?

Diary, you seem to speak, "Go there, Juanito."

Well, I can always burn you when I have written this. You're just vellum, no longer living flesh and blood. I strain my eyes to glance at the past now. I see that we were never safe, a family of secret Jews in Valencia, for we were always looking over our left shoulders, waiting for the day that the king's axe would fall and the bundles would be lit under our feet.

Dark waters seem to cloud my memories as if protecting me from the pain. If I try hard enough, I'll be able to see through them. What was in our secret place, the cellar of our granary? Mother was there until the plague got her. Before then, teaching by example, she'd quietly welcome our guests, taking away their dark cloaks and shawls to reveal silks of bright purple against a sea of white. She gave the men their yarmulkes from a cavity behind a loose brick. Sand was strewn on the floor. Hushed tones reverberated off the walls until it felt like the walls themselves, not the mouths of our guests, were talking.

"Why sand, Father?" I asked.

"Oh, my clever boy, to remind us of Moses's wandering in the desert."

I'd thought it was to muffle the sound of our footsteps in the secret places. And if we had not feared the rap on the door, would our guests have meant so much to me or would I have been bored, like my pupils at Mass? I do not know. I must get to work soon. First, I have to find a way to rescue my father and three sisters who still live in Valencia. Then I will find us all a haven—somewhere, anywhere. If not here, perhaps in the New World.

"Father, why don't we go to Salonika or Venice, where we might be safe?" I'd ask when I was fifteen and all my siblings were younger than me.

"Hush, my worrying boy. It will all be over in a year or two. The king and queen are not so stupid as to lose all their best doctors and financiers. It will all go back to how it was. Just be patient."

He believed this, and despite all the evidence to the contrary, he still believes it today.

So, diary, will you be a tool to help me? Will you be my counsel on these matters? No, not yet. You have not proved yourself yet.

But neither have you betrayed me. It seems cruel to put you on the flames, as my aunt was. That was the terrible event, you see, that made me leave when I was seventeen. And so, under you go, into the hessian sack beneath the floorboard, between two walls bricked up on this side and with cloth placed either side of the loose board so that it will not creak. Away!

1 December 1522

It's a shame, but I can't quite keep away from you. You're like a girl that's got me under her spell, or a new batch of wine I can't help but drink. Perhaps you're just that certain someone I can share nonsense with. It's true. I could write instead to my youngest sister, Leonora, the artistic one, the poetess. She'd love to hear about the winter frost that's climbing up the windowpanes like the sharp hands of an assassin, but by the time the letter gets to her, it will be spring and long gone. So, I'll write to her in advance of the season about blackbird chatter and snowdrops while sharing the business of the day with you.

It was but a few days before the great man, Johannes Van der Poel, arrived at my door. He's tall for his age, like a spring vine that's shot up too fast and is a mess of spine and limbs. He's got a strong jaw, though, and if his face had not been pitted with scars of the pox, he'd be impossibly handsome. That he survived at all when most did not is a sign of great strength. His heart's desire is to command armies and work for the king, but I'll beat that out of him. He is but fifteen years of age, and he is my brightest star.

A firm rap came on the door then, and I uncrossed my legs, put down the quill, and picked up the lute. "Enter, Johannes."

"Have you started writing yet, sir?" he asked with a hopeful glint in his blue eyes.

"How do you think my great works get here, Johannes, if I'm not always and forever writing? On a magic carpet from the Orient?"

"No, no, sir," he said as he scratched his face. "Your diary, the little book I gave you. Remember? It would be rude not to use it, sir. I had to save up to buy it. It's for your secrets."

"Don't pick your scars, boy!"

He stopped, but he looked at me as if demanding a reply to his question.

"Well, if I had started writing, I wouldn't tell you. And if I did, I'd hardly confess what I'd written. That's the nature of secrets, eh?"

He relaxed with a deep and contented sigh and laughed. "So, I'll have to break in when you're not here?"

"You wouldn't understand it," I replied, rising from my chair and strumming gently on the lute.

"You're writing in Hebrew, then?"

"Why are the sun and the moon round if the earth is flat?" I asked, holding the lute tightly with one hand, fiddling with my grey worsted jacket with the other. He was a sharp tool.

"If Magellan has just circumnavigated the world, then it must be round."

"But why don't the people on the bottom fall off?" I asked, putting the lute in a corner of the room.

"There must be a giant magnet in the middle," he declared.

I nodded. "Must be."

He changed tone. "Why do the Spanish want the New World all for themselves?"

"Greed and power blind the mind and kill the beautiful. Men have always used scripture to justify such deeds and—"

"Scripture," he interjected, "my favourite topic. Why do you go to Mass if you are a Jew?"

I stopped pacing and started searching his face for a hint of kindness, a sign that this was jest. I found nothing but a steady gaze.

"Well"—I checked myself as if recalling a long-lost memory— "Grandfather mentioned that his great-grandfather perhaps was a Jew? And there was a crooked-nosed fellow, a pedlar in Barcelona—perhaps he was a Jew?" I stopped and thought about my father. Did he still make sausages from rabbit and chicken, spiced so heavily that they seemed to be made of pork?

"Will they kill you if they find out?" he asked solemnly.

"There is nothing to find out," I replied in a deeper tone, leaning against my chair.

"But Rhodes has just been taken by the Turks." He walked around the room, waving his arms as if scything off the head of a Greek peasant. "They massacred them without mercy."

He came to a halt and picked up the brass astrolabe that Father gave me the day I left Spain.

"I hardly think that's true, Johannes," I replied with a frown. "Yes, Rhodes may have fallen, but the Turks are a merciful race."

"You had better be careful. Our kings will be in no mood now to protect a crooked-nosed Jew or an Arab-o-phile." He laughed out loud uncontrollably.

I asked him to conjugate four simple verbs: to gain, to learn, to lose, to survive. Then, absent-mindedly, I asked him to do another: to die.

I paced around the small room, catching a glimpse in the copper mirror of swollen veins in my temples. "I am not a Jew. I will have no more talk of it."

He nodded.

"Johannes, do not tell anyone of this conversation. Agreed?"

"Of course not, sir."

Diary, are you my friend or his?

May God quell my energy and my chattering mind. May I steer clear of the trap. May I burn you, diary, and stop this.

*   *   *

And then the day of the great man was upon us and, though I needed to focus, I was consumed with thoughts of those long summers days when my brown skin glowed and I played with my pandalla, my gang, in our short breeches on the long stone quay. I was always the last to turn home. Instead, I'd sit behind lobster pots and listen to the fishermen mending their nets and to the sailors swapping tales of the New World. I heard that all men are like the fish that swim in the ocean, for there are great fish, middle fish and little fish. Someone shouted, "What type will you be, Juan Luis Vives? A great fish?" All collapsed in laughter. I'd made my intentions clear, without even trying.

Born a year after the Jews were expelled, I thought that I could never really be any kind of fish at all, for if I became a great fish, I would surely be exposed, and then what? But one day a man who had dove for pearls, called Margaritas, at the behest of the queen spoke of another kind of fish. This one swam with the big ones, cleaning their fins and gills, and was never ever eaten. By their close association, the little fish journeyed to underwater palaces and caverns of silver and gold. This would be me. If I could be that kind of fish, swimming alongside the great fish, perhaps I could rescue my people from the abyss.

And if ever there was a great fish, it was England's Sir Thomas More. And when asked by Erasmus to be his eyes and ears in this ancient city, how could I refuse? It's true he is all for Catholicism, but an enlightened Utopian Catholicism in which I hoped my people would find a place.

On the day he arrived in Bruges, a company of Englishmen marched me quickly along the streets as if there was a pikestaff up my arse. I approached the house with the Dutch gable that was his lodging in Bruges. The door was opened, and I was thrust into the beating heart of the drawing room. But, where was he? No sooner had I arrived than we were away again. The great fish had tired of waiting for his little companion and was gone.

This time, down the blowy cloisters we marched through the icy streets of Bruges past men with loads of winter kale and carrot until I saw his silhouette on the steps of the Duke's palace. I prayed to God that his body accompanied it, but I would not have been at all surprised if this was a jester's act! As we drew closer, he turned, the contours of his face highlighted by the pale sunshine. I thought that he must have been posing for a celestial artist. There was the smell of lanolin sweat and a vague scent of frankincense. Finally, I was with the great man, my big fish.

There were never any formal greetings with Sir Thomas More. He always started with a question. I was not ready for it, and he knew it as I climbed, puffing, up the steps of the palace.

"My man, Spaniard, I have forgot… Vives, is it?" He laughed at my red face and the breath coming out of my nostrils. "What's your view on the education of a woman?"

"In Spanish culture," I said, "the education of women is very important." I cursed myself for saying "my culture," hoping that I hadn't given myself away. Every inch of my crooked body was aching to engage him eye-to-eye, man-to-man, but he would have turned away.

'Yes, Isabella, the deceased queen, was so enlightened," he laughed.

"It's not her I'm thinking of. I would not teach a woman cruelty or greed." My heart was still beating like an executioner's drum.

He touched my left forearm and whispered, "Who says they should be the equals of their husbands, fathers, or their sons?" His brows were furrowed, and the creases that marked the pouches of his face deepened. Then, in a flash, he let all expression disappear, and his face became like an even millpond. This was a grand dance, but where was it going? Three years earlier, he had written *Utopia,* in which men and women were equal citizens.

'Come, Vives," he said. "This way."

I followed the party into the palace and found the Duke of Alba, stony-faced and tottering from wine, next to the one-eyed Grand Bailiff, Louis de Praet. They were surrounded by a gaggle of awkward merchants and sat at a long table laid with a gold cloth. If they hadn't stood up, they would have been lost behind giant jugs and pewter tankards. Although a grand chair had been prepared for Sir Thomas, he made straight for a lowly stool at the end of the table. I quickly ran to sit next to him at a right angle.

I was with the great man, a gold chain of office draped over his crimson velvet shirt. That he didn't remove his black woollen cap reminded me of Father at the Shabbat table. I caught another whiff of frankincense as I spoke.

"Education is the means by which we progress as a race. With it, a woman can give birth, not just to babies, but to a unique language, a new philosophy."

Men fussed over him like flies around sugared fruit. I lost attention for a second as my eyes strayed to the chestnut-haired serving girl. She carried two pitchers under her arms that elevated her breasts into voluptuous pillows where my head longed to rest. I snapped back to the moment as thin-faced Louis de Praet sidled over. As ever, he wore a yellow feather on his black cap so that he looked like a wasp.

"And Suleiman, he welcomes the bloody Christ-killers," Sir Thomas said. "Better they go that way from Spain than to us, eh de Praet?" Sir Thomas said looking my way, for he knew me for a third generation New Christian.

De Praet, sitting upright like a statue, his eye glazed from an attack from an owl whose chicks he'd tried to steal, nodded in excitement. As he replied, he turned his head so that he could catch me with his one good eye. "Ya! And so, I have good news. Charles V sends officers to the Netherlands to root those secret buggers out."

Sir Thomas answered him as de Praet stroked his red badge. "Pray, sir, ask the Spanish king to send a physician or two to England, for we have a problem with scurvy there, too. We'll even give them their own house of conversion"—he leant towards me—"and?"

I wanted to grab him and shake him. Scurvy? The scurvy of Judaism? In *Utopia*, he called for religious toleration. Perhaps with the advance of the Turks and Martin Luther, his heart was hardening? I blocked what I had just heard and returned to our previous matter. "It's a pity that a woman can't sit in the privy council and pacify the decisions of those who can."

"And?" he asked again, his face an unreadable manuscript.

My voice became a throaty stutter. "In the fa-family, the educated woman can s-stimu-late debate among her children, and new ideas can be formed." I paused as he raised his left eyebrow. I continued, clearly now. "I am surprised that you do not see that."

He opened his eyes wide, so that the white showed both above and below his iris.

"Dear God, man," he said, standing up to push me on the left shoulder with such vigour that I toppled in my chair. "Whatever possessed you to think that I do not see that? Are my daughters not the best-educated women in England? You should hear Meg sieve through the bollocks of the court like a mudlark on the banks of the Thames!"

"Who is Meg?' I asked.

He smiled at me as if I were the court fool. "Mea culpa, Vives! You passed the test! The education of the princess is of the upmost importance. England's future depends upon it."

The princess? Who else could he be talking of but Mary, the only living child of King Henry VIII and the queen, Catherine of Aragon?

He looked up to the beamed roof as if summoning divine energy for his dream of a new Catholic-led golden age, and all listened intently: "If she is to rule the country, in peace and war, prosperity and famine, then she must understand languages, history and philosophy." He was silent for a minute. "The king won't get another child by the queen, and so the education of the woman is everything." He caught my smile in an instant. "No, Vives. Don't ask who I have in mind. I have in mind the best."

This was to be my catapult to greatness, the chance to realise my dream.

Patience deserted me. I had pledged to do all I could to find a safe home for my people. Even though he called us a scurvy, perhaps England would be such a place.

"Can I bring my father and my sisters?" I asked. "And the woman I love. Will it be soon?"

He came towards me, a smile on his face.

"Of course, they can come. My table is their table. If anyone knows the meaning of this next word, you and your family do, señor: B'yi-to."

It was the Hebrew word I recited daily in my prayers; it means, "in its proper time." What did he suspect? I didn't have time to ponder this, for he transformed into a debating demon, the perfect advocate for his nation's interests. He displayed his verbal skills like a strongman throwing logs at a fair. He asked briefly about the progress of my latest work, for faith, not politics, is what was truly in his heart.

"It's a translation and commentary on St Augustine's *City of God.*" For I'd do anything to convince the world what a good Catholic I am."

Before we parted, he gave me the name of an expert printer and bookbinder. He would help me with publishing it and with learning English. The printer was a fellow Spaniard, Álvaro de Castro, with whom he had worked in London.

"Please," he said softly, "give him employment and dedicate that book to King Harry, the great king of England."

Argh! If I can play this king, then I can save my people. But first and foremost, I am El Toro Bravo. "Hasn't Martin Luther recently defiled a king named Harry as an oaf and a pig and declared that he should be covered in his own excrement?" I laughed until all chattering in the room stopped. Sir Thomas looked serious, but I didn't hold back. "You know that my work speaks against tyranny and torture and that the king is known for both? I have paltry funds for a clerk, however brilliant."

"Please, sir," he implored me. "This king is a good king, the noblest, the kindest. And de Castro is the Cardinal of Burgos's page, a great and clever man."

Everyone knew what a zealot the Cardinal was and what he gave his pages—and what he took from them. I didn't need the old Cardinal's boyfriend looking over my shoulder, vetting me for signs of Judaism.

Sir Thomas fixed me with his eye, a cold, brown pebble. I knew in that moment that I'd have no choice, for I had to get to England.

"Just do it," he said. "It's your road to success and greatness." He thrust a purple velvet purse into my pocket. I opened it carefully, marvelling at the jangling mass of silver inside.

In his scheming, brilliant mind there was a plan, and in that plan, he saw London as the power-horse of Europe, a new Rome. He saw that from there, new lands with his strong ideals would be settled. But I know from the mouth of Martin Luther and from the torches he has lit, Sir Thomas's dream is receding, for this is a new age in which empire and religion will be tested and new voices will be heard. Only those able to exploit the new age will survive.

As for me, diary, I am his eyes and ears in this town, but like a cunning little fish, I am not truly with my master. By evening's light, you'll find me in taverns and barracks, jostling with the English militias that are marshalled here for the final onslaught against the peasant's revolt. I hear among them their new dreams, the true word of God, that all in that land is about to change. What then of my people's place, the sons and daughters of the lost homeland, the children of Israel? And this king, I have never heard of him torching a Jew or speaking up against them, unlike Sir Thomas, unlike Luther, unlike Louis de Praet.

I departed with three kisses on the cheeks, one for him, one for his king, and one for his Meg. As I left the great hall, I kissed my own hand three times, once for Mother, once for Father, and once for the one I love.

I trudged home, wine-slow, through the ice and snow piled around the tying posts, disturbed for a moment by a man in rags shivering by a doorway. I tossed a coin from my new purse and gave him my grey woollen jacket. I rushed home after that, for it was freezing. All is now quiet in my wood-panelled room, which somehow feels like a glorious tomb.

I grab an apple, too soft to the touch, the skin starting to wrinkle, and I compare it to my own skin, still tight, thank God! It reminds me that life is short and that I must act fast before I, too, am wrinkled and softened. I ruminate on every sentence, for my meeting with Sir Thomas was indeed just the last movement in a well-rehearsed gavotte. The seeds that I long ago sowed seem at last to have born fruit. He is convinced that I am the only one who can bring the princess to an enlightened version of her faith, but little does he know how enlightened my version would be. I see that if she is to be queen, then I must be the one to turn her away from the pain that her grandparents, Ferdinand and Isabella, have wrought.

*   *   *

England is a pretty name, but what do I know of it? In the court of Queen Claude in Paris, there were two English sisters, beacons of charisma. There was fine music—a flute and a harp—tapestries of crimson and golden thread, dancing, laughing, drama. The younger of the two girls sat on my knee, black hair pulled back with two shell combs as she twisted my beard. She tried to teach me the English verbs "to be," "to do," and "to love" and then chuckled at my Spanish accent. She spoke to me in perfect French. "Señor Vives, you are surrounding the words with wool." She wore green, a pearl necklace, a crimson hood, and smelled of sandalwood. I was drunk on her, although hers was a beauty like no other. She brought me out of my rapture and asked me, "Is the pope truly our spiritual father?"

Before I could answer, her sister, fairer and more buxom, took my left hand. She ran me through the long halls, past courtiers and lute players. She wanted to bring me to the queen's attention, but her sister held her back. "What is your name, my pretty one?" I asked her.

"It is Mary Bullen, sir." Her older sister grabbed and shook her. "Never say that! Your name is Maria Boleyna!"

Then, cheery Maria Boleyna approached Her Majesty and spoke to the queen in English. "Look at Señor Vives. Is he not the biggest smidgeon of Spanishness?"

The queen nodded. "The greatest thinker, ma petite Boleyna. Think of his mind first when you describe his virtues."

Anne looked at her older sister. "You're a fool, sister. You will never keep a man if you do not appeal first to his mind."

Maria replied, quick as lightning, "If you think you can outwit a great man, then you'll lose everything."

Anna turned her nose up and laughed. "Sister, you know nothing."

* * *

The wine of the dinner proved too strong. I must have drifted off, diary, with you open for anyone to see. A dream slipped by, but I managed to grab it. In it sat my father, sanguine, reposed, beside still waters, reciting in Hebrew the words of the Twenty-third Psalm.

In the dream, I was in the jasmine blossoms, and their strong scent in late summer was replaced by the lavender that pervades the winding terraces of La Juderia. I was sleepy, but I dragged my head forward and wished in my haze that I was a merchant. I could trade the coarse words of the drunks in the street below for the gentle tinkering of the silversmith, Eduardo, working by early light in his salon behind the bedchamber I shared with Jaime, my brother. I contemplate how I would trade this rough earthenware inkpot for the brightness and beauty of what de Pinto created. There were silver monkeys and birds fashioned into inkpots, thimbles and brooches, shiny and smooth to the touch, if only I had been allowed to touch. This was a place where I practiced silence as I looked at their creations.

Eduardo's son Nathaniel was the leader of the gang called Los Pandallos de Pinto. He was our life's blood, and we adored him like a false messiah, with his chin jutting like the overhanging storey of a townhouse, his hair long and tied back like a girl's. Only fifteen, he had a beard. Nathaniel, say you are not gone, waiting in a foreign land.

It was the month of Nissan. I woke up one day without the tinkering of brass on silver, and there were no more fine silver monkeys and ornate brooches. Father, what did you say to try that might mend my broken heart? What was that note nailed to the door with a drop of blood and a red, waxy diamond seal? You said they had sailed for Africa in the dead of night to a new shop in the city of Ceuta. What, dear father? You are sure? Why then did the women of the neighbourhood talk of shouting and screams in the middle of the night? Why did they take nothing of their silverware with them? Why, a week later, was the shop commandeered by the family Garcia, who bashed and thrashed the silver, more like loggers than craftsmen, and failed the business within a year?

No, today is a day for the future and a day to forget the past.

But my mind won't stop this cursed thinking just as my blood won't stop circulating. Please Juanito, if you are El Toro Bravo, stop this thinking.

What is that now? Boots on the wooden boards close to my room, and a knock on my door shakes me out of Valencia. Am I discovered? Is this the officer of Charles I, the grand order of the Holy Inquisition? I am undone as I scratch the chair on the floor to rise. I will lock this diary, throw it in a pile of books. They know I am here. They know.

But it is only letters that have arrived. The first is from Sir Thomas.

"Great scholar, Vives. I believe that's your name, no?"

I sat frozen. Was he alert to the fact that this is not my true name?

"'Tomorrow, I'll be gone, but soon to return. Be ready. When I call for you, you will come, and you can bring your father and your sister and your love. Our home will be your home."

He calls the Jews scurvy but would have an infestation of them in his own home, so he can't possibly think we're Jews. But why send the Cardinal's boy to spy on me?

There was another letter, beneath his, from de Castro the scrivener at Antwerp. The lettering leapt off the page with a square-ish script, almost Hebraic.

This is perhaps a clever trick. If they're trying to pull the net over me, I must be ready.

9 December 1522

Out you come, diary. I have things to say, so listen.

It was after the fair, with the boys' parents among the bank-side hog roasts and red and yellow canvas tents on the iced-over river. Moving quickly, we huddled inside the tents. Inside were cards and dice and jugs of mead. We emerged to find children with wooden skates dodging us, grabbing for a purse. There was a man on stilts with a false beaked nose and a skullcap chasing the children across the ice.

We walked past Douwe's apothecary, which is exactly when I heard it. It was so shocking that I fell back into his arched doorway and let them walk on without me. I pushed the door that creaked like the tooth he was extracting, and instinctively I made sure he was using clean hands and silver needles, as if that would take my mind away from what I had heard in the street.

I stumbled out once they had gone and walked home, where the fire now spits and roars, as if to tell me, "Slow down, Vives." The flames reminded me that I must confront the reason I slipped into Douwe's. It was Johannes Van der Poel's father, the blundering, slurring merchant, who let it slip.

"Who'd not be proud of one like that? Johannes is your best student, yes?"

"The very best," I replied. "Tongue like a razor blade."

His father smiled. "Listen to this. I saw to it myself, by de Praet himself, to be a spymaster one day, to root out traitors and heretics."

"Young Johannes, a spymaster?" I stopped dead in my icy tracks and looked around to see who else was listening in.

Johannes must have noticed something. From shop windows, the street was lit by candles that cast an eerie, silvery light on the ice and snow. The whole town seemed suddenly silent, as if all noise was muffled by the snow until, proud and upright, he broke the silence and declared, "Yes, sir, and you can tell your Friday night friends that the eyes and ears of the Spanish king are open."

My Friday night friends? Eyes and ears? I cannot let you lead me to them, diary, to the one I love, just coming of age, whose hair is black and wavy and yet somehow almost blue in the light. Don't let me mention her name or where she lives. No more talk of the one whose skin is olive but soft like butter. Diary, you may root me out, but you won't lead me to the others. The words you force me to write are my chains and shackles, no? This young Van der Poel, the clever student, whose fees keep me here—he has you on his side? Well, I'm not a clever little fish for nothing. I'll find a way to play this.

*　　*　　*

The town feels empty now that the English militias have gone. They marched east in their meagre boots across the muddy landscape to finish off the Arumer Zwarte Hoop: brave men and women who are fighting to shake off the yoke of the Spanish king. Will there be any mercy? How will mothers be able to feed their children if the fathers are lined up and hanged, just like the sons of Haman in the Book of Ester? It's a cruel world, but the only way to change it is to stay in it. To do so, I must jump through hoops. I must be one step ahead.

After classes, then, I strolled through the *geldmuntstraat* and the *kraanplein*. I found some comfort from the lacy stonework of the city's churches that seemed like familiar old clothes. The carvings, the gargoyles and griffins—they said something new, though. Was it a warning or a comfort?

Walking slowly onwards, a mother reined in her children like a sheepdog. How odd that God blesses her with so many when he blesses the king of England with just one. The windows of the grand houses caught a reflection of weak sunlight that glinted across the cobbled squares where I bathed in the warmth outside the tavern. It took me home to the endless summers, the embrace of my mother and the laughter of my sisters.

Once inside the tavern, I sat down at a quiet table and called the girl whose name I never remember, the one who leans her bosom right into my face. I asked for some chicken broth and beer. But what was I getting into? This was the place where I'd arranged to meet Álvaro de Castro. Although I arrived a whole hour early for the sake of casual spying, I was already too late.

He sat there in the corner, grinning. He was in his early years, dressed in a dark-green brocaded shirt, a dark man with lightly curled black hair, taller than me and leaner – not what I'd been expecting.

"Valenciano! I am de Castro, but you can call me Álvaro, late of the cities of London and Antwerp, but a Burgueño, a Spaniard at heart and looking to spread my wings." The light of youth shone through his dark, expansive eyes. His olive cheeks were narrow, but his jaw was strong and prominent.

"Very good," I replied cagily, taking everything in as the pretty girl thrust the comforting broth under my nose. She let the flap of her skirt fall open around her leg so that I could feel the sweet touch of female flesh. "Bring him some too, please," I mumbled. I offered de Castro my wooden spoon and my broth, and he took it and ate.

"Ha ha, I see you want me to talk." He laughed and gave me back my broth. "Tell me, Master Juanito Vives, what is life like for the secret Jews here in this pretty town?" I thanked God he spoke in Castilian. "Sweet son of Abraham. I am looking for work!"

I tried to hush him up, but he continued.

"Got a pretty Dutch girl into trouble, I did, blonde as Spanish sands with a Venus mound to lose your face in." He grinned, and though his front teeth were slightly twisted out of place, they did not take away from his handsome looks. "Her family don't want a Spaniard, much less a *Marrano* for a grandson. They are demanding I be drawn between two horses!" After a sigh he asked, "What are the girls like here, my friend Juanito?"

He was a stallion, the power of his late youth charging at me like a horse that had bolted.

"And how is the Sabbath here?" he asked. "Is sand thrown on the floor? Is there a Kiddush cup of pure silver, or is it merely pewter? Pray tell, is it just a hollow wooden bowl?"

What cruel trick of Sir Thomas was this?

"Quietly, señor," I said. "Sir Thomas sent you, but this is nonsense. You know we are third generation Cristianos? You are the Cardinal's page, are you not?"

It had finally reached Bruges. I knew the Inquisition had reached Utrecht and Ghent, where New Christians were rooted out on old accusations.

I asked him what he knew of my work.

"I know you challenge Aristotle, that you champion the new learning, and that you elevate merchants' sons to be new and better nobles."

He was right, but that was not what I was asking.

"I also know you write Torah without ever mentioning it," he continued. "I know you are a soul in torment."

"You do not know that."

"I do," he muttered with a chuckle.

"What are your skills, my Burgueño? Why would I take you under my wing for a printer and a clerk?"

"Sir Thomas More has already paid you, and if you don't do as he asks, you'll be stuck here forever."

"Madre mia!" I exclaimed. "And what have you got on him that he pays you to spy on me?"

"Do you think he's the one who's controlling this game? Do you think he's cleverer than one from our tribe?"

"Just tell me who you are and what you can do for me."

"A bookbinder in Antwerp, an illustrator in Amsterdam, a translator in London. In London, with my Cardinal's recommendation, I became known to Sir Thomas and his five lovely daughters!"

"Meg, of whom he talks so sweetly—is she one of his daughters?"

"The brightest and sharpest, with eyes like the night sky and a tongue like a viper," he replied.

'And pretty, too?'

"You'll have to find that out for yourself, my friend."

"Enough of this talk. You're one of the Burgos boys. They're famous for what they're willing to give and take."

He didn't defend himself, but recounted the struggles of the de Castro family, a story I did not believe for a second. His father sent him for an altar boy at the grand cathedral to quell rumours and to find out what they say about us, to get recommendations and references. And with those references, he ran away to Amsterdam, London and Antwerp.

He smiled and, bringing his elbows forwards, as if drawing an invisible prayer shawl over his head, he regaled me with stories of streets of silver and gold, of inks and copper plating, of antimony and of lithographs and printing machines as heavy as olive presses. He hailed from a long line of scriveners who translated Castilian, Arabic, English, and Hebrew.

"These are common skills, though. I really don't think Sir Thomas gave me enough."

"You want to know what else?" he said, expressionless, like a cat about to pounce. "I've learned that the future is among the English and the lands in which they'll settle."

That set my mind buzzing with possibilities. Perhaps this was the future of our people. Perhaps I was sent here to help accomplish this.

"Take me in and I'll write you sonnets to win the hand of the girl you love. You will not regret it, my good Nuevo Cristiano," he said with that warm Spanish grin that I had not seen for a very long time.

"I need to see your work," I told him. In that instant, I felt that here was a person who, after many years, might see me buried in the proper way and might know what prayers to say at that time every year afterwards. But I was getting carried up in his spell, and I couldn't have this.

"You see, Valenciano, good son of Ferdinand! I knew you'd want me!" He threw me a song sheet, with black ink on fresh vellum and red and green on either side of the flowing script. It was from the pen of the great Jewish-Spanish poet Ibn Gabirol. Reading it in that smoky tavern brought a salty tear to my eye.

> At dawn I came to you, my rock, my strength;
> I offer you my dawn and evening prayers.
> Before your majesty I stand in fear,
> Because your eye discerns my secret thoughts.
> What is there that man's mind and mouth
> Can make? What power is there in my body's breath?
> And yet the songs of man delight you; therefore I
> Will praise you while I still from God have breath.

He turned to me. "When do we start our great work?"

The sudden softness of his words seemed like the brush of my father's hand against my face. I was no more than five, jumping up to him, full of piss and vinegar. He turned and swathed my face in the tassels of his love.

Now the memories come, unlocked.

Father, bent in the middle, chin like a ship's prow, skin bleached white by the candles beneath him, is in the cellar, with the sand on the floor that made him think of Moses in the desert. He is kneading his tassels with the six hundred and thirteen knots for each of the commandments.

It is early, before the sun lights the Plaza de la Figuera and the Calle de la Cerrejeria. We gather, hearts pounding. We are the Viveses. There are our neighbours, the de Pintos, and last to arrive are our friends, the Elazars, now known as López, who are here from beyond the mountain. The prayers have finished, we've drunk a sip of wine from a silver Kiddush cup, and Beatriz, my middle sister, the fiery one, the one who threatened to assassinate the king and poor hot oil on Torquemada himself, starts singing:

A la una yo naci,	When it struck one, I was born,
A las dos yo en grande si,	When it struck two, I grew up,
A las tres con mi amanté	At three I was with my lover
A las quatros me case	And at four I married he.

A tear runs down Father's cheek, for what happened to Beatriz's lover a week before the wedding—well, no one could ever talk about it, the medical dissection of a living man. Mother rushes to wipe away his tear, as if showing emotions would be risking too much. Eva and Leonora join in the melody, and we cannot help ourselves. Tears and smiles come at once, but we move to happier songs and are in a circle, holding hands and dancing, laughing with hands over our mouths until our ribs hurt. At the hour before dawn, silently, they disperse in cloaks of black, like bats.

"They are magic cloaks," my mother, with whom no man would dare disagree, says. "They will not be seen in the darkness."

Fourteen hundred and ninety-three was the year of my birth, just a year after Columbus sailed to the New World and swapped Spanish disease for Aztec gold. Mother whispered in my left ear, curled tight like a seashell, "This possession is a theft," and her words became ingrained in my conscience. The other calamity of the year before my birth was The Alhambra Decree, the edict of the expulsion of the Jews:

Dare they return, so much as to take another step…

They say that Columbus could not get a ship out of Seville because too many of us were moving eastwards to welcome the Sultan, or westwards to the respite of Portugal. Some of the braver ones went to the northern lands: places with strange names like London, Bristol, Antwerp. Should we have taken a ship, too? Or were we wise to sit in Valencia and wait for the monarchs to change their minds and see the error of their ways? We made an outward show of Mass while inwardly keeping the past alive.

*　　*　　*

But that was then, and this is now, and I had no choice but to take him under my wing. Sir Thomas had spoken to de Praet and they'd already prepared the empty room next to mine. In those early weeks, though I always kept my door locked, he would just turn the handle and try to get in. It was a rigid surveillance, and everything in my world changed. I couldn't be seen visiting my Friday night friends. I wouldn't risk leading him to the home of the one I love. I would not be drawn on my Nuevo pedigree, and I'd take him to Mass at St. Donation on a daily basis. The tzitzit tassel of my great-grandfather's prayer shawl, perhaps woven in the fourteenth century, had to go. And so did that fragment of an ancient Mishnah, the white yarmulke Mother gave me. But you, diary—the written evidence, the clever trap—I couldn't put on the flames. And neither would six weeks of suffocation get you, for you are like the lover I have no power over.

Let's be quick, diary. I have a chance. He has gone to chase a girl or a boy, and I have you and the evening to myself. He accompanies me to class and teaches me English. He works with the zeal of an expert and a skilled man, sitting for hours as he works with vellum, leather, brilliant inks while concentrating with the will of a monk at daily lauds and matins. Yet he also makes the boys laugh until they sweat and then calms them with a glance, and after lessons he plays games with jacks, balls, and bright polished stones of carnelian.

It seems that I wrap envy up in my bag along with my books and wear a thin smile. He is better at being me than I! He holds them in his grasp, and they return their affection for him by calling him Señor Álvaro. When I have only ever been addressed as Master Vives.

I throw them a discourse on ethics, a lesson in Greek, a book from Homer, and with a "Thank you, Señor," they run from the hall laughing, one clipping Álvaro's ear. He catches one under his dark green cloak and stabs a finger into his ribs until the boy convulses with laughter. I pretend I have to work, but instead I strain my ear at his door to hear the muffled, indecipherable chanting that is like a babbling brook.

Against this chanting, blackbirds start to chatter, singing songs of courage. Small white flowers emerge from winter's frozen soil, dangling a promise of less bitter weather. They seem to tell me, "You can trust him." There are days of clear glass-blue skies that promise a new life, a new way. Then, as if on celestial command, the clouds appear again with a sudden squall that seems to bode warning: "Tell him nothing—never." He asks me of my friends in the town, but I will reveal nothing.

Earlier, when I saw him dart into the streets below, I got into his room that he had, for once, not locked. I turned over papers, trying not to disturb anything. I found it beneath his translations of my *City of God*, a tightly set Castilian sonnet.

> Mi Primavera Burgueña, por verte, lo que yo daría…
>
> Si, por vivir en esos claros días, sentarme con mis gentes, ay…que alegrías!
>
> Pero No! Lamento la libertad perdida, vidas desintegradas, agonias malditadas!
>
> Alerta! Alerta… a las escuras…. sentinelas, caras mascaradas, con sus manos cenizadas!

Hijos de Israel, encarcelados, humillados...
quemados!

Hijos de Israel, esparriados, pero en fez...
fuerte y agrupados!

Si, juntos, lado a lado, nuestra hermandad
otra vez prosperara...

Con tan solo encontrar al Salvador, que será
un hombre sagrado.

A-ti-ri-ti...A-ti-ri-tando! El Señor Vives,
Kabalista, a nuestro lado!

Si! Lo proclamo desde todas las alturas y sin
ninguna duda...

Porque su pluma, humanidad y sabiduría
formaran canales...

Regando los jardines de mis gentes
convertiendolos en eterna hermandades!

Y, yo, y los Hijos de Israel, seremos los
pequeños granos de arena...

Y, el, sera El Pastor de mis gentes, como fue
también, El Gran Moshe, el profeta!

My Burgos Spring, to see you, how much I
would give...

Yes, living those clear days, to sit with my
people... what happiness to bring

But no, I lament freedoms lost, disintegrated
lives, damned agonies

Beware, beware... in the shadows...sentinels,
masked faces, ashen hands.

Children of Israel, imprisoned, humiliated…
burnt alive!

Children of Israel, scattered, but in faith,
strongly bonded!

Yes, together, side-by-side, our brotherhood
will again prosper!

Together in search of our Saviour who will
be a sacred one.

A-ti-ri-ti, A-ti-ri-tando! Señor Vives, the
Kabbalist, at our side.

Yes, I proclaim from on high…there is no
doubt!

Through his writings, humanity and wisdom,
he will form channels

That will water the gardens of our people, to
again create our brotherhood

And I, and the children of Israel, his flock
of lambs,

And he, the great shepherd, as our great
prophet Moshe.

Dare I let myself believe this is real, or is it like you, my
diary—a spider's web and the cleverest trick of all?

14 March 1523

Time passed in this "not knowing." I barely recognised that I
hated it because I was so familiar with it. The winter that should
have given way to spring stayed a while, and we did our minstrel's
dance of truth and half-truth, deftly stepping over the lies.

In early March the snow finally melted, and the dreaded news
came. There was a man from Ghent named Mendoza who was

caught in a mourner's Kaddish and a yarmulke on his head. As there is only an edict against us, and no Inquisition, he was carted back to Spain to face the auto-da-fé. Álvaro was unmoved as he told me. Louis de Praet openly rejoiced.

Then it happened. He found out the name of my Jewish family and where they live. Everything is now changed. As I sit here in the candlelight, the diary speaks to me. "Wake up, Vives. It's time for action. The stakes are raised."

"Stakes? Don't talk of action? Let me wallow in words." But the diary responds:

"Get to the house of the one you love, if it's true you love her, and get there before he does."

"Yes, diary, but first let me tell you how it happened."

It was the holiday of St. Ansgar. We decided to get out of the city.

"Who is he, anyway?" Álvaro asked on that grey-skied morning. Muddy puddles dotted the street, cold water seeping through the cracks in my boots.

"Just the man who made the heathens here Christians," I replied with a snigger.

"Perhaps he shouldn't have troubled himself," he said.

On the St. Ansgar's Day, with the university in recess, we mounted two fine greys that trotted out of the cobbled city as if they knew exactly where they were going. We passed the muddy fields that had been frost-locked for months and two hours later came to the port city of Ostend. As we entered, he asked, as if trying to trip me up, "Must we attend mass even here, Juanito?"

"Of course," I replied. "Why wouldn't we?"

It was strangely quiet in the streets, usually bustling with salt seadogs, fishwives, and pickpockets. I breathed deeply and felt liberated by it. I decided, too rashly of course, that we should ignore Mass and go for a hearty drink instead. The sea-wall tavern was empty except for a pair of ugly dogs, scrapping for remnants of bones. A chandelier hung precariously by a single chain. The fire barely crackled as we huddled close together, our scarves and jackets still ruffled around us. After a minute or two, a balding, beer-fattened landlord arrived and sat down with us, breathing through blocked nostrils and oozing pus from a wound on his left cheek.

"So, you're from the university, are you? Spaniards?" He had a thick guttural dialect. He scratched his wound and smelled his own fingers. "And you are paid for that? A waste of money."

"Shouldn't we bring the light of humanity to even the darkest corners?" I asked.

"Well," he said, swallowing phlegm, "as for Spaniards, we had an interesting party the other week."

I tried to laugh it off. Álvaro smirked and his eyes seemed to light up on cue.

"A family came from Bruges for a shipment of silks, and the old bugger's daughters wore silver rings on their fingers and diamonds in their ears. You must know them if you're from Bruges."

I stood up and downed the last dram. "No, we do not know them, and we must go to Mass. Here, take a coin."

The landlord grabbed the coin but continued. "There were two daughters with dark eyes to dazzle any man." He glanced from Álvaro to me. "If you gentlemen like the womanly form, that is."

Before I had a chance to speak or act, Álvaro jumped in. "What are these good Spaniards – if that's who they are – doing in Flanders? What is their name and where do they live?"

I had to stop this but was unable to speak.

"Why they came here, I don't know. But if you young men are seeking company from your own sort, head for the tallest house on the Verversdijk and make yourselves known."

"And the family name?" Álvaro demanded.

"It is not our business to know!" I said.

It was too late. The landlord had already found his guest book. "A groat for the information, and another to keep my mouth shut."

In an instant, Álvaro flung him three.

"You can read the name better than me," he said.

Álvaro grabbed it. "It is Valldaura."

The doors swung open and a rabble of men and women fell into the inn. Thoughts of my intimate Friday nights with the Valldauras flooded my mind – the secret prayers, lit only by two candles, with the windows boarded and the doors bolted. And the lovely girls with braided black hair and smiles that could surely warm the heart of even Torquemada, the Grand Inquisitor. And there in my thoughts was my girl, lovely Marguerite. I could not put this family in danger, but how could I resolve this? The inn became louder by the minute, and my thoughts grew cloudy. A rowdy party of young sailors from England threatened to tear the place down with their laughing and storytelling:

"On dear old Bessie Blount, the good king took his mount," one said.

An involuntary twitching overcame me, and I was on the floor. Then there was nothing.

Álvaro got me back here and laid me in my bed. A damp cloth dampened my brow. When I opened my eyes, I found a soft pillow had been placed under my head while the firmest one had been placed between my knees. I was lying on my left side so that the curve in my spine had the short side down so as not to strain my back. A Bible, open at the first psalm, lay on the bed. There was an apple chopped finely and steeped in honey on the table beside me, and as I lay there, I was aware that he sat in silence, watching as loyal as any parent or pet dog.

During the next few days, I was in torment. I was lost in thought, paralysed by the seizure. I couldn't get out of bed to visit the tall house. On the fourth day, I felt my strength return. You're right, diary: now is the time for action, so get back to your hiding place. I must go.

* * *

Like a monk, I dressed in a cassock and made for the tall house on the Verversdijk. I had always known that I'd be safe, for Señora Valldaura was my mother's cousin, and her cool bony fingers had the same comfort as my mother's hands. Bernardo of Toledo, her husband, was an expert in diamonds and a dealer in cloths. He was publicly baptised in Toledo at the age of ten. Still, fires were lit, the smell of burning flesh filled the air, and the screams of victims reciting Hebrew prayers were heard across the town.

On a moonlit night the family Valldaura locked the door of their house one last time, taking special care of the iron door key in case one day things changed, and they could return. On that night, they got past the city walls via a tunnel and passed through fields and forests and finally struck the mountainous road to Portugal. The road, they say, was shared with many a Nuevo, or a Morisco. All they had was what they wore and could carry, sacred possessions sown into their clothes.

"What sacred possessions?" I asked one Shabbat night.

Valldaura got them from the attic. There was a ruby rosary and a silver cross with pearls inset. There were diamonds and ingots that had been sewn into his wife's dress until she was heavy, like a snow-laden cherry tree. "Not sacred to a Jew, these things," I scoffed.

"Choose life," he replied. "Don't you remember that commandment?"

"Yes, but..."

"But nothing. If we must bargain for our lives, we will, so shut up."

That was the way he spoke – quick, sharp, and always one step ahead.

Once in Lisbon, in a favela shared with rats and shit-strewn gutters, families still went missing in the dead of night. In the year known as fifteen hundred and six, three thousand Jews went to their deaths, and though they pledged loyalty to the king, his ears were not open. The Valldauras, who escaped by hiding in the coalbunker of a monastery, left on a sea that promised only a faint hope of survival. I have to think it was God's light that directed them here, to Bruges, to save my lonely soul.

He is a little over five feet tall, with the big face and tarnished skin of a man who has truly lived life, and with the bulbous nose and sagging eyelids of a drinking man. It is not of Bernardo, though, that my heart sings, but his eldest daughter, Marguerite, my door marked "summer."

She is nine years my junior. Her long-brocaded hair, black and shiny, tumbles down like waterfalls around her neck, and her dark skin glows by candlelight. Her pretty eyes do not betray the fear that has been the backcloth to her short life. When my eyes meet hers on those Friday nights, she looks away. I hardly ever hear her voice.

We recite *The Song of Songs*, and she is allowed the part "Comfort me with apples." I am lost in the magic of a safe land, and I promise myself that I will one day buy her a whole orchard full of apples. I always find an excuse to get up and brush past her, and as I do, I get a scent of wild poppies in a wheat field, for she is my future, my little bit of heaven on earth.

When I rapped on the door dressed as a monk, it was she who opened it. She peeled the door back and scanned me cautiously before she realised it was I. A deep dark male voice yelled, "Quiens es?"

"Father, its Señor Vives," she called without taking her gaze away.

I bowed then took her hand and kissed it. Did she giggle? I think so, for surely, I am a gnarly branch on an old tree to her. But I can show her that with her loving hands I can be fashioned into a sleek arrow shaft to be prized, treasured, and loved.

Bernardo came out and took me to the long kitchen table, stained with six years of feasting, and asked Marguerite to bring me some bread. He put his thick hands around my shoulders as I sat, pinning me to my chair as he spoke. "Tell me where can I find a man to build Spanish looms. Which town is best to buy yarn by the hundred weight? Would it be Liege? Ghent?"

"There is a man here named de Castro. I'm not sure if he's a friend or foe, but we have to be more secret than ever."

The young whippet dog nudged his wet nose to my palm, and I give him my portion of bread, for how could I eat it in the presence of Marguerite? Maria, her younger sister, painfully shy and buried in her embroidery, balked at the name de Castro. Her father noticed it and, like a rabbi or great sage, cautioned us all.

"Spies are everywhere. Vives, keep your wagging tongue silent and do not falter."

I told him of the fated trip to Ostend, the innkeeper, and the apoplexy. To ease my discomfort, Nicolas, his fourteen-year-old son, lunged down the stairs on a piece of sackcloth, making enough noise to raise the dead. In the distraction, I addressed Marguerite.

"What does your day bring, Señorita Valldaura?"

She looked at me and reached for an orange, a rarity in these lands, and a knife. She was silent for a minute before peeling it and looking for her father's approval to speak, though he did not give it. There was silence. Finally, she said, "I haven't yet had the day, have I? So how can I say what it brings?"

"Good answer, daughter." Her father banged his fists on the table so that we all sat upright. He threw a scrap of bread at me, and all laughed as it hit me on the brow. He sipped something of his *agua da vida* and fought to keep it down. Yes, I was the object of derision. Yes, we were in upmost peril, but it was worth it just to see her smile and laugh. I saw in that moment that however hard the stony road and the burdens of the favelas were, they had not yet tarnished her smooth face with the bitter lines of vengefulness. Neither had they dimmed the spark of her pupils or sullied the whites of her eyes.

"But, if you had your perfect day, what would that bring you, Señorita?"

"Is there such a thing as a perfect day? For is a day not just a series of moments in the present." She looked at me with a grin. "What are you talking about, señor?"

"Excellent, daughter. You have it!"

"Señor does not understand, does he, Father?"

"No, he does not. You can see that he is weak, daughter, not sharp like you."

"I'm not sure if he's weak, Papa, but I'll find out one day and let you know!" She took off, kissed her fingers, and put them on to the door post as if saying a blessing to an invisible mezuzah. She was gone with a rapid, "Adios, señor," and I was empty.

I departed, for I didn't have the slightest interest in looms or yarn. I stumbled through the damp streets in my cassock. I realised we hadn't spoken fully of the danger of de Castro, for he was the reason I had gone there, but the coward in me didn't turn back. When I got back to my room to contemplate the smell of her, he stumbled up the stairs and knocked loudly. Entering, he shouted through with laughter in his wine-touched voice.

"How's the day, Father? Never would have picked you for a Benedictine!"

He must have seen me in the cassock, even though it is heavy at the hood, and I had walked bent forward like a man twice my age. Did he see where I went?

The word "Father" brought me back to the greater task: I must get my father and my sisters from Valencia to here or to London. Why didn't I go there? In his stubborn detachment, would push me away again? Is this a justification for my cowardice? Oh, my foolish and noble papa, if only you'd let me in.

He was baptised at the age of twenty-seven, in the terrible year before I was born. Yet he remained in every other sense a man of the golden age of the Muslim-Christian-Jewish concord. In fact, he was devoted to the study of the great Arab scholar Ala al-din Abu al-Hassan Ali ibn Abi-Hazm al-Qarshi al-Dimashqi. The Arab had compiled three wondrous works on anatomy and philosophy, and those books were what my father had a relationship with. The books had exquisite illustrations, and each vellum page became a family member. Father would turn them with all the respect of an angel dusting the throne of God. Every page was inked with brilliant gold, with blues and shining reds, and the colours flew off the pages to strike me, a child of six, like arrows. Each page described the intricate secrets of the mind and the metabolism, the complexities of the circulation. Each page inspired me to learn more.

From the profitable sale of woollen yarn, my father kept us safe in our whitewashed house in La Juderia, certain that the golden age was coming back as soon as the monarchs realised what they had lost. With his trusting mind, what else could he do? For time immemorial his forbears had walked these streets in peace, though it was impossible for him, when he became a man, to be who he was. So, he lost himself in study, and I lost myself in watching him. He would recite aloud, in Arabic, the wondrous words, as if by doing so he could keep the magic within himself. I didn't know what he was saying, but I marvelled at the sacred voice and followed the shapes and the circles, the dropped spirals and raised verticals and the carefully placed dots of the Arabic letters. Those letters became entrenched in my soul long before the coarser Hebrew or Roman ones did. Even at that tender age, they raised my thoughts skyward to the heavens and to God.

The books disappeared as quickly as they were produced. To be found with those texts in the house would be enough to consign the whole family to the flames. They were the work of the infidel; knowledge in our kingdom was then, as it is now, considered satanic. And so my father would hide them every day, sometimes under a floorboard, sometimes between two walls, sometimes beneath a floorboard, and sometimes in a tin box in a secret ledge inside the grand fireplace, as if tempting and defying the very flames.

*   *   *

I take a sharp breath as I realise my new and difficult situation. Will Sir Thomas come for me soon, or should I just leave? There is a sudden tightness in my chest, close to where Father's texts showed a beating heart. And I remember here, in my isolation, him comforting me with the words of the Ninety-First Psalm: "Together with him am I in distress, and I am safe again, sheltered beneath the angel's wings." Surely, Lord, he's right, and one day soon this madness will be over? You'll see to it, won't you, Lord? That men will be allowed different truths as the world changes, and if you will not give it to us in Spain, say you will give it to us here in Flanders or there, in the place they call England.

*   *   *

There was a loud knock on my door.

"Let me in, Father Vives! Give me sanctuary!"

"Go away!" What could I do, though, but let him in. He marched through, picked up the brass astrolabe, and started playing with it. I could smell the red wine on his black beard.

"Your friends, these Valldauras, you must take me to them this Friday," he said.

"I will not, Señor de Castro, be given orders by you." The hair on my neck bristled.

He walked to the front of me and giving me the astrolabe, said, "Nice Islamic piece, this. You'll find you have no choice, Juanito— if you and your people are true to your commandments, that is."

What was this some kind of blackmail? "I won't be lectured on commandments. Leave me."

He grabbed me by the shoulders, piercing me with his dark eyes. "Sir Thomas brought me to you for a reason, and he will know of your secrets. There will be grave trouble for you and for yours if you do not share them." I could feel his warm breath on my face as he went on. "As will the Duke of Alba and Louis de Praet." He turned to leave, but before he did so, said, "This Friday."

What could I do? Murder him and make it look like an accident? Don't laugh at me, diary! You know I've no stomach for a knife or a rope. I sat for a while and then knew what I had to do. I scribbled something, and when I could see beneath his door that his candles were extinguished, I went out in the cool of the evening and knocked again on the door of the tall house on the Verversdijk. In an instant, there she was: imperious, divine, dwarfing me as I stood on the step beneath her.

"Father's has gone to Utrecht and won't get back until Friday," she said, giggling. "I'm not permitted to talk to you."

I had to let them know that I would be bringing a strange guest this Friday and that we must not, under any circumstances, reveal who we are.

"Señorita, sweetness, you must give this to your father. It is imperative."

She looked at me with doleful eyes.

"Our future depends on it," I said.

She sensed my urgency as she grasped the note, making sure our fingers entwined, if only momentarily, and then turned away. Just before she closed the door, when it was too late for me to reply, she said, "I am not sure I can give it to him, for he cannot know that I have spoken alone with you."

The door was shut and bolted; surely. Surely, she would pass this note on to her father so that we could have Friday night dinner safely.

20 March 1523

It wasn't quite dark as we made our way to the home of the Valldauras on Friday evening. There was a heavy shower of cold angled rain in a day that had otherwise been one of intense sunlight. Álvaro used the squall as an excuse to pull me into the tavern; he had to, after all, give the Flemish girl a special message. He came down ten minutes later, ruffled and sweaty and laughing, I could not see the funny side of this. Later, we entered the tall house on the Verversdijk.

Senor Valldaura greeted Álvaro like a friend. I imagined the purse strings of the trap were finally drawing in, that my years of secrets and lies were over. The dining room smelt of fish and saffron and freshly baked bread. Those lovely girls had their hair down around their shoulders. Marguerite averted her eyes as I looked at her. Had she given her father the note? Did Bernardo know him? Had he been paid enough money to sacrifice me?

I was rigid as we sat at the long table. Bernardo had placed himself between his two daughters. The three of them sat there and muttered something unintelligible, then Marguerite left for the kitchen. Clara, Señora Valldaura, sat opposite me with a face ashen grey. I became transfixed by the purple and blue patterns of circles and spirals in her dress that gave the hint of an autumn bramble. Álvaro just sat there with half a smile.

Inge, who had long been the maid of the house, stoked and filled the fire with logs one last time. She then gave us all half a lemon, producing them from a silver salver as if it was something that had once belonged to God. Before she bid good night, she placed a double-handled silver washbowl and linen cloth on the table. With rounded cheeks, kind eyes, and auburn hair, she seemed impossibly pretty, but as she left us in silence, she turned to give Señor a nod that said, "I know you." This sudden and complete lack of faith overwhelmed me and became only more paralysing as the doors were barred. Who was upstairs? Were we about to hear marching boots, the clinking of chains? Startled, I prayed to God, albeit quite a hollow prayer. *Praised be the Lord, sovereign of the Universe, who keeps our secrets safe.* Only then did I become aware of green-eyed Nicolas dressed smartly in black velvet breeches and a white shirt with a cravat.

"Señor Vives," he said, "I want you to quiz you on Rabbi Moses ben Maimon."

I wished to talk about anything but the Rabbi-philosopher known as Maimonides. Inside, my gut was twisted, and yet there was something in me that loved this; there was something strangely comforting about being in the abyss. Álvaro watched my every move, his eyes like shiny pieces of black marble.

"Rabbi Maimon," I said, "talked about the oneness of God, what is called in Hebrew the *echad.*"

He replied with an angelic smile as if to ask, "What more?"

I stepped into the abyss. "That the true messiah, or at least messianic times, will one day come."

The very breath seemed to go out of the room: we were timeless, frozen in the moment. Clara Valldaura smiled. "Go on, boy."

"And you, Señor Vives, do you believe the messiah will come?" Nicolas, with his unblemished skin, asked.

The weak sun must have finally descended at that moment and another level of darkness arrived. We had gone into the Sabbath with no candles lit to welcome it. Although I was certain that I was now walking into the arms of the Inquisition, I couldn't stop."

"Messianic times will come."

Bernardo Valldaura stood, staring at me with his bulging eyes. "Let the axe fall. Do it quickly."

Marguerite re-entered from the kitchen full of smiles, a bowl of hraime—spicy fish that only a Spaniard could make.

My heart was pounding. Could they hear it? Could they feel it? Was Álvaro mentally sealing the deposition? Had Inge or the one from the tavern called the guards of de Praet? When would the rap on the door come? Out of nowhere, tiny Clara Valldaura brought out two candles as if she had manifested them from the ether. With a voice like a sparrow, she broke the silence with the Hebrew blessing: "Baruch atah Adonai eloheinu melech ha olam, asher kidshanu be mitzvotav vetzivanu le hadlik ner shal Shabbat."

"Blessed are you, our lord, sovereign of the Universe, who has blessed us with your mitzvot and commanded us to light the candles of Shabbat."

Two challah warm loaves, plaited to signify the binding of all our peoples, were then brought out. Bernardo threw salt on them, explaining that it was to preserve our relationship with God. There was a collective exhalation as we touched the loaves while the blessing was recited. I looked up, my face shedding every crease of fear, for I was at home. Then he leant towards me, kissed me on both cheeks, and called me "brother." Tears rolled down my cheeks.

Instead of pain and isolation, here was unity and strength, the absolute safety of family. Laughter erupted; shoulders fell back, and old songs were sung. If this life was soon to all be over, then at least I had this moment. After talk of our homeland, the warm nights and sweet-scented days of the Sepharad, I was myself again. "How did this happen?"

Álvaro looked at me like the secret rabbi of my childhood used to and, forgetting platitudes, launched into an attack. "Do you think you're the only one clever enough to live a secret life or that I'm not working for the same aim as you?"

I looked down, shame-faced.

"Is it you alone who is able to save our people?"

I began to think the unthinkable, that, together, we could achieve what I could not achieve alone. Álvaro studied the room, the sticky buds on the cherry branches in the vase, the silver candlesticks with crowns embossed on them. He seemed to grow in stature as he stood up.

"We must work patiently and stealthily," he said. "All can be gained now, but all can be lost. We need unity and faith."

We talked late of fast days and feast days, of establishing a secret synagogue that, they say, exists in Antwerp. Álvaro told his painful story of being a prized altar boy by day and of studying the Aramaic Talmud and Zohar by night. He spoke of an ancient rabbi who lived as a beggar, or at least pretended to, one who taught him secrets of Kabbalah even though he was far too young. But what he learnt he wouldn't reveal. There was the horrible abuse by a cardinal, Álvaro poked and prodded from behind with a rag in the mouth. He went jigging up and down while the cardinal sweated and snorted until Álvaro thought his sides would split. All the while, he recited the sh'ma, and from this suffering and that sh'ma came his chance.

"How so, Señor?" Nicolas asked, wide-eyed, and Álvaro didn't spare the details. To get away from there, the young de Castro, whose true name was Jacob ben Manasseh, bargained with the cardinal—with his own smooth body—for a commendation from England's Queen Catherine. The queen, virtually penniless now, took pity on him and sent him to Sir Thomas. Working for Sir Thomas, de Castro slowly won enough trust to vet me to be absolutely sure of my Christian credentials and that there were no vestiges of the faith of my forefathers. If I was to be tutor to the Princess, as Sir Thomas had already decided, there could be no shred of doubt.

"Juanito, will you go back for them, soon, for your family?" Clara asked me as she offered me the bread that smelt of home.

"Of course I will, when the time is right."

She covered her ears with her hands, and all at the table, with wax now dripping over the cloth and crumbs strewn here and there, looked at me as if a coward.

"When I get to England," I said, "I will provide them, and you too, with a new home in a safe place. I promise."

"Might be too late, boy," Bernardo said with a tired voice.

I knew this like I knew the veins of my own hand. I couldn't have it posed to me again. I stood up, throwing my arms around like a banshee. "Don't worry me with this. I have plans."

They looked, one to the other, Clara to Bernardo, Nicolas to Marguerite, and Maria to Álvaro. In that terrible moment, I felt a greater judgement than if the officers of Louis de Praet had handed me over to the Inquisition. I held my head in my hands and there was a painful silence in an otherwise beautiful place and time.

Álvaro came towards me then, put his strong hands on my shoulders, and whispered to me like the father I no longer had in my life.

"Enough. Just focus on your breath, which is the soul trying to speak." In that moment, I felt comfort and solace despite the terrible decisions I had made. Within the very essence of the souls, here together, was the sacred unity of oneness. I became aware that the thing I craved most was neither the breasts nor the tassels of this beautiful woman before me, but the freedom to share my soul with other loving souls, to regain for a short time that lost sense of family.

It was late and time to depart, but we would rather have stayed as the fire slowly died, for when again would we feel this? To delay our departure, I spoke a little more of the great plan to create a new world. Señor Valldaura whispered, "Are we are a hermandad? A brotherhood, a fellowship?"

How could we be anything but? Tonight, I had experienced true brotherhood.

As we left in black cloaks by the back door, I turned to him and, like a fool, said, "Señor, now that she is of age, may I court your daughter?"

With a backhand, he cuffed the top of my head so that my cap flew off.

"No, not my girl!" he cried. "Get, go on, blackguard. Valenciano, get out of here!"

Álvaro laughed at the spectacle and put his arm around my shoulder. He walked me home through the poorly lit streets. "Oh, Juanito, you've got a lot to learn."

"Not me, Álvaro. I'm not like that, but I should be with her. I—"

"Settle down, brother. What do we say every day, twice a day, as we pray?"

I looked glum, scanning the cobbles of the dark pavement. I felt like a scolded child.

"We say, "B'yi-to, in its proper time."

*   *   *

Here I sit by the light of this candle and wait, as I always wait, for the proper time. But I relive every second and commit it to memory. Whatever happens now, this magic evening will be mine. And, diary, if those filigree spirals are neither eyes nor ears, then I need to tell you that Álvaro is sitting there, as if in meditation in my own private room. For the first time, we have a witness. Shall we watch him, his eyes closed, chest slowly rising and falling, his face a harmony of something we do not understand? Shall I copy? This is like falling down a well blindfolded!

"Everything will change now," he whispers, face lit golden by a single candle flame. "I have seen it."

27 March 1523

Álvaro de Castro was not wrong, because everything changed. A few days later, when I arrived from vespers, there was a note on coarse parchment stuffed under my door. Was it from my love? It had a waxy, familiar diamond seal. Who could it be from but Louis de Praet? With sweaty, fumbling fingers, I pried it apart to find a lyrical poem in perfect Spanish.

'Malditos rumores, Senor Vives, existen rumores...

Murmullos, que se practican las maneras de Judios!

Con Corazon pesado, asin mi saludo a los desafortunados…
Que Los Judios, Los Judios, no son bienvenidos!

Fue pajaro de mal abuelo que un ojo me robo,
Con el otro, veo todo claramente, Si Senor.
Como agente de La Sagrada Inquisicion, se lo digo yo…
Sin ninguna duda, unica y pura, asin mi religion!

Se olle del platero golpeado, descuartizado, del Judio descubrido!
Y que de aquellos que volaron de sus nidos?… ninguna pluma se les dejo!
Suerte a los escapados? Pues no! Para nunca retornar!
Si, Judios nunca mas! Pajaros de mal abuelo a derrotar!
Que no haiga ninguna duda! Asin me despido…

Judios, Judios, No Son Bienvenidos!'

Damned rumours, Senor Vives, rumours exist.
Murmurs that the ways of the Jews are in our midst.
To those unfortunate beings, so my greetings must be…
To those Jews, those Jews, never amongst us to live!

A cursed owl, one of my eyes, indeed, he did claw.

But be warned, with the other, clearly, I see all, yes, sir.

I tell you as agent of the sacred Inquisition…

Without any doubt, supreme and pure, so must be my religion!

I hear of the bashed silversmith, body carved up… a Jew was exposed!

And of those who flew their nests… we left them without a feather!

Lucky, they escaped!… But they are never to return!

Yes, Jews never again, cursed owls forever forlorn!

I tell you, let there be no doubt… and so I leave you…

Jews, Jews, Never Again to Live!

Were the walls moving in, as if peering to read it, too? It all makes perfect sense: Hildegard checking all around my desk as she polished it with beeswax until the very grain almost came out of it. Young Van der Poel was impossibly quiet when not long ago he swathed around these rooms with an invisible scimitar. And Inge, who seems to know Bernardo Valldaura so very well. We must move fast. We can't wait for Sir Thomas's call, and Bernardo said that he'd come with us across the stormy ocean if he could get Spanish looms.

What to do? There was no comfort in my plans for my hospitals or in obsessing about Plato or even the Torah. I was all thoughts of escape, of taking her, at least, if no one else would come even if it meant absconding in the dead of night on a horse to Calais. I went out into the streets where I knew that, today of all days, I'd find her.

It was the festival of Purim, you see, and I knew it wouldn't pass without mishloach manot, a delivery of food to the poor. Dressed in my monk's cassock, I waited for them, pretending to swap clipped coins for beets and turnips, as if I should know what to do with them! They finally appeared with their wicker baskets, hair tied back and faces whitened with nightshade, and I made the men in the market laugh as I, the worshipful monk, had my eyes on the two girls in front.

"At least it's girls, not boys, that this priest is looking at," one said.

In an instant, they turned away and disappeared around a corner.

"Don't go, my love," I called in Spanish, drawing attention from the garlic seller.

I did my best to run, sliding on the wet mud, cursing a couple of drunks who got in my way. Running faster around the next corner, I caught them again. At a distance, she was stepping deftly over sacks of grain. I was closer now and so stopped dead because I couldn't let them see me. Men looked at them with eager eyes, and I wanted to smite them all with a scythe.

Everything became quiet as I saw that she was giving from her basket to the children and the beggar woman. I hid behind a moss-covered pillar that supported the market arcade, lost in the wonder of her, for where does she truly go as she gives freely from the basket of stored apples? Does she think of herself forever as a grape forming upon the vine, with all of life ahead and with no knowledge of the autumn? In my mind, the sunbathes her eternally in light, and she will never turn russet.

People must have thought it odd—the motionless monk with a tear in his eye, staring at a girl. But lost I was. What is it that you really feel? When the candle is out and your sister is asleep, do you hold the pillow close and imagine that it is El Toro Bravo? Do you place the fingers of your left hand between your legs and enter? Do you imagine that it is me inside you? Do you think that one day we may be allowed back home, that by a miracle of God we will be raising children beside that pool in my father's courtyard?

Someone slapped me on the back. "Wake up, Father!"

There I was, like a sleeping horse standing in the field, hidden deep within my cassock hood, and I became suddenly aware of a strange and distant murmur, like a hum. Something was happening in the distance, and the hum grew louder. It then became clear that here was a gang of five men joined by chains around the necks, moving forwards with heavy, wounded limbs. A cry of "Groote Pere won't save you now" rang out from a gaggle of town boys. These were peasant rebels fighting the Spanish oppression in their own right. I went to chastise those boys for taking the peasant hero's name, Great Peter, in vain. But I saw one of the boy's red hands, swollen from dragging vats of cold water from a deep well across the cobbles to wash carrots and beets, so I couldn't bring myself to say anything. The groaning of the men in chains was closer now, and I saw two girls on the other side of the street.

I ran up to the soldiers as the townspeople made a parting for them like Moses at the Red Sea. I stood there, holding up the crucifix around my neck, and shouted, "Stop in the name of Jesus!"

They did, and the church bells rang out across the wintry marketplace. One of the captives, with a bloodied head and dirty face, uttered, "Bless us, Father."

The soldier pulled his right hand across his sullied breeches, grabbed for the sword in its sheath, and yelled at me: "Ha! A Spanish priest tries to save these bastard souls. Out of the way, ingrate. It's for your king that we do this."

I knelt in front of him with my arms crossed over my chest and prayed out loud. "Dominus, dominus…"

I looked up, and the soldier's eyes now seemed crazed, but I could see that my words had hit him like a cross-current from a rocky point. I continued. "Lord, have mercy on their souls."

The second man in chains, the tiny one, cried salty tears, shoulders convulsing. "Father, help my wife, Claudia. Help my baby boy. They're in the village of Eelko, by the church. I beg of you."

The tall soldier put his sword back in the scabbard. He grunted deeply, spat in my face, and lifted his boot to my shoulder.

"You meddlesome priest, get back to your own land. I am losing patience."

He pushed his sodden toecap underneath my clavicle, and it went *snap*! I groaned but didn't yet feel the pain. He kicked me aside, and I was sprawled across the dirty street, not knowing whether to look up. I heard the marching continue away from me, and in the pain of knowing that this was to be these men's last few minutes on Earth, I heard a soft voice, like that of an angel.

"Father, here is some spring water."

I struggled to my feet, enmeshed in a sea of bodies. Someone drew my cassock back from my eyes, and I found myself looking deeply into hers. She didn't balk. Unflinching, she said again, "Father, you must drink."

"I didn't want you to see this, sweet girl."

"Drink." She held my head and brought a leather bottle to my lips as young Maria tidied my cassock until my body's shaking slowly eased. The soldiers with their captives had gone. Her face came into focus, and I felt that I had seen love itself.

"I was wrong, wasn't I?" she said. "I thought you were a weak man, like papa said, but I can see you are not at all." She smiled, and it looked like a spray of white lilies. She turned to young Maria as if to leave. I wouldn't let her, reaching for her wrist, but finding I had a sudden crippling pain in my shoulder and had no strength in my grip.

"Come, my love, to England. We will be safe there, and we can be wed.… Don't shake your head like that. Stay and listen for a minute. I'll meet you tonight at the ringing of the last bell of St. Donatian under the window of St. Luke, and we can take horses to Calais. Please."

She wrenched her wrist back so hard that my clavicle popped again.

"Señor, even if I secretly loved you, I wouldn't leave my family for anyone."

She turned, and with her arm in Maria's, started marching off, and then she stopped dead.

Had she changed her mind?

"Look at me and listen, Juanito." She called me Juanito, which in itself was enough to cure me of my broken shoulder, my broken heart. "Get to Douwe's, the apothecary, get calendula and arnica, and get the shoulder bound tight. Adios, my secret."

Did she really say that or was it the mirage of a dying man?

* * *

Back in my room, I try to work out what happened. How could I have left my own father and my own sisters? What ghastly, self-serving thing am I? For penance, if I can't get to England, I must get to Eelko, to a woman named Claudia and give her the money I had set aside for my escape to England. I determined that I would do it on the morrow. A pain pierced my left shoulder, and I knew I'd have to get to Douwe's soon, but that pain—it took me back to the place that I hate most of all, a place I can no longer avoid.

Here, there is a whitewashed wall, an oven always baking, a row of copper pots and measuring spoons that only a woman would understand; and here there are the cool hands and the scent of Mother.

"Do not show yourself," she would say as I made my way to school and attended Mass every day with a confused mind. I held on to my urine all day until I got home and rushed to the courtyard and urinated for two minutes, the waters gushing out of me and smelling like a drain. Why not show myself? I asked one day and then found out why. Miguel Fernandez declared it to the entire school.

"Here come the filthy Jews."

However many Hail Marys I said or how many times I genuflected and praised the Lord Jesus Christ, I was ever more regarded with suspicion, ever more rattled and bullied. "Jew scraps" were held down; I was kicked around the grounds like an old leather ball. I vowed at the tender age of thirteen that I would fight the bullies and expose them, that in time I would see that the wrongs were righted.

Nevertheless, in my family group, in my closed circle, I was not bullied. In fact, I was known as El Señorito sin Reglas, The Little Lord without Rules. I led my gang of rascals, La Pandalla do los Vives, through the streets and to the quay of old Valencia. Moshe, known as Miguel, and Elijah, known as Enrique, would run to the Passé Caro and the Calle del Barco, always behind me, and I panicked when they raced to my shoulder. I determined there and then that when I was grown, I would never run behind. I could not perform, with my east-west hips and backwards spine, the cartwheels, back flips, somersaults, and twists that brought the others into the very heart of the quayside's deep waters. On those days I would advocate fishing at the end of the quay and then, quickly bored by our fruitless endeavour, we would climb slowly to the tops of the towers and declare ourselves kings of the city and, on brave occasions, kings of the Jews. I would crave to sit on Father's knee, and sometimes he would let me. I truly felt like the King of the Jews. Father would tell me about the great Moses ben

Maimon and the thirteen principles of faith. He would get lost in the telling and mother would continue. She came from knowledge, and however hard he studied, he could not escape the fact that, first and foremost, he came from wool and commerce.

"First, my son, there is the knowledge of the mind, and second there is the knowledge of the soul." In her telling, something awoke deep in my spirit, and it was there that the will to learn, to be recognised for my learning and to disperse the truth of the Torah to a deaf world, was born. How, though, was I to be recognised if I was a Jew? My dilemma arose, my struggle and my conflict. I vowed to fight it all my life. I would not let being a Jew hold me back. The world would hear the voice of a Jew but would not know it until we were safe.

The diary speaks to me: What happened next, Juanito? *Delve deeply, revisit it. Find the strength.*

All right then. All went well until the summer of fifteen hundred and four. There was an inquisition. There are those who go missing, but I hardly saw it, blinded by my parent's love. At the age of twelve, it all changed.

*   *   *

There are muffled laughs and jokes along the way, but I know this is not a day for laughing, and for once I do not lead. At the front of the monastery of San Cristóbal, we take our stand. The priests stand on a raised platform, with the hated cardinal bedecked in red, bejewelled in gold from the New World and pearls from deep inside Asia. There is an audience of four hundred townspeople—students, merchants, holy men. There is a drum roll, and then, helpless and hapless, six men and four women are brought before the priests. Each has a chain of iron around the neck; each has a shaved head and a towering hat known as a sanbenito and is wearing a white tunic with a yellow Magen David on the chest. I become dizzy and almost fall. This could easily be my own mother and father, my cousins and the sweet townspeople of La Juderia.

In an instant, the drum rolls cease and the cardinal, dressed in a hat fashioned at the gates of hell, takes over the proceedings. There is little that I can hear, but I make out some of the words: synagogue, Sabbath, Jew and the name, Rabbi Bahbout. I look up, startled. Bahbout? The quiet man who leads prayers in my cellar? Scanning the backs of these men and women, I see a man, sixty, stooped with age, a crease in the back of his neck. It looks like an axe wound and there is something familiar about its look. Then, Amalia March and Jacob March, my mother's sister and my sixteen-year-old cousin. This cannot be. Please God, if you exist at all, intervene and stop this.

"Blessed be the Father, the Son, and the Holy Ghost." With that, the accused men and women turn around, and in his face, I see the creases of the eyes and the withered mouth. But the eyes are still shining. I realise that I am looking at my own rabbi, the man who behind oaken doors blessed our courtyard with its ever-flowing fountain and its tiles of red and blue, the man who performed my own circumcision.

There is a chorus replying to the chorus of "Blessed be the fathers." The drums roll again and there is more silence. Thoughts spiral through my head; my forehead meets my left hand as a kite meets the earth. *Thud.* The fear in the air whizzes like flies in summer. I know this will not end with a penance and a warning. These men and women will be sacrificed to teach us all that this is now the era of fear. The cardinal stands up and speaks with a snarl.

"In the name of the Holy Father in Rome, of the children of Christ, I pronounce you guilty of Judaising. There is but one punishment that befits you all, the punishment of fire."

The nuns, the brides of Christ, smile and jump for joy. Then she looks at me, the one I fear the most—Sister Concepción. She looks at me with a sly sideways look that says, "One day this will be you."

I cannot go on, but the diary speaks again. "What next, Juanito?"

It is one week later. There is not a bird in the sky. Has the horror of what is about to happen frightened them away? There are nine stakes that have been raised overnight, bundles of sticks all around them. There are pigs' heads nailed to the stakes. Luis Velasquez, shoulders rounded like the dome of a minaret, is physically sick. I do not want to look but cannot turn my eyes away. Out they come, the nine convicted Jews. They are chained to the stakes, their heads next to the pigs' heads.

There are clouds of smoke and a groaning as Rabbi Bahbout, the first to feel the flames, tries hard to disguise his pain. There is the scream of Amalia and the smell of burning human hair, followed by the screaming of my cousin, Jacob, only a little older than my sister, Beatriz. Next is the terrible unified screaming, the Hebrew words, the licking of the flames stoked by the afternoon winds until that screaming becomes a chorus of death. I cannot avert my eyes or control my shaking. Moshe comes to me, puts his arm around my shoulder, and places his hand across my brow, but the smell of the crackling flesh reaches me still, and I can control myself no longer. My knees give way and I crouch, curled into a ball, speaking to the shiny cobbles. "No, dear God. No." I do not care who sees me. I look up as the last scream peters out and there is nothing but ash and the charred bodies chained to the stakes.

Now, from somewhere, somewhere deep inside my head, I can hear the words of the ancient rabbi. "Juan Luis Vives. Can you hear me? Our suffering is over. Now you must live."

But I must not listen to ghosts.

I am standing in the Plaza Mayor. I am twelve years old and Moshe, my cousin, touches the nape of my neck and tries to pull me away, but I will not be moved. A Sister of Mercy comes to me and points her walking stick against my left ear and says, "Get up, child." I obey her and hate myself for it. What can my face look like? Contorted and disfigured. She looks deeply into my eyes and says, "Learn well from this day."

I renew my vow. No one will know the truth.

Is it any wonder that I do not want to go back? Perhaps Catherine of Aragon, if I can befriend her and mould her daughter, could guarantee me safe passage there so that I can bring my family to England? Although it may still be a secret life, surely it would be a safer life? In the future, if it's true that the king is more flexible than ours, then there is hope. And if England is not safe, perhaps a new Jerusalem lies in the New World?

* * *

And so, we wouldn't go to the tall house after the letter arrived, even dressed as monks, for who was watching us and who would take a bribe for giving false evidence? Every step we took had to be a step in the right direction, had to be witnessed by the right people in the right places, for who knew when we might need an affidavit? But a new thrill coursed through me, for I was getting closer to her, and I knew that on Thursdays she went to the Graskampf tailors on the windy street known as the Konewinkel.

I found myself there, searching for lace to send home to my sisters. Finally, she arrived with the ringing of a bell above the shop door. She wore crimson and black, hair in a neat hood, and her mother nowhere to be seen.

"What chance, Señorita!" I said. "What are you looking for? These are beautiful. Feel them." I grabbed a silk scarf and put it into her hand, making sure I touched her soft fingers as I did. She chuckled as I asked her, "Will you let me buy you that one?"

"No, you cannot, Señor Vives."

"Please, it's Juanito."

"No sign of your suave friend today?"

Why must she mention him? Did I not exist in my own right?

"Forgive me, my lady, but what is in the recesses of your heart and soul?"

She looked at me as if she thought me insane, which very possibly I was.

"What nonsense! What a question!" She thought for a moment. "But I can see you've thought long and hard about it. I'm here for a new gown."

I was mesmerised by the long hair peeking from her hood, her piercing dark eyes.

She blushed and continued. "I am for my parents, for my sewing, my cooking... my faith in Jesus." She said the latter very loud. "I'm... for my sister and my brother." She stumbled over her words, so I stopped her with a finger to her lip, took her into a quiet corner, and spoke in Spanish.

"No, Marguerite. What are you really for in your heart and soul?"

Did she realise that I was asking as if my future depended on it? Then her breathing changed as her voice became enchanting, like the voice of God in female form.

"I am for integrity, for what is real and what is humane. But I think I am mostly for love."

"I, too, am for love," I replied, taking her hand.

"No," she replied, "what are you really for?"

"Yes, first I am for love, second for my people, and then for my learning and my teaching, for spreading the truth of the word, not these horrible lies."

"As I thought," she said. "You are for you."

"I am for me?"

"Yes, before your family. You are for recognition, for fame."

Could she see into the recesses of my soul? As I'd tried to understand what was truly her, she had exposed what was truly me. I wanted to scream, "No!"

"In this precious moment, I am for you, my sweet," I said. "Can't you see that?"

She shook her head. "Yes and no. I still think mostly you are for you."

"But if I could sweep you away to a magic land, to a safe place, then I would."

"Then what you will not do for your father you will do for me? Fly, señor. Fly!"

"One day I will just do it. I'll prove it to you. I promise!"

Her mother, sister, and their two whippets entered the shop. Clara called in her high-pitched sparrow voice, "Marguerite, where are you?"

What could I do but hide behind the acres of linen, scrambling along the floor to the back door. Marguerite was all giggles, and Maria clearly saw that something was going on and spoke to her quickly in Flemish so that her mother would not understand. I squirmed my way to the door, the giggling of the shop girls seeming like a hive of bees chasing me down.

I ran all the way back to my room, where I found Álvaro in a sea of inks and quills. I told him what had happened, and he laughed as roughly as an English sailor. "You should play her like a lute, not attack her with questions like, 'What are you for?' "

He began teaching me from his repertoire of lovemaking skills, for I had been stuck in the safety of books all these years, suppressing the thing that I needed most of all: love. First, he showed me how to move towards a woman so she would get a scent of me and ache for me to get closer. Next, he showed me how to pull back at exactly that moment to keep her guessing. When she thought all was hopeless, I would calm her and make her think I was the gentlest, most misunderstood thing on Earth. And when she was alone and frightened, I would comfort her with a "shhh" and a gentle kiss.

Who is the master here? Does it really matter?

Later, he removed himself to his room and bolted the door. There were muffled tones, sacred words. I pressed my ear to the hard oak-panels and strained to hear, but I did not recognise the words. Was it Aramaic, the language of the Zohar and the Kabbalah?

As I sit here, tired, with the candle burning very dimly, I ask myself what is his mission, his true purpose.

30 March 1523

Early the next day, just as the sun was up and the spring pollen was in the air, I travelled to Eelko. After asking at the marketplace, I found Claudia with a son, Zeek, perhaps three years old. He sat on the back step of the cottage, playing with a wooden soldier. As I approached, he looked at his front gate as if expecting to see his father.

"Where's Papa?" he asked. "Have you got him, mister?"

How I wished that I had, that I'd come here to bring his father home, or at least his body, which had been thrown into a pauper's grave. I think he somehow knew that his father was not coming home, now or ever. I sat with them, mostly in silence, until Zeek's shallow breathing changed, and he started telling me about his toy soldiers, the ones that would one day fight and defeat the Spanish. I gave Claudia what little coin I had left from the silk purse of Sir Thomas More.

"If you need me, go to the tall house on the Verversdijk and ask for the teacher, Master Vives." I kissed her stunned cheeks and bent down to kiss the boy on the head and was gone.

I found myself back in the cold and bleak lecture hall. Sadly, it was time to discuss Leviticus, with all its "you shalls" and "you shall nots." Johannes Van der Poel, pockmarked face and blond hair, stood up, tall as a sunflower.

"I've got one for you now, master. A tricky one. You shall not be a Jew in the Netherlands. Should we add this to the list of commandments?"

"My, what a strange question. A relevant one, though, now that you're celebrating a Jewish Sabbath with Jewish friends. Doesn't it say in this very book that we must make the foreigner welcome?" It was then that I broke into a stammer. "Is it not na-na-tural for one to sp-sp-end one's free t-t-time with the people who come, not only from one's country, but also from one's hometown?"

He pinned me with a cold, confident stare. "Actually, I heard that the Valldaura family is from Toledo, not your hometown, and yes, we must make them welcome unless, of course, they are really furtive Jews trying to persuade others to join them. You've been taking de Castro there to persuade him to join them. Even a maid can tell the difference between Hebrew and Spanish."

Is it Inge or stocky Hildegard? Do they hide behind the heavy drapes or underneath the stairs? Are they really trained emissaries of Torquemada and the auto-da-fé?

I dismissed class, but the dizziness and the shaking sent me to the cold, stony floor. Thankfully, this was just a petit mal and I got up, stumbling back to my room. Then it began again, the same uncontrollable shaking in my toes and twitching in my fingers. Then my forearms and knees started. My head rapidly rotated left then right, and I heard groaning, but I was not making the sounds.

Sometime later, long enough for the fire to die, I woke in the darkness. I crawled to my bed and saw in my shiny brass mirror the bruising around my eye and the ten years on my brow that hadn't been there that morning. I felt like a driven nail, hammered time and again into the brick wall. I denied it, but eventually gave in to the solitary pitiful thought, *Why me? When will the good Lord take this away?*

An hour later, I was asleep again but was awakened by Álvaro, shaking me furiously.

"Up, Juanito! There's no time. You have to go. Señor Valldaura is accused and arrested and taken in chains. Quick. Gather your things."

There were voices outside the window, a troop of men.

"I have to go," Álvaro said.

I jumped up, dazed.

I tried to put you on the fire, cursed diary, but the cursed fire was cold. Then the banging on the door came.

*   *   *

Well, diary, if I'm still writing this, back in the cold sarcophagus of my silent room, I must have survived? Survived, perhaps, but I'm barely able to scribble. Why's that, you ask? Because the nerves and sinews in my fingers are stretched and tremble even to hold the quill. And how about the dislocated shoulder, the same one with the broken clavicle, now strapped close to my chest that throbs like a badly infected tooth. If I move it, I experience waves of pain that have me ricocheting to the floor. Oh, and there are the blue bruises that travel all the way down to my elbow. That's why, diary.

Do you remember how I bound you in cloth and threw you over the bookcase and lifted the board quickly to put you there before the bashing on the door? Did you hear me get the identical diary from its hiding place? Did you hear the murmuring of de Praet, who was outside the door with his glassy eye and diamond badge? Did you hear the laughter of de Castro?

Welcoming them with a calm smile did nothing to warm their hearts because they tied my wrists behind my back with rough ropes that bit so hard into my tender skin that the marks are still there. They marched me through the streets in front of my students and their wealthy fathers, just like the peasant rebels I'd seen a few weeks earlier. I was dragged up the steps where I'd once engaged Sir Thomas More. Where was he now? Wasn't he supposed to come for me?

Once inside, I was shoved down the long corridors from one chamber to another and finally cast into a large cell that smelled of dampness and decay. There was no sunlight, no window, and the only sound was the distant cries and groans of other captives.

Gradually, in the quarter-light, one by one, their faces took on form. There were two aldermen of the city and the Count of Flanders sitting behind a table. The door opened again and in came the wasp-like Louis de Praet. One man stood behind me, like an ogre; he had a leather mask on his face. I could hear his heavy breathing, and I could smell his unwashed beard and putrid breath. With one hand, he held the ropes that bound my arms together, and with the other he held a lit torch.

Their faces, poorly lit and gnarled, were more frightening than the faces of the gargoyles on the churches. One broke the silence. "You have betrayed us."

The man behind wrenched my arms higher until my shoulders cracked and jerked forwards. I yelled, "Please, sir, do not... hurt me... more. Please. I have not betrayed you."

De Praet sat back and laughed. My eyes were adjusted now. He was wearing a dark tunic with white-ruffed collars and sleeves and a silver chain of office. He peered with his good eye, as if scouring my soul. Then there were words, rapid like drumbeats—hard, hammering words. With Bernardo Valldaura, I had been accused of Judaising, and like Socrates before me, of corrupting the youth of the city. I took small comfort that I was in good company. I was commanded to explain my Friday night visits to Verversdijk and my recent absence from Mass. Each question was accompanied by a yank upwards of the rope and a brush of my beard with the torch flame until the air was filled with the foul stench of burned human hair. I hardly caught the words that followed. Why did I encourage free thought in my pupils? How dare I discuss the contradictions of the bible. What was the nature of my friendship with de Castro, the page of the Cardinal of Burgos? Had I been Judaising him? Why publish anti-Christian manuscripts?

I was strangely calm in the fate that had befallen so many of the children of Abraham. I felt the soft, warm hand of my

Aunt Amalia on my left shoulder, and I swear that I smelled the bergamot and rose she always wore. Next, I smelled the sweat of my cousin Jacob, with whom I would run to the end of the Calle del Barco and jump into the shining waters. As with all who had gone before, they went to their fates confessing loyalty to the king and to Jesus Christ, but it did not save them. I felt compelled in those moments to sanctify their memory and confess to everything. But another yank of the rope pulled my left shoulder clean out of the socket, and the pain ran up to my skull and down to my fingers until I was sure that I would convulse. Sadly, that release did not come. A bucket of icy water was thrown over my face as my interrogator yelled, "Talk!"

My heart changed. I would not confess. If this was to be my end, I would not consign others to the flames. I denied what was at my core, the faith that gave me meaning and made me whole. The pain subsided into numbness. Was I suddenly accompanied by the angel of my aunt, who took away my fear? I had to safeguard the family Valldaura and Álvaro de Castro, if he was still on my side, and in this moment I thought of the Viveses of the old Juderia of Valencia, going about their daily struggles in a world more difficult than this.

What could I do but lie? New Christians celebrate the end of the working week after evensong on a Friday. It's what we've always done. Whom does it hurt? Is there a better night for a long drink than a Friday night, with the university in recess on Saturday? We sang songs in Spanish, of course, but perhaps some Hebrew crept in, for our great-grandfathers may have been Jewish long ago.

"I am sorry for their sins," I said, "and though I do not ask you to forgive them, I ask that you do not hold us culpable for their sins and for what they taught us. I have been visiting the Valldauras to teach them Flemish and French so that they might employ people in this struggling town. My mother was Clara's cousin, and both women were baptised before a priest long before the edict of Ferdinand and Isabella. Call us what you like—conversos, marranos or Nuevo Cristianos—we are not Jews, but servants of Christ. What anti-Christian document have I ever produced? My latest work is a translation of St. Augustine called *City of God!*"

Louis de Praet got up. "Put him in the basement cell. Take him away!"

Were all my words meaningless? I yelled an almighty, "No!" as the pain returned, and I was dragged down stairwells into the bowels of the earth. The ropes were finally taken off, and I was thrown into a new cell where there was moss and water running down the walls, as well as the stench of corpses, of piss and vomit. There was a distant groaning, as if somewhere near someone was slowly being starved to death. A torch lit the darkness, and for a moment I could see inside—straw in one corner, a bucket in another, and a pile of bones that something was crawling on.

The door was slammed shut and then all was darkness. I stumbled to the straw and collapsed. What had I done? With the promise of England, I had allowed an imposter to lead me. I cursed de Castro with his double-talk and Johannes Van der Poel, who trapped me with you, diary. I cursed love itself for weakening me and opening the door to my prison cell. I tried to cry, but tears would not come. I uttered a prayer, Adon Olam, and found comfort, convinced that my soul would soon be with my mother and my cousin and my aunt.

There was no sense of time in this living death. I was there perhaps two days. A half-loaf was thrown into my corner and water placed by the door in a rough wooden bowl. Sleep found me periodically, giving me brief solace, but then the pain from the burning chin and the dislocated shoulders woke me. At last there was the sound of boots, and I struggled to my weakened feet. The door swung open.

"Vives, it is time."

They helped me up the stairs, blinded as I was by the light of the fiery torch. I was led back to the hall, where six of them sat on cushioned velvet chairs, a table full of wine and hogsheads before them. I stood there, impatient for the onslaught.

"You give a good account of yourself, Juan Luis Vives." Was there a hint of sympathy in de Praet's tone? "Your intellect has a growing renown." He looked to the others, some of whom nodded, while others shook their heads. "You're not frightened of challenging the greatest minds of our age. We are no match for you there." He was honest at least. "Our sons have learned much from you. Look at Van der Poel, as an example. What a clever lad. He gave you this diary, yes?" He slapped it on the table. "As if you'd go for that trick! Seems you just filled it up with the Book of Psalms and praise for St Paul."

I was jerked upright by the pummel of a sword. De Praet continued. "These friends of yours, it is true, bring employment to the slowing city." His tone changed, and I braced myself. "But make no mistake, our lot is with the king of Spain. This city is not Venice, where anything goes." De Praet buzzed around the room, flapping his arms, muttering into his thin beard. Then he returned to me, and his eyes seemed like bulbous tubers. "But no, we are not Spain. We are Flanders. They don't own us—not fully, not yet."

I breathed a long sigh of relief. I remembered Mendoza of Ghent, whom they'd sent back to Spain. Would they spare me?

"It's confinement to your rooms for one year. You are to have no contact with these Spaniards except de Castro, the cardinal's envoy, and Sir Thomas's man, who must stay by you at all times."

Confinement? Sir Thomas's man? Thank God for Sir Thomas.

"You can continue to teach, but no more talk of this nonsense— what men learn from the beasts or from other faiths. No talk of your pathetic tolerance. Now go."

It was over. I could breathe, and as I made for the door, Louis de Praet, with something of a glint in his one good eye, called me back, whispering, "Vives, I have tried the Inquisition, but I have no stomach for it for now, so I'll have a book for this in praise of my humanity."

"Of course. Your humanity, sir. Anything."

"You might not think I have any, and you might be right."

"No need to explain, Master de Praet. It's already done."

And so, I find myself at my desk. The guard is outside. Hildegard the unsinkable brings me an abundance of food. She checks that no one is looking and pinches me silently on the cheek. Can I trust her? Can I forgive her? Is there anything to forgive? My right hand can barely function and my left hangs listless.

In the cloisters below, young men play games with wooden skittles, and blackbirds sing songs of freedom. *Pink pink. Pink pink pink.* But my own heartbeat and my own song are now nothing but a murmur. The old questions come back. Where is the danger in us? Where is my family when I need them the most?

I remember in the agony of self-pity that this isn't all about me, for what of Bernardo Valldaura. Where is he? Did he survive? And where is Álvaro?

* * *

I was grateful that I had my wounds to nurse and my dressings to change, albeit one-handed. Hildegard dropped me a vial with oil of hypericum that she snatched from between her massive bosoms so I could clean my wounds. I burned the old linen bandages, as an old Morisco once taught me to do, and replaced them daily. Then I was lost in the silence. There was no word, no letter, from the tall house, not a glimpse of de Castro.

At the end of the third day, he breezed in, as healthy and quick as a young buck. He kissed me on both cheeks and stood back to look at my face and shoulders. "Not as bad as I had thought," he said.

"What the hell are you?"

"Quiet, Juanito." They hadn't suspected him of being a culprit, with his letters from the cardinal and Sir Thomas. "It was all explained by your obsession with Marguerite and the promise of what was between her legs."

"You take me for a fool," I replied.

"Such a fool to remind them of England's response that you were to be taken to trial with a sanbenito on your head?"

"What could England do, even when she is married to Spain?" I asked.

"Sir Thomas might take his trade elsewhere."

"Tell me, what of Bernardo and the groans and cries I heard in the other cells?"

His face became white like a sheet, and he held his head in hands. "Fat-fingered Bernardo, greeting his interrogators with silence, was stretched upon a rack until every joint in his body cracked and popped. It was the driving of a wood chip into his fingernail bed that got him to open his mouth, but in a cry only. Then he was bound in rusty wire chains, left to die in a corner of a cell."

"What happened next?"

Clara Valldaura marched out of confinement, threatening her guards with a sharp knife, and drove a cart down the streets yelling to all to get out of her way. With a sack under her arm, she strode up the steps of the Princenhof and demanded to see Louis de Praet. There, she cast a sack upon the long table where I had sat with Sir Thomas not so long ago and threw him the ruby rosary she had brought all the way from Toledo.

"Am I not a Christian woman?" she screeched.

He appeared unmoved until she took out the silver cross with four diamonds. "For the sake of your humanity, give me what remains of my husband and my daughter's betrothed or cut my throat with this now!" She handed him a sharp knife, like an Arabic dagger.

She was given a twisted ball of old limbs and a body that somehow connected them. In the back of the cart she took him home, where he now lies.

"We must visit him!" I yelled, realising that he was my gaoler. "It is a commandment."

What can I make of this? How much is truth; how much is a lie? I hate him for a minute and then he recites an ancient poem, a quote from one of our great Spanish rabbis, until I fall asleep at his side. "Choose your friends from the good at heart, those who grew up in waters of love and nobility, those who bring joy to friendly conversations and songs, those who are always truthful in good and evil."

I awoke with a start and asked out loud, "Where is she and what is she feeling now?"

Clara called me her betrothed, no? There will be a wedding under a chuppah, the breaking of the plate, and I'll share my bed with her when the year is finished. For now, I find peace by losing myself in the past, for the present is torture and the future unknown.

*　　*　　*

The University of Paris welcomed me after fleeing Valencia with my father's endowment. Nights were red, vivid, sometimes crimson, drunk with rich burgundy wine. We sat up all night, reciting verse, challenging one another. Le Maverick, l'inconformiste they called me for challenging Aristotle, Plato, the pope. We strode through the dark overcrowded streets, sang in St. Germaine, and caroused the nuns of Notre Dame, tempting them with flesh, promising them danger.

Her name was Adeline, the flower girl from Montmartre, rich with the scent of the land and a glint of country fields in her blue eyes. We spent the nights in a tiny, moth-eaten garret, plunging into one another's bodies like we were diving into the ocean. There was a pregnancy, talk of a marriage, and then such bleeding that I never thought possible. Mama's words came back to me. "Do not love them, son. Let them love you."

I blocked the blood and the tears, thinking it was a weakness to suffer so. In the shame of my tears, I found the energy to become brilliant, and instead of diving into her body, I dove into my reading and spoke at the university until I got noticed, first by Erasmus and Queen Claude. She was young then, so I taught her to read bibles in French and Hebrew, and one day I introduced her to a new word: humanism.

"There is no greater thing than the study of oneself," I said. "There is no greater thing for man than education."

She still quotes me, and I wonder if the English sisters I met there, Anna and Maria, still quote me also, safe in their homeland of England. Anna, the precocious younger one, sitting on my knee, never tired of asking questions.

"How can the pope know he's God's advocate on Earth? Why do people believe that? And why is no one brave enough to stand up to a king. Are they too frightened of losing their precious lives?"

We whittled away for hours, her black eyes burning into me. They were unafraid, those eyes. It was as if they saw a very big picture indeed. She expressed an idea repeatedly. "What sense is there in being another forgotten woman in a world where so many women are forgotten? Better to risk everything than to be forgotten."

She ate up the Spanish I taught her, and although I lusted for her, I could see she was too young and too ambitious for me. The professorship at Louvain manifested, and I left the French queen with la petite Boleyna. In my confinement, I do not expect to see either again.

21 April 1523

The days of my confinement turned into weeks. We weren't allowed to even open the windows. As the days grew longer, the stench of the room grew stronger so that even thick-skinned Hildegard pinched her nose as she entered. Álvaro, calm but distant, urging patience, accompanied me on my way to the lecture halls and gave me faint reassurances that Bernardo was recovering. Like me, Bernardo's wounds were healing, and he was getting stronger. This was some relief, but now that Marguerite was old enough to be courted, how could I survive this incarceration?

When I least expected, it seemed that hope became real. This is how it happened. It was a sunny day. All I wanted was to open the damned window, and then I heard shouts from the guards in the street below. I remained oblivious to it, forcing my attention into stacks of parchments and books. But there were footsteps on the stone stairs, and without warning there was a rap upon the door.

There he was! It was the mighty man, the great fish, the Englishman, Sir Thomas More, but with a face more solemn than Yom Kippur. There was no smile, just the sense of something new, something that needed to happen fast. Álvaro woke up from his chanting, ruffled.

"Good God! What is this? Caritas Christi. Open the fucking window."

"I can't open it, sir."

"For the love of God." He walked across the room and dislodged the metal bars that had been placed across the window. He opened the window and threw the bars into the street. He didn't even look to see where the bars fell. He came back into the room, ignoring the shrieking in the street below, and said, "That's better. How is the great scholar and his treatise for *The Education of a Christian Woman?*"

"*The Education of a Young Woman*," I said, correcting him.

He raised his left eyebrow as only he or Álvaro could. "Vives, for that's what they call you, I believe, don't mess with my semantics when your life is dangling by a thread." He looked at the bandages that held me together, peered at my pale face, and shook his head. He looked to Álvaro for answers. "What on God's earth happened? Surely it's not true that he lapsed into his old ways?"

Álvaro looked him in the eye. "No, sir, it's just a cursed rumour, a lie. He simply tried to court the daughter of another Nuevo. There's nothing of the Jew left in him."

"So why the hell this incarceration in his own merde? That's a punishment fit only for Martin Luther and his cronies." He threw the back of his fist against a tapestry and stuck his head out of the window. There was a growing audience below, but all I could focus on was the spring air that smelled so sweet. I moved towards the window to join him and instinctively took a mighty breath. Sir Thomas spoke in a voice that would have bettered Zeus himself.

"For the love of God, what has this town done to this man?" When he had an even greater audience below, he bellowed, "Hopeless fucking Flems, imprisoning this one, the only one among you with a mind for the future world."

"Please stop or things will get worse," I cautioned him.

"Don't tell me to fucking stop when I'm here to save you."

I rushed through an explanation, but it was nothing he did not know already. He strutted around my room like the courtroom lawyer that he was and then returned to the open window.

"You imprison him for visiting the house of a New Christian and for courting his daughter. What kind of a barbarous jack-in-the-arse puppet state is this?" He looked down at his audience and, gripping the sandstone window ledge, shouted, "Piss off, the lot of you!" He pulled the window down, charged around the small room, and I feared that he would swipe my mountains of papers off their shelves. Instead, he grew quiet and gentle, a bit like a father. "Let me tell you, Vives, that as a younger man, full of life, I tempered it. I spent four years at the monastery in Charterhouse. Every day was contemplation and meditation, but even there, in that most holy order, I was allowed to leave my cell. If that had not been allowed, my mind would not have grown. You must be allowed that."

He looked at me with those huge eyes, and I became aware of the milky complexion that could only belong to a man of the town, not of the fields. His words seemed like a kindly admonishment, for he knew all about de Praet and how he played the Spanish powerbrokers. It soon became clear that he could use English trade as a bargaining tool, for Bruges was waning with its silting river, and he could bargain with that.

"I will be back in three weeks," he declared. "I expect you to be ready. Cardinal Wolsey has a place for you at Corpus Christi in Oxford. I have great things in mind for you."

Lost in my obsession, my love for Marguerite, I had forgotten that.

I pulled him back by his left shoulder as he charged towards the door. "Sir Thomas, I will consider this, but there are others in this town. I've left people behind before. I can't leave these behind now."

He looked kindly at me and then transformed into a gryphon about to take flight and strike me down. "Pish and tush. Stay here with *these* for a living death, bring them with you and have a future life, or don't mention them again. The choice is yours!"

I stepped back and my eyes settled upon Álvaro, who'd sat in the corner watching everything with a sly, otherworldly grin. What part of his master plan was this?

Sir Thomas looked deeply into my tortured eyes. "Vives, life is short and uncertain. Love comes and goes, and thousands lose their voices. Don't allow yourself to lose yours."

"But who will provide for me? And where shall I live?"

"As if I needed another excuse to ridicule you," he said with a shrill laugh.

I couldn't help but smile on the inside, for here was a new day and an escape. Here was a chance to make my mark on life.

"You'll live with my wife and me in London as our guest, and then you will be in Oxford. You'll be taken care of by the cardinal, for he's richer than the king as long as you stay on his right side."

A cardinal richer than a king? So, this was the world I was entering. I accepted the offer. I felt the breaking of my heart to be leaving Marguerite and her family at a time when they needed me most. I sat at the desk then and wept as he slammed the door and was gone.

I sit here with my magnifying glass, writing smaller script than ever. I left my father and my mother once, and now I am leaving those who love me and need me again. Perhaps I should go to Spain first and ask Sir Thomas for armed guards to bring my father and sisters to England. But I cannot face the fires, and so I pray. The strength does not come.

I begged Álvaro to write a poem from me to Marguerite. Couldn't he play a woman like a lute? "Let her know that I will be back for her, that I'll never forget, that the pain in my heart is like a knife."

There was a juvenile exchange of "You do it" and "No, you do it," but in the end he grabbed a sheet of parchment and began.

Later, it appeared, and I called the poem "Leaving Lament."

My love,
I know who I am,
Where I am going,
What I want for us. Have faith,

Steal yourself
Though I must leave.
I am not running but fighting.
El Toro Bravo, your faithful, your own.

Believe.
The day will come
In its proper time, the *b-yi'to*,
When I shall return, when we shall be one

In a heaven on Earth
As has been promised.
As our forefathers once said,
A peaceful place: *"Ha'shamayim el ha'aretz."*

And though today
Our bones may be broken,
The brotherhood is not crushed.
So, I tell you this: have faith, have courage,
for I love you.

Farewell my love,

JLV

What would she make of it? Would she hear my heart? He captured it and understood it.

I dedicated my *City of God* to the English king, but what else did I know of you, England?

Álvaro said, "They call London the flower of cities, where the streets are paved with silver and gold."

"I've heard that one before. Come on, what's the truth?"

"There's a magic there, a sense of the future, that these are the people we must nurture and cajole, however difficult and lengthy that process may be."

"I don't understand."

"All will be revealed, *B'yi-to*, in its proper time."

"Right, the proper time. All right, let's talk of King Henry then."

"He grows tired of his Spanish queen. He blames her."

"For what?"

"For not producing a son—one who lives. That he's only got one legitimate daughter. He thinks it's divine retribution."

"Funny how a daughter's life is worth less than a son's," I said. "What does he propose to do about his situation?"

"Juanito, our chance is in exploiting it, not in questioning it. We should get to know the king and the Protestants. We should try to move him in their direction."

I hadn't considered this. "You mean in the direction of a break with Rome?"

He nodded unconvincingly.

"Álvaro, the cardinal and Sir Thomas are all for Rome. They despise the Protestant cause."

I clutched the desk to steady myself. In Álvaro's plan, I was to play the clever little fish. And if my quest sounds abhorrent to you, my diary, remember that there is no greater abhorrence than the flames I saw in Valencia and the fears that haunt my people day by day.

The king coveted the wealth of monasteries, and unlike his counterpart in Spain, he had no wealthy Jews to plunder.

"And what of the Tablets of the Law and the folks who guard them?"

He was quiet for a minute, deep in thought. Slowly, he opened his mouth as opening a hundred-year-old jewel box, not sure what he would find.

"I have heard them say," he said, scanning my face for the trust he craved, "that there are secret synagogues in the purlieus of the city. Without question, there is a domus there, a house for captured and repentant Jews."

Fear and thrill coursed through my veins as he referenced the word "synagogue," a place I had longed for all my life. I, too, had heard of the Spanish and Portuguese merchants in London who lived as good Christians while adhering in their hearts to something far more ancient.

"What else?" I asked.

"There are English brothers and sisters who have kept faith alive some two hundred years since the English expulsion."

Mysterious as ever, he would not speak of their whereabouts. He merely said that England would one day have her own empire in the New World. In that empire, he told me, we could one day create a safe home.

He put an arm around me and said, "Juanito, it is not just your work. It is not just about your family, so don't take it all upon your frail shoulders. We are a hermandad, a brotherhood, a fellowship."

When the sonnet would be delivered to the door of the one I love, and when Sir Thomas returned tomorrow, I would be gone.

PART TWO

A NEW WORLD

Bucklersbury House, Home of Sir Thomas More, London, England

6 June 1523

The last day in Bruges was like preparing for the final day of Earth.

Soldiers, papers, and affidavits flew around the streets and across the courtrooms. I felt like I was watching children in the street scrambling for gold coins. The problem was that my liberty, my very soul's breath, was the coin. The officials were in and out of my room. The troll-like man with the stinking leather mask reappeared. He stood over me as I sat writing a pleading letter to Erasmus, to the English queen, even to the pope. When the activity had stopped and the silence of the deep night became overwhelming, Louis de Praet entered. He banged his fist on my table and demanded once more an academic paper in his name and let me go.

We had one night to organise it. Álvaro took the sonnet, and as soon as he left, I unstitched the pages from the diary and put it in my secret place. One minute, all seemed to me to be lost, yet in the next all seemed to be gained. On the one hand, I was cast into the abyss. What joy could I have away from the adopted family that I had come to love? On the other hand, there was hope that I could create a new world in a golden age.

It seems that God has given me a moment of peace. Here I am in this sturdy home in the middle of the city. Here I can breathe again. As I gaze out the open window and look across the knot gardens, I take in the scents of English roses and honeysuckle. If only I could pluck them and send them home.

I didn't think I'd see such a day, though, as I set out on the boat from Ostend.

It was the sixteenth day of May. The winds blew against the small sails and the creaking ropes. We rolled first this way and then that before a sudden gust threw us out of the harbour, like a stone from a catapult. That open ocean, though—what horror! The thunderous rising and falling of the waves crashed across the bow and spilled through the cabins. The men fought with the masts and rigging, but their shouting was muted by the storm until their work became like a telepathic movement, like the communication between a school of fish. Álvaro placed an arm around me inside the tiny sodden cabin, next to a crying woman reciting Hail Marys. Álvaro grabbed a post with his other hand, and we huddled together, humming *Adon Olam: Lord Eternal.*

The sky seemed to collapse into the ocean as it rose into the sky. Rain fell like arrows. Gulls hovered over us, shrieking. A strong westerly wind caught us, and we were forced into the stony harbour of Dover, in the lee of the wall of white chalk and flint. I said a blessing to every deity I knew: Mithras, Isis, Minerva, Cybele, Julius Caesar, even Jesus Christ.

The dizziness, the double vision, the ringing in the ears, the weak knees—these were with me a whole day later. But why were we in Dover, not London?

Sir Thomas, with his characteristic scratching of the back replied, "I've business in Canterbury that I'd like to share with you."

We mounted the stout English horses: Canute, Ethelred, Sigdur. I held the ropes for dear life with my right hand, my left bound to my chest. Faster than seabirds, faster than windstorms, we charged along the old Roman road and entered the city, scattering dogs and children. Along the uneven and noisy cobbled lanes, we trotted, slower now, as the passages got narrower. The timber buildings jutting across the street looked like gossiping old women with pointed chins. We pulled up by the east wing of the grand cathedral, with its wave of fine stonework and wondrous glass in blue and red and gold. The kind expressions and round faces of the monks were the perfect antidote to our journey. They led us through a maze of cloisters and grassy lawns. They sang, "Moreños, dark ones, Israelites, they're back!"

A new smell of a different kind of bread pervaded the candlelit passageways. We were truly in the beating heart of the church in England. We were shown to our cells, for that's what they were, with straw mattresses on the floor and a ewer of water. Here was the honorary brother of the king and the cardinal, lying in a stone coffin. But there was a peace and beneficence about him that I'd not before seen. Was this true humility? Was this peace that surrounded him the reason that he defended his church so strongly? Was this the thing he feared losing the most?

I settled down and tried to sleep, but I still felt the swaying of the boat. For comfort, I imagined that I was cradled in the warm arms of Marguerite. As sleep welcomed me, my door swung open. It was Sir Thomas, barefoot and dressed in his cassock.

"Come with me," he whispered.

We entered the main church, a vast, cavernous sea of candlelight, bunches of hops hanging by the pillars. A monk led us with a lantern up a stone staircase, and each step we took was worn in the middle with the tread of years. We were in the triforium, ringed with stone arches and gargoyles. I looked to Sir Thomas for reassurance but found none. We sat there for several hours until my buttocks were numb, listening to the chanting and then to nothing but the silence. He leaned over to me at last, touched me on the shoulder, and whispered, "Can you feel his presence? Can you see why I must keep the faith at all costs? The light of God lives here."

I nodded as a strange thought came, though I banished it. Should I record it here? But it won't leave. All right, here it is. I thought about abandoning everything and living like a monk, for who would challenge me or drag me from my bed at midnight to face false charges. It was only a thought, just a fleeting one, and thankfully it is gone.

The next day, at mid-morning, we waited in line with the pilgrims. There were a hundred at the shrine of St. Thomas Becket. Some were in rags, others in silks, but the tomb seemed to be a great levelling spirit, as if all clamoured to be equal before a higher power. It almost felt like idolatry. The place was getting to me, touching me, making me question everything.

Sir Thomas whispered, "See how even the king's greatest friend, his most favoured subject, can fall? But if God is with me, whom should I fear?"

I nodded and tried to reassure him with my eyes.

He continued. "Things are changing so very fast, and perhaps my time, like his, will come, and if it does, señor, then stay with me to the end."

*   *   *

Well, Juanito, if ever you read this in a future time, if all your hopes and schemes here have come to nothing—if you're living safe and old with Marguerite and a houseful of grandchildren and have forgotten the spirit of these people, then come back! Travel in your mind once more along this scarred and sacred road in England! Here were pilgrims moving east and west, bending to pray and singing songs that I didn't understand. There was a seething mass of icon-makers and penny-bakers, of shoe-girls mending the last of road-weary shoes, of wheelwrights fixing the wheels of less-than-sturdy carts. Men with long white plumes danced and jumped to the sounds of chopping sticks and a brass cymbal, all for a clipped coin or a clap and a cheer.

The day was long and warm, and everywhere Sir Thomas was greeted like a king himself. At the end of the long day, we arrived at the manor of William Owen in the town of Chatham. He fawned over Sir Thomas and then made directly for us, speaking loudly and slowly.

"My sweet Spanish gentlemen!" He poked me in the chest as if to see what a Spaniard felt like. "Be sure to remember us when you meet the gentle queen! Long life to you and welcome."

Was there healing in the smell of freshly cut grass and the gentleness of the evening sky? Nearby were haymakers in fields, working late. It was almost sunset as I walked through the rose garden. It looked so simple and so perfect, so very safe. Then the thought came back to me, and I wished that I had always been one of them, that I hadn't chosen such a tortuous and impossible task. I breathed deeply as if absorbing their energy, receiving it from across the fields. It felt for a moment as if I were in the bosom of my father's home, like I was six years of age.

At dinner, Abigail, daughter of Master Owen, sat on my left side at a long oak table, her breasts like a pair of milk buckets around her neck. She carried the spirit of the fields with her with her wheat-coloured hair and bale-shaped face. With an encompassing smile that swallowed me whole, she was the very fruit of the land.

"And how do you make a living, kind sir?" She laughed as she spoke.

I couldn't help but smile and laugh with her. I replied in my slow and heavy English. "With words, with books, with my mouth."

She tossed her long hair back and breathed deeply, heaving her bosom up in its red-and-cream dress. "I can see you are skilled with your mouth, sir."

Something stirred within me; something moved between my legs. The girl's father looked to me as if to say, "Take her and then you can really put our case to the queen." What was I to do?

"My mouth is not the only thing I am skilled with," I said with a grin.

"And your friend, the handsome one, is he skilled, too?"

"Not as skilled as his wife, who cut the tongue out of the last woman to touch him."

"I see that you want me all to yourself."

I stopped. It was as if a whiff of lavender hit me, and I was transported to the gentleness and scent of Marguerite. I stood up but realised I had exposed myself. Álvaro was in hysterics. Sir Thomas looked scornful. I had to stop myself, for there was one love for me and one love only. I made my excuses and left the table.

The next day we were off at dawn.

"Remember us to the queen," Owen said as we left. I nodded, but he wasn't satisfied. "And tell her, please, señor, that we are sorry."

"Sorry?" I said as we trotted off, but he had gone.

We moved on, passing ancient villages with strange names: Strood, Darenth, Blackheath. In the distance, the city looked like a broad swath, with a grey haze piercing its middle by what could only be a river. Nearer to the city were villages: Camberwell and

Kennington. We were storming, kicking up dust. Álvaro leant over to me and shouted above the din of the horses and the cheering.

"Have you ever felt this, Juanito?"

I turned and shook my head.

I got my first clear view of the city from Southwark near the great church of St Olave. There it was, London Bridge, with shops and houses so dense that the area was almost a town in its own right. My excitement was not thwarted by the smells of tanneries on the riverbank or the reek of horse dung, only by the begging children whose thin grey faces were so different to the ones we had seen on the road. Upon crossing the bridge, we were greeted by the distorted heads of traitors on poles. Surely none of them could belong to my own people?

After crossing the north arch of the bridge, we moved into the city with a clatter. Carts were stuck in the poorly paved roads—not paved with silver or gold. To our left side was a fish market with its small fishing boats and skiffs, some moored, others casting off. Men were on the streets, in the gutter, in the pavements, sharpening knives as flower girls traded and sang songs. A drunken woman bound by the hands, face down, screaming obscenities and thrashing violently, was carried off by four soldiers.

We trotted along streets with names like Corn Hill and Cheap Side. In the distance were the tall spires of St. Paul's Cathedral. To our left, the streets seemed to roll downward towards the river like unravelled ribbons. Then we were at Bucklersbury, the house called The Barge. And what a fine house! Three wings jutted from the timber-framed building like welcoming arms. As we walked through the wrought-iron gates, the grand front door was flung open. Four young women ran towards us, chased by a group of barking dogs and an older woman with a stick. With their arms wide open, they shouted, "Daddy, oh my daddy! Home at last. We missed you!"

I wanted to be among them; yes, in that split-second, I wanted it forever. The girls became slowly aware that there were guests in their father's party, one of whom they recognised, one of whom they did not.

"This is my wife, Alice." Sir Thomas introduced me to a short, plain woman who was mother, or at least stepmother, to his bounty. Her face was like a storybook, and each of her lines seemed to be a chapter for each of her children with Sir Thomas.

"And these are my daughters: Margaret, known as Meg, Elizabeth, and Cicely, and this is my ward, Anne Cresacre. And this is my stepdaughter, also Margaret." They all curtsied with no sign of a sly eye. He looked around. "And where's my boy, handsome John, huh? Must be away making sailing ships from sticks."

Was I right to think that here humility had found a way to reside among magnificence?

The supper—goodness me! It was the first of many alive with its many languages and poems in the great hall beneath a minstrel's gallery. If only Marguerite had been there beside me. If only Papa had been there, regaling them with stories and the words of the great Ibn Gabirol. One day, I pray.

There was a smell of something, rose perhaps, from the six-pronged siphon that drew a scent from a burning candle under an ancient pewter bowl. We drank from Venetian crystal glasses, red and blue, and ate from French tableware, dishes in green and yellow and patterned with snakes and eagles. Sir Thomas stood to carve the side of beef, and the rich smell of the roasted joint and the meat juices made my mouth water. There was no talk of fashions or cloths of gold, of courtly gossip. This was talk of commerce, architecture, and universities.

It was elder Margaret, dressed in dark blue that looked almost black in the half-light, who caught my eye. She had light brown hair, a full bosom, and two keen front teeth that protruded slightly. Was she seventeen, eighteen? And already with a gold and ruby ring. She leaned forward and asked me of Erasmus's translation of the New Testament into Greek. Should she undertake the same project and translate it into English? I was too pre-occupied with her to answer. *Has ever a woman been so alive?* I thought. Álvaro kicked me awake, but Sir Thomas had already beaten me to the answer: "Not if you want to keep your head, Meg. That is not going to happen in this land, never mind in this house."

She ignored him—what pluck! She looked at me and nodded, as if demanding my answer, which was, of course, "Yes."

"Erasmus has done a commendable job," I told her with a smile. She seemed completely unaware that she had a bosom. It was as if she thought of herself as a girl with a flat chest. I was lost in wondering of how long her breasts had been there, pert and ample, curving gently upwards. I got another kick from under the table and remembered my Marguerite.

"It is my heartfelt belief that only through the discourse of many ideas in many tongues that we may progress," I answered.

"Oh, he does have opinions, not just observations!" she said. "Do you believe the bible should be translated into English?"

Of course, diary, the bible should be available in English and Hebrew and Spanish and any other language, but I was not going to incriminate myself on my first night there. I replied, "The bible is revolutionary, Mistress More, for within it, men challenge kings, and kings challenge God."

"Roper."

"I'm sorry. Roper?"

There was a wave of laughter, Álvaro included. The laughter felt like a sudden gift of God, but it unsettled me. What had I missed?

"I am Mistress Roper, a very married woman, señor!"

Did I look disappointed? Relieved?

"Señor, are the English people not allowed to know that biblical heroes usurp biblical kings unless their particular priest sees fit to tell them?"

Thankfully, young Elizabeth More started singing an English ditty about King Harry. All laughed, but my respite did not last long. When it was over, Margaret struck again. "And what of Ferdinand and Isabella? To give us our queen, there must have been great monarchs of Spain, yes? To wrest the land from the Moors and the Jews, they must have been magnificent leaders, yes?"

I took a deep breath. Escaping from one fire, I found myself in another. "I'm very tired, my lady. I am sure they achieved much."

My avoidance fooled no one.

"Do you say that they were great leaders or not?" Margaret asked impatiently.

"Answer the question," Elizabeth ordered, a tooth missing in the upper right of her mouth.

"They have given us a daughter, the great Queen of England."

"Come on, Juan Luis," Álvaro chirped as if siding with them.

I went on, for what else could I do? "If they had united our country, then they would truly have been great monarchs. But with every victory, of course, there is a loss."

"This sounds rich," said Sir Thomas, scanning the faces of his daughters. "The Spaniard's true colours are about to be shown. Listen."

All at the table leaned forward as if drawn by a puppeteer from the minstrel's gallery above.

"The Moors, not the ones gathered here at the table, of course, but the Arab ones," I laughed. "They taught us much about science and astronomy. Medicine, too." I was not brave enough to mention the achievements of the Jewish people. "Our nation, which once consisted of many nations and many voices, now consists of just one. You see, I am for many voices, a pluralistic world. To banish these people and others does not make Spain great, but makes the nations to which they are banished great."

"I sometimes agree," Margaret said. "In *Utopia* we would tolerate the Moors and the Jews, would we not, father?"

"We would indeed, but we are not living in a utopia, my child." Clearly, his views had shifted since he wrote his great work. I looked at him with a quizzical glance. He turned away and uttered, "Here we send them to the Domus Conversorum." A chorus greeted his last words as the girls sang, "To the Domus, to the Domus, we'll send them to the Domus."

"What is this Domus?" I asked, already knowing the answer from Álvaro.

"The house to where we send them,
To live for all their days,
Punished for blood-libel,
And their crimes against His ways."

Elizabeth gave a stronger voice to the sentiments. "Unless Reginald Pole gets them first, then it wouldn't be the safety of the Domus, would it?"

I couldn't hold my tongue. "Is Reginald Pole one of the king's men?"

The girls tried to talk over one another with hurried explanations. No, he was not a favourite of the king—more of the queen—and was studying in the Vatican, a Plantagenet and a potential royal pretender.

"Stop!" Sir Thomas yelled. "Honestly, girls, the way you get animated over a handsome and clever man."

"Sounds like an ally of de Praet," I said.

"Don't make me laugh, Ludovicus. He's cleverer by a country mile! Look at what happened to the Duke of Buckingham!"

"Yes, Father, you're right," Elizabeth said. "This country is a place for neither Jews nor Moors. That's why we sent señor, the cardinal's man." She looked at Álvaro knowingly. "Sent him across the water to make sure he was not a Jew, as people said he might be."

"I am God's servant," I said assertively. "I believe God brought me here to bring his true message to the princess."

They all stood and cheered, and then the pretty one, Cicely, spoke up. "Please, Daddy, the song about childhood, the one you wrote that's in the nursery."

He stood and let out a throaty laugh and, with each line, recited his own verse:

> I am called childhood, in play is all my mind,
> To cast a quoit, a cock-stick, and a ball.
> A top, can I set, and drive it in his kind.
> But would to God these hateful books all,
> Were in a fire burnt to powder small.
> Then might I lead my life always in play:
> Which life God send me to mine ending day.

There was much cheering and clapping, and then Margaret asked for a song of love. Sir Thomas, with a twinkle in his eye for Meg, obliged.

> Whoever knows not the strength, power and might,
> Of Venus and me her little son Cupid,
> Thou manhood shall a mirror been a right,
> By us subdued for all thy great pride,
> My fiery dart pierces thy tender side,
> Now thou that before despised children small,
> Shall grow a child again and be my thrall.

At the end of that first night, Margaret Roper looked at Sir Thomas and declared, "I like him, Father. Seems he's a good man."

"I like him too, Daddy," Cicely added. "Can he stay here forever?"

Sir Thomas looked to the minstrel's gallery and said, "None of you likes him as well as I. I flew over that bloody ocean, incognito, to get him back, and Cicely, beloved, yes, if God is on our side, he will stay with us forever."

As I write by the early morning light—not by the flickering of a candle when the rest of the town is sleeping—I feel that anger and gratitude are two uneasy bedfellows. Sir Thomas's family are clearly not friends of my people, yet they welcome me like one of their own. They rescue me and give me a chance, and by doing so, give my people a chance. I am here on a quest, but God, if ever you grant me anything, grant me this moment of peace in the golden light of this new land. Let the birdsong and the roses imbue me with all their strength and light for the journey ahead. The path may be rough and full of broken branches and stones, but let me have this time of healing, of plenty, first. Amen.

10 June 1523

Well, diary, as I arrived in London, the monarchs departed, for they are bankrupting, it is said, every large house in the land. I wonder if they'll go to the Owens in Chatham so he can apologise himself? As for me, I am left to sit and write by the window in the upstairs library, or in the pergola with its climbing roses that somersault and back-flip, just like my busy mind.

There are no letters yet from Bruges. I've no word of how she is or of the boy, Zeek, whose mother, on the day we left had brought him to our back door, with the simple words, "take him." We arranged for him to go to the house of the Valldauras. There was no word of Señor Valldaura, with all his bruises and wounds. with all his bruises and wounds. There is nothing from Spain either despite my letters inviting them here, with my description of the hospitality and the length of the summer days. I'm left with the moment, and the moment, mostly, is a sense of joy. But this joy, this safety, it dulls me, and I need to shake myself awake. But it is hard when peace happens. What, diary? I am disloyal? I am selfish. All right, but let me illustrate my point clearly and show you how hard it is.

Yesterday, I walked out in the early morning, with its golden light peaking from behind the red-tiled roof, to the small pergola in the rose garden. There, amid the aviaries with their sweet finches from the land called Cuba and chattering green parrots from India, I sat down to write. I was deep in planning when I heard footsteps and a gentle *tap tap* like summer rain on a window. It was Margaret, known as Meg.

"Señor, would you care for tisane of hyssop to sharpen the mind, or cool cider to cloud it?"

"Both, of course!"

She laughed, for she'd found me unprepared.

"That's funny to an Englishwoman—to ask for both?"

She smiled through her great front teeth and nodded. Then, like her father, she changed demeanour. "What of Erasmus's work?" she demanded. Margaret was off and running with her conversation! "How will you raise a tax to pay for your colleges? And an English bible—you support it, don't you? Think of the discord, the revolts. What hope for the unity of the church if the poor can read it in their own homes without understanding it? They could not contextualise their own learning."

"Well, my lady, that's precisely it."

"Precisely what?"

"Precisely the problem. All should have enough education to be able to discuss the teachings of the"—I almost said Torah but stopped myself—"the bible."

Our conversation became a battle of questions while I sipped on her strong cider, ignoring the bitter hyssop. I tried humour. "What of the guile of Jacob? The stealth of Abraham? Shouldn't the English themselves learn some of that? They could challenge the might of Spain?"

She took me from the gazebo and grabbed a rose. "Pretty, no?" She smelled it while looking at me. "Do you like to smell roses?"

Where was this leading? I needed to break her spell. "What do you know of the *kol ishah*, my lady?" I was testing her, but also risking my neck.

"I know little Hebrew, señor." She sensed my change, declared that she must leave, and began to walk down the gravel path.

"But, Margaret Roper, what of your work?"

She stopped like a sheepdog that had remembered a lamb left on the mountain. Without turning, she took a breath. Had I won? I could see her shoulders rise and knew that her breasts would follow. She faced forward as she confessed that she was working on a translation into English of Erasmus's *Precatio Dominica,* known in English as *A Treatise on the Pater Noster.* She calmed her breathing, turned, walked back to me, and placed her very white English hand on the radial aspect of my left wrist as she whispered, "The voice of the woman that in this world is little but a vibration."

"That women like you will change into a song," I said.

She would not be further drawn, but something in her relaxed. She softened as if my words had touched her.

"Señor, you must know me as Meg."

I paused. "But would your husband allow me to call you such?" The man of commerce would surely not allow it.

"Probably not, but nevertheless you must call me Meg."

Silence ensued. Was this a temptation I'd do better to refuse? Was this a step on the path to infidelity?

"My lady, Meg, recite for me your work and help me with my poor English."

She smiled and took her hand at last from mine, allowing herself a deep breath. She let the words out like a man at court. She seemed to be channelling her father in all his strength:

> For thy glory as it is great
> So neither having beginning nor ending
> But ever in itself flourishing
> Can neither increase nor decrease
> But its skills yet mankind not a little
> That every man it knows and magnify
> For to know and confess the one very God.

Though my knowledge of English was yet imperfect, I could see beauty in her work. The one very God, the concept that we shared but that divided us so, as if the one very God would judge in which language the bible was allowed or would bar citizens from comprehending its words. I could see why her father called her "Marguerita charisma."

So, diary, this is why it is hard it is for me. I am ashamed of these thoughts, but if I cannot talk to you, then to whom can I talk? How can I come to know myself if I don't get it down, even the shame? How beautiful she looked today in her long gown, green as a yew, and pulled tightly around the waist by a cream stomacher. There was just a glimpse of light brown hair beneath her simple English hood, and as for her teeth—they fascinate me, beckon me. But enough! I am here for a reason. This is not it.

Later that same day, when the burn of the cider had worn off, she and her stepsister, Anne, took me by carriage to the hospital known as Bedlam. There, among the dank dormitories and viewing platforms, live the invalids, the insane. Men and women of the city pay a penny or two to watch these poor souls grubbing about, talking to themselves and crying in their distress. This, the girls told me, was where we need to put God. This, I was told, should be my work until Oxford is ready for me.

I could not disagree.

Back home again and before supper, William Roper, with the stomping of steel toecaps, arrived. He bid me a muted "Good evening," a welcome fit for a pauper with early signs of leprosy. Brown-bearded, thick in the eyebrow, and sallow in the face, he is a little younger than me and carries the odour of opportunity. Surely, he allies himself with this family of scholars just to raise his profile in the upper echelons.

It was an uncomfortable dinner. Sir Thomas was strangely quiet. "There will be no poetry tonight," he said. Elizabeth, being the youngest, sulked like my sister Beatriz. Álvaro did not join us at the table as lately he has taken to staying out late at night.

The music was played quietly, just a harp. All around was tension, forced postures, a concentration on the knife and the food. Finally, Sir Thomas spoke up.

"Ludovicus, daughters, I've news from the north. The king continues to obsess about the queen's relations with his long-dead brother, Arthur."

"I have heard this," I told him.

"The king believes this is why not one of their sons has survived," he said, his face contorted.

Elizabeth tried to lift his mood, making light of the king's fanciful thinking. Sir Thomas spoke of the king's growing arrogance and that he would challenge even the edict of the pope. "But this talk stays in this room," he said.

"Divorce?" Margaret said.

"Yes, a divorce. There are factions, bastards at court, that suggest the very worst if he does not get it." I saw that Sir Thomas was deeply troubled by this.

"The very worst?" I asked, knowing full well that the very worst could be the very best.

"A break with Rome, an alliance with the Protestants—or worse."

"Worse?"

"Yes, Vives, worse."

"What could be worse?" I asked.

"A Turk, for one. Or worse still, a Jew."

Sir Thomas got up and left. Without his guiding presence, the remnant finished quickly and left one by one until it was only Margaret and me and her skulking husband at the table. She looked at me as if scanning my body for signs of something not to like. "As long as I live," she said, "the Protestants will not find a home in this land. It is father's dream, as it is mine, to keep England united and Catholic."

My eyes closed like the scrolls of the Torah in the granary, not knowing if or when they would be opened again. And then I was left at the giant table alone, and I retreated quietly to my room.

Álvaro returned to our chamber by midnight, smelling of summer sweat.

"Álvaro, tell me where have you been these late evenings?" I needed to know, and I was not above playing innocent to get his answer.

"I have been to the stews, my friend—to the stews of Southwark, where I have made the acquaintance of more than a fair Scottish lassie."

"The stews? A lassie?" I asked, not understanding the meaning of his words. It was not long before I found out that a stew was a whorehouse, and in Southwark there were many, hemmed between the bear-baiting pits and the cockfighting rings.

"My God, what are you doing there? Haven't you learnt your lesson from the harlots of Antwerp?" I spoke quietly, though I wanted to shout about creating a good impression on our hosts and spending wisely the money they gave us. I stormed around the room, wanting to throw candlesticks and smash chairs.

"Calm yourself, my friend. I can handle myself in the stews. Besides, as for the harlots, I have taken precautions."

"What precautions?"

He produced a six-inch-long hollowed-out piece of tortoiseshell as thin as a fingernail.

"It is amazing what you can pick up in this city," he told me.

"Not the clap I hope."

"Precisely why I use this little beauty," he replied and then sat cross-legged, murmuring his barely intelligible chants in Hebrew.

Something stirred in my memory, something I recognised from Father: Elohei neshama shenatata bi, t'horah hi—the soul God gave me is a pure soul.

Álvaro de Castro, what game of chess are you playing? Whose side are you on? Am I just one of the pawns that you're moving on the map of Europe that seems to be your chessboard?

16 June 1523

I couldn't get an audience with the king or queen or even meet with the princess. There was a note from Bruges, but not the one I'd hoped for. It had the diamond seal of Louis de Praet. "How goes my paper?"

I'd nearly finished it, but there was a city here that I hardly knew, and I wanted to run from that diamond seal. With three silver sovereigns in a leather purse attached to my breeches, we set out into the day.

"Beware of the cozeners and the coney-catchers!" Sir Thomas yelled as we sped out of the gates, but his voice was drowned by the energy of the streets. St Paul's rose above the timber houses like a giant cliff. Álvaro rolled his shoulders as he walked, strong as a blacksmith. I tried to copy him until he doubled over with laughter, like someone had put a sword into a sack of grain.

Outside of the west door was a group of young men, and although it was another warm day, they were gathered about a brazier. There was the sound of shrieking and cheering: they were burning books and pamphlets.

"What are they burning?" we asked a skinny boy not more than fourteen.

He smiled, tossed back dirty mouse-coloured hair and replied, "The pamphlets of Luther and English scriptures." He seemed frightened. Traitors have smuggled 'em in."

I played along. "Shocking news, intolerable."

"Such blasphemies we can't 'ave."

There was a rhythmic cry of "Burn them!" and my mind turned again to other burnings in other lands. I leaned down and whispered into his left ear, "Remember, if you English can read a bible in your own homes, then you can challenge what you live with."

He backed off and ran away as if Lucifer was after him.

Álvaro and I walked into the cathedral and threaded our way through the monks and handsome clergymen laughing like girls. We climbed the two hundred or so steps to the top of the tower and looked beyond the city. To the east was the Tower of London.

"That's where you'll end up if you don't keep your mouth shut," Álvaro said, his black hair flowing in the wind. "I believe this is the old Jewish quarter," he said, pointing.

I looked at his trajectory. There were crowded streets packed like piglets at a sow's teats.

"See that building with its high walls and tiny windows?" he said.

"What is it?" I asked.

"Juanito, close your eyes and listen to the wind. You will find the answer."

I stood there, at the turret of the poor old cathedral, blustery clouds and strong winds above, chiming bells and murmuring streets below. I closed my eyes, and pictures of dark rooms, men in hoods, and prisons overwhelmed me.

"It's the Domus, isn't it?" I said. In that moment, I felt his pain and his passion. "Álvaro, we must do something now." He made to descend the two hundred steps, but before I could catch enough breath to stop him, we were out into the fresh air again. Outside, we were accosted by a group of young men and greeted in broken Spanish.

"Mi señores Espanol, you must be hungry. Come to the Black Boar for snipes, partridge, and English ale."

We followed them to the rowdy, raucous tavern that smelled of hops and old beer.

One of the men shouted, "Tell us about Spain, sirs. Is it true that you sleep in the afternoons and stay awake all night? And what about the Spanish girls, with their curly hair and big breasts?"

"Yes, it is true," Álvaro said, "but if you want to see big breasts, go to Amsterdam and you'll have a feast."

A chorus of laughter erupted. "Amsterdam it is!"

Dark ale arrived, known as bitter, and bitter it was. This was more food than drink, and more medicine than food. A little later, our meal arrived, but I was already dizzy with the ale, and the food had no appeal.

"Sirs, we must play some dice now," said one.

Remembering Sir Thomas's words, I sensed a trap. Despite protestations, we stumbled out of the tavern, bid our hosts goodbye, but found they were gone, as was my purse and the three sovereigns. It had been cut from my breeches.

"Álvaro, my money," I cried desperately.

"Do you think I am that stupid?" he laughed, tears running down his face.

"What will we do now for money, and how will I explain this to Sir Thomas?"

Álvaro pulled the three sovereigns out of his sleeve.

"Let them have your purse," he said. "I emptied it of its contents."

"How?"

"With the skill of a de Castro," he replied.

Slightly dizzy with ale, we meandered through the narrow laneways that radiated away from the cathedral. The uneven cobbled streets of the Old Jewry greeted us with suspicion.

"Do they hide here still?" I asked.

"There were Viveses here," Álvaro told me in his worldly tone.

"How do you know this?" I asked.

"I just know."

"But that's not our real name," I countered.

"I know that, too."

We entered the church of St. Lawrence Jewry, the church of Sir Thomas, where he meets his living muse, William Grocyn, the most learned preacher in the land.

But what horror! There was a painting of the saint being burned on a gridiron, and it sent shivers down my spine. In the confines of the red-painted walls, my eyes suddenly misted up and lost their focus. Where was the door? I had to escape. Then I smelled it. No, this could not be, not again—the fire, the singeing of hair, the crackling of flesh, the groaning, the cheering, the screams. I raised my hands to my ears. Sweat ran down my brow as I trembled.

I felt a hand on my arm. Was it the officers of the Inquisition? No, it was Álvaro, guiding me out, one arm around my right shoulder, and we were out at last. I was back in the moment.

"What would I do without you?" I said.

He took me in his arms, like a brother, and held me tightly. "You'll not have to find out."

The air was dank and humid as we emerged into the streets of the Old Jewry. A great cart swung around the corner and rolled past us, kicking up thick dust.

Back at Bucklersbury, they commented on my silence. Voiceless for the next three days, I was unable to offer anything but silence.

On the third day, Meg took charge. She took me back to Bedlam in the open carriage that sprayed mud and dung so that I had to cover my face with a scarf. I kept it over my mouth as we entered the hospital, for the putrid smell of faeces and unwashed bedding was too much to bear. She spoke with the warden like a counsellor. The patients needed fresher air, clean clothes, and running water. He looked dumbstruck, with a nose that looked like a small rotten apple and skin red from years of ale.

"My Lady Roper, there are no funds."

She looked at me as if egging me towards the land of words, but no words came. She spoke for me.

"This man has an answer."

The warden looked at me kindly, perhaps wondering if I would one day be an admission here.

"My father and Cardinal Wolsey ponder these questions, and there's a new tax, a subsidy on the wealthy. If all goes well, we can direct funds here and elsewhere."

"Oh, my sweetest lady," he replied, with the foul odour from the abscess of a rotten tooth.

She stepped backwards before remembering her manners and spoke again. "There's a new breeze in the air, sir, if we can catch it, and then great things will happen here."

He smiled and nodded as if to say, "Good luck."

Back in the carriage, clarity, my wandering friend, returned. "A new breeze, eh?"

Her breasts rose a bit. "Are you with us on the breeze, señor, or are you just a cuckoo in the nest?"

"Every part of me is with you."

*　　*　　*

One night, I cornered Álvaro before supper and asked, "What of the Domus? Who's in there? How can we help? And what of a dramatic rescue or a letter to the king?"

"You do your work and I'll do mine," he said with a snarl.

Although I was dissatisfied with his answer, I had permission to bask longer in the light of this safe place. The next week was spent immersed in the company of women, so much so that the tiny hairs on my arms and on the nape of the neck bristled. I would not have them think of me as a cuckoo in the nest, but with them on their quest for a more enlightened Catholic realm that our people could also enjoy. I started talking of it to Álvaro, but what silence greeted me! What a scolding came! What of my immediate duty? What of my father in Valencia and my new family in Bruges? Clearly, those bristled hairs had been noticed.

Perhaps I had forgotten my obligations in Bruges and in Valencia. But what of their obligations to me? There has been no letter from either place.

"But Juanito."

Who said that? Was it you, diary? Was it you, conscience? Whoever it was, go on.

Nothing. And so I sat here with the window open and the garden breeze wafting through it. Sunlight bounced off the light rosewood panels. The candle flickered but did not reveal a shape. Time passed. I listened to the silence and got a clumsy draft of "On Assistance to the Poor." Álvaro printed it and sent it to de Praet with a dedication that sounded sincere. Perhaps, then, the drawbridge will be lifted, and I'll get a letter back from my love?

26 August 1522

Is it such a bad resting place, what's left of you, diary: ripped-up pages from that thing that looked like it had eyes and ears etched upon it, wrapped in Bruges lace, under the false bottom of the hammered leather trunk? I was going to leave you for a while, lost in the shame of love for my new life, and I will, but first I've got to tell you about this, the greatest show on Earth—Bartholomew Fair!

We arrived early dressed as country folk in long, loose white trousers and flowing red shirts. Hysteria was in the air. Even Álvaro began to laugh again. Alas, one of us was missing: Sir Thomas, who'd been called to Woodstock to be with the king. He did invite me to go, and I could plead my case and that of my people, but I chose this instead.

There were stalls and stages, canvas tents and groups of prancing men, street urchins and women from the stews. There were the merchants from St Katherine's, Dutchmen wearing clogs and flared justaucorps, and Frenchmen wearing blue-striped hip-length breeches. Margaret Roper told me that even King Harry sometimes attended the fair in disguise. One year, he would come as a monk, the next as a strong man from the circus. Where would he be this year? Was he there amongst the Morris dancers in their smocks and hats, leaping up and bowing?

"More Moors, Mores, Moriscos and Morrisers," Álvaro remarked. Casting his eyes towards Margaret More, he added, "But, please, wayward brother, no more amours."

He calls me wayward!

Cicely begged Lady Alice that she might get her fortune told, and so we entered the tent of an ancient gypsy woman. Gnarled like an old tree, she sat at a table with a glass ball, some dice, and a stack of cards. Cicely sat in front of her, but the gypsy pointed at me.

"Spaniard who is not a Spaniard," she said, "prepare for the fires of hell!" She gazed down and then flung her head up and cried, "Your dead mother will be killed." I was petrified by her chilling words.

"What do you mean?" I demanded.

"You know very well what I mean" was the venomous reply. "There is one who knows more than you, but no one would believe it. He sees everything that you do not see." Who could she be referring to but Álvaro? Who but the frequenter of late-night taverns and stews?

"And what do you have to say to my little sister?" Meg intervened.

The gypsy snarled. "What to say to the one they'll call the cleverest woman in England, as if such a thing was possible to tell! You're cleverer than the next queen, who'll hate you for it and try to take him from you. You are loved above the others, but you are not loved."

A tear appeared in Cicely's eye and, after a pause, the gypsy spoke to Meg in a softer tone. "Do not fear when the night grows cold. He will be with you, and he will be watching you. I've seen the depths of your daughter's love. You'll not leave him, even in death."

What could she mean in saying *Your dead mother will be killed*? What did this bode for the future, and what did it say about my family, still living there? And what of the next queen, who'll hate Meg, and who will she try to take from her? Is it me?

Exhausted, we sat by the ring for a wrestling match between the giant of York and the ogre of Oxford. It was nothing but show, and we lost a few groats in the game they call shove ha'penny. The girls were overcome with excitement as we passed a stall selling puppies and kittens.

"Mummy, oh, Mummy, look at that one." Meg beamed like a six-year-old. Even to my eyes this creature was beautiful, a black bundle of fur with a wet nose and eyes, dark as pieces of polished coal.

"We simply cannot have more animals," Lady Alice said.

"No, we can't, but Juanito can."

My heart sank. She called me Juanito, a word reserved for family, for Álvaro, for Marguerite.

"But I am leaving for Oxford," I countered.

"He needs a family in his new home," Meg declared.

Before I knew it, the deal was done, and in a wicker basket at my side was a bundle of fur and sharp teeth.

"What shall we call him?" Elizabeth asked.

"Why Henry, of course," I replied, "for the great King of England."

We made our way back, weary now, through the side streets of St. Bartholomew's, passing the ancient hospital and the monastery, the one where Sir Thomas had studied and prayed. The puppy in the basket, slung over my shoulder, whined his earth-shattering, almighty "I am."

Once at home, with jugs of lemon and rose water, we gathered on the patio of the garden. Álvaro played Spanish music on the lute that took me to other places, of Mother dancing with Father and of a sweet girl named Ana from Andalusia. Lost in the memory, I fell asleep.

It was dark when I awoke but for the candlelight, and found that it was just Meg and me, the two of us on adjoining cushions, neither awake nor asleep. Her face was lit from her left side, and I could see every curve of her face had become beautiful, every lock of her light brown hair lit with the magic of the candle flame. She reached her hand towards my elbow and said with her eyes still shut, "Will there be another evening as blissful as this one, Juanito?"

"I hope so, Mistress Roper."

"Meg."

"I hope my family and yours can live honestly in a fair land. I hope there are many more summers together like this, many more fairs. Can I share my secrets with you, Meg?"

"Please, yes."

"How I'd love to show you the palaces and the whitewashed houses of my home. I hope I take you there as…" I hesitated.

"As your love," she said.

I could not stand because of the bulge in my pants.

"I see you are in conflict, sir," she said, eyes cast towards it.

We lay there in silence and giggled. Every moment felt like an hour. Eventually, she rose and touched my hand, and I got up and followed her to the stairwell. It was only then that I realised I was still holding her fingers.

"Good night, my lady."

She did not turn back.

Drawn like a magnet to my bed, I slept soundly in the bliss of the moment, imagining I was still on the pillows, that my breath was mixed with hers.

In that summer, corn was billowing, oak trees were murmuring, and from the oaks came shadows. I ran into the oaks, and she was in a ruby dress. I grabbed her. She turned, and it was Marguerite of Bruges, of Toledo. I hugged her with my body and soul.

"When will you fly over the seas to come for me, señor?"

"Someday soon, love, and I will bring you back here to make a home."

The magic was broken, and I woke up with a start.

8 September 1522

So, my fickle friend, consisting of vellum and coded letters, where did you go? We were leaving, and with a heavy heart, too, but as we agreed, we'd always leave together. So, where were you? I searched the trunk a hundred times over. I took out the false bottom, went through my clothes again—pockets, wallets, more false bottoms. Was I going mad? Had you become invisible to me? On the morning we left, I searched one more time and you were back.

Don't worry. Who could understand the secret code: Hebrew-Arabic-Spanish-Greek written sideways, right to left, sometimes in a mirror? Perhaps you're right. Perhaps my worry is the figment of an overactive imagination. Perhaps it's the pain of leaving Bucklersbury, of getting back to the task I've come here for.

But perhaps you've got a new master? In any case, you know me well enough now, so why stop telling you what's truly in my heart.

There I was, as flat as the unleavened bread I had taken as I left London for Oxford. Meg, too—she had the same look. I guess that's because her husband was there. I kept my goodbyes brief. And with you strapped tightly to my stomach with a bandage, we were off, a train of academics, a secret Jew, his impenetrable companion, and the undersheriff of London. Henry, the poodle pup, growing so fast, was tethered by four leather leads in a cart and protested with his razor-sharp teeth. At each stop, he looked to me for liberty, imploring me with a cocking of his head and those obsidian eyes.

Like a war-weary captain, Sir Thomas rode with me, mostly with his head down, deep in thought. I sensed that secrets were for the taking. I tried to draw him out, and when I thought I'd never succeed, he cracked.

"He's been deceived by a family of chancers, worming and squirming and thrusting their daughter on him," he said.

I knew of whom he was talking, for the girls cannot help but gossip. Who else would it be but the one I'd met in Paris: Mary Boleyn.

"But he takes a new lover every year. It'll pass, the infatuation, no?"

"And well she knows it, so she tries to get a son on him while she can."

"But she's no true rival to the queen," I said.

"You know her?' he asked, halting.

"Just by reputation."

Even the crows in the ploughed fields seemed to stop searching for scraps.

"God save our Catholic queen and all she lives for, who never flinches from her duty to Christ and his message," he proclaimed.

My mind was in a different place. Christ was a Jew, a great rabbi. How would he be disposed to her parents' cruelty to the Jews?

He waved the party on and rode close to me.

"The king has listened to her family and others," he continued. "They tell him that the holy book condemns the marriage. I know your people follow Deuteronomy in this. I mean your father's people, of course."

A flock of starlings chattered past, a cloud like a dark portent. The road was tortuous at this point. Thick mud lay in the furrows better suited for pigs than horses.

"Ludovicus, my friend, you must draw on all your knowledge and superior wisdom to strengthen the position of the queen and the princess."

This was, after all, the reason I had been brought here. But it was not the reason that I myself came. In that moment I felt the break from him and from Bucklersbury. I was following higher orders than those of Sir Thomas More. Álvaro must have caught my thoughts on the wind as he rode up beside us.

"Juanito, se acerca el invierno, no? Hoy en dia es brillante, y podemos sembrar las semillas para la cosecha de primavera, no?"

"Winter is coming, no? But today is bright, and we can sow the seeds for the spring crop, no?"

He laughed like a clown and raced off. Clarity, that transient friend, spoke again. I was back on the quest to save my family and to save my people. I pointed to Álvaro, bucking his horse in the distance: "Crazy Spaniard!"

Sir Thomas laughed.

"And what of Mary Boleyn and her family?" I asked. "Where are they on theology?" I hoped he would never discover that it was I, in Paris, who had stoked the fires of reform in the Boleyn girls. I wouldn't let him know that it was her sister, Anne, who was the real threat.

"Can't fault them on wit and learning," he replied. "Perhaps this nonsense came from Paris. They are secret reformer champions of the new church. But the king will tire of Mary Boleyn."

"A tolerant bunch then?"

"Too fucking tolerant," he yelled. "I'd cover them all in pig shit and throw them in a tar pit, and their English bibles after them."

"Let us hope so, Master Thomas!" I said. "Let's ride!"

That, my diary, was the journey from London to Oxford, and here, now at last, is this town of history and scholars. The towers and spires loom high above the cottages and townhouses, as if holding a promise of greatness, a whisper on the wind that says, "This is where you will make your mark, Vives." At dusk, long shadows fall across the town like the arms of Barbary apes. There is so much sandstone here! It is like a golden city, a warm place teeming with young scholars in black robes carrying books through the ancient streets. I heard the wind calling my name, telling me it was time to take my place among great men, that the little fish had grown up.

My college is known as Corpus Christi, The Body of Christ, and you can still smell the sawyer on the wood panels, the blacksmith on the bolts, the currier on the leather. On one side of the quadrangle is a dining hall that seems forever anticipating a feast. On another is a well-stocked library that smells of knowledge, and there is a lofty tower with a neatly finished chapel. The president is a famous student of Pliny, known as John Claymond, a well-built man. He wears a stunning sapphire ring and has eyes of the same colour.

'Señor Vives," he says, "we've already decided you'll be known as John Lewis, and your famous discipulus, the cardinal's boy, what shall we call him? Alan Castle? Welcome to your new home."

"Please, sir," I said, "tell us more about your college funded by the cardinal."

"The butcher's son," he said, as if remembering something. "From the subsidy tax on the rich. And there's more funding to come from the dissolution of a few unnecessary religious houses."

Perhaps Cardinal Wolsey would be my friend after all? Sir Thomas looked down and shook his head as Claymond went on. "For our revival of Greek and for our Hebrew library, we're called the Renaissance College."

We may fit in well here, diary. It may be just the right place to bring this princess into the light. There is a warm and well-furnished room of reds and green, one high bed for me and a truckle for Álvaro, now called Alan Castle. Sir Thomas has already explained that I must have a constant companion for the apoplexies lest I harm myself, as well as a dog also to tell me when the attacks are coming. They do not realise that somewhere, in a place of his mind he still can't name or understand, he still suspects I am a Jew. And who better to be his eyes and ears than the Cardinal of

Burgos's boy? That way, every gesture, every prayer, every kiss of the sacred book will be noted.

Not a very successful strategy, is it? His eyes and ears, having meditated with a gentle chanting of Hebrew words, are now closed, asleep. His chest rises and falls like a gentle ocean. I light a candle and cover my head with a silk cloth to say a prayer, *hamapil*. Away now from the strange spell of Meg Roper, my thoughts return to Marguerite Valldaura.

I must have lapsed into a dream in which there was a voice that sounded like Mother. What she said, I do not know, but it was good, and it was warm. We are here where we wanted to be, and though I haven't heard a word from my hermandad, from my brotherhood, the quest is still on.

And these Boleyns, they push things on, eh? Perhaps it can be exploited. Is that treachery or just stealth? Whatever it is, I must pursue it.

1 October 1523

I'd been here only a day or two, and then one morning, just as early light spliced through the gap between my curtain and its pole, there was a knock on the door, and I was up. I'd been summoned. I reached the destination, a room with no air in which I had to open my mouth to.

"My Spaniard, my scholar, here to tread the funambulatory path of rightfulness."

I knew at once who had spoken: the famous physician to both this king and the last. Five feet tall, he was stooped and withered, though he had a spark in his eye, full of love and kindness. His face was angled like a dreidel. He smelled of old books, but one whose pages are still turned, whose pages will forever be turned. I did what Álvaro told me to do: listen to the silence, which told me that God was close to him on the final leg of his journey. He drifted into an oratory about the future of the college."

"Recently obtained funds, Lewis, for the Royal Charter of the College of Physicians where I am president. Not bad, eh, hom-hum, ho diddley dum." With the vivacity of a man thirty years younger, not frayed by the journey of life nor the proximity of its finality, he said, "Things move quickly with this great prince and his friends, Wolsey and More, who will see your plans a reality, eh, señor? For you understand the psyche, my friend."

I nodded and smiled.

"Just as well," he said. "We've got work to do yet."

"Indeed, sir, and you are?" I knew who he was but wanted to see his response.

"Sir Thomas Linacre. Whom else could I possibly be?" He laughed before his face went blank. Then he was off again. "This is wonderful! We will have hospitals built. We will make England fair and free. I will have more of you, Lewis, more indeed." He moved to the door, his old bones creaking like a ship setting sail. "Stay here. I'm going to get the princess."

After a long wait, the door swung open, and there she was, my great work, an angel in human form. She walked with tiny steps, barely making a sound on the polished floor. She was like a midget woman, face made up white like a statue of the Virgin Mary, slight of frame even for a seven-year-old. Her hair was between red and brown and tied behind her inside a Spanish hood far too heavy for so little a girl. I approached her and bowed.

"Your royal highness, it is my greatest pleasure," I said in Latin.

"Señor, the pleasure is mine."

That was all I was to going to get as she turned and said, "Good day, señor." Linacre opened the door, but she suddenly stopped. Her two ladies-in-waiting walked into her, and the princess was thrust into the guards before her.

"Your highness!" I rushed over but was pushed away. She turned and brushed down her dress, too old and too grey for one so young, and then told the guard to leave me alone.

"I can see that you're a good man. Will you help me be a good queen?"

My heart melted. How I'd love a little one like this to love and nurture, for though she had privilege, she seemed lonely and old for one so young. Álvaro had found his way to Linacre's room and had seen everything. He didn't bow, but mouthed, "Do not promise her."

But didn't I owe her something? This little girl was the reason Sir Thomas had wrested me from the grip of solitary confinement and the hands of Louis de Praet. I bowed long and low.

"Para siempre, para siempre." She got closer and blinked away a tear. She trembled and then composed herself, as a future queen must.

"Señor, will you promise, as a Spaniard, that you will stay with me and Mother, even if your life depends on it?"

Here was the granddaughter of the inquisitors, the zealots, the ones who'd instigated the terror, commanding me to pledge my life to her mother, the fruit of Isabella's womb. In an instant of realisation, the walls came in, the ceiling lowered, the shaking began. I tried to stammer a reply but could not.

I am scared. Are these episodes happening more frequently now?

Six hours later, Álvaro brought me water and sugared fruit. He muttered that the prophet Elijah had saved me from swearing a lie. My throat felt like it had been force-fed road-soil. Henry, the poodle pup, nudged gently against my hand. Álvaro, who was through with caretaking, had the *yetzer hara*, the evil inclination within.

"What about her maids?"

I looked up, my head too heavy to lift. "Good."

"Do you think they would like a Spanish cock to remind them of their loyalties?"

"For the sake of our fathers, Álvaro de Castro, son of Abraham, do not say that again."

"I will," he replied, "when you least expect it."

The next day, a young boy thrust a parcel into my hands as I made my way to the lecture. He ran away like a pig that had escaped the slaughter. I opened the letter, and though I already knew who it was from, I cried for joy when I saw Papa's slanted writing, for he had sent me a Spanish book concerning the martyrdom of St. Cecilia. There, between the seventeenth and twenty-third pages, was his piercing of the letters, vowels omitted—one of our codes. He tried to disguise it, but I could smell the scent of desperation, as I decoded it.

"Son, my greetings and prayers. Remember words of Rabbi: those accepting exile demonstrate faith, a belief in the unity of the one, a brotherhood. Look at Abraham and Joseph. Here, various people disappear and every day more are taken, mostly just for questions. I myself was brought before them twice. You'd laugh, mainly from other cloth men, some of them conversos. I have beseeched your three sisters to leave, but I am safe, so fear not. It will be a happy outcome when the king comes to his senses. I will take my chances within these city walls and its narrow streets. Padre."

What insanity! Can I bind his feet and hands and drag him out of the city that has become his prison cell?

There were two other letters with this one. They came from Bruges. My heartbeat doubled. The first was in a man's rough hand, and I recognised it, although this time there was no diamond seal.

Master Vives,

Your work is good, very good. You write with the hand of God.

I thank you,
Louis de Praet of Bruges.

Does he mean it? Can I use this?

There was a scent about the second letter that was inescapably light. I felt something on my cheek, like a breath. I ripped it open.

My dearest Juan Luis Vives,

It has been several months since I received your letters, all together, delivered by Master de Praet, smelling of the camphor of your own cuff. I trust you have received all of my letters and the clothes. As I have said, Father grows weaker, Mother stays strong and does her very best at continuing the trade, but money is becoming sparser. Zeek grows daily and is learning to read a bit. As for Nicolas, he's studying in earnest to one day be a physician and make us proud. Each day, I think of the happy times at the table and in the shop, of your bravery. We say prayers for your safety and that one day you will fly across the ocean and sing the old songs with us and pray with us, your family, on the Sabbath.

Your best friend, M. V.

De Praet had been the gatekeeper of my correspondence, as I suspected. There was no more time to waste. Although I may be the tutor of the seven-year-old and the best friend of Sir Thomas More, it is the king and queen who I had to get to, and fast.

20 October 1523

I found myself in the midst of dark shadows and early nights, cold winds and early frosts. Even my lecture hall was alive with the voice of change. Did the boys feel that something was about to happen in the land? And could I be an instrument to direct that change for the good?

"Would we not agree that the relief of the poor is the task of the state and not of the church?" I asked. "That the problem is not simply of the distribution of wealth, but of the availability of opportunity?"

A few eyebrows were raised. I'd already decided that I would find a way to make them believe in this Renaissance age.

"One man must regard the distress of another as if it is his own." I looked to their faces, making sure I had their attention: "So what say you? Speak, boys. Speak!"

"Where can we begin to relieve the conditions of the poor?" Walsingham, uglier than a gargoyle, stood up. "That's a massive undertaking, sir, for if their condition improved, they'd be demanding everything! English bibles, new lands. There could be a revolution, a new civil war."

"We'd begin by making a proper survey of every institution in every town and of every hovel where they dwell. Above all, we would understand their journey and that they are as clever as us—that they are one with us."

"And when you had a new doomsday book?" Walsingham said, his smirk belying the thought that God was indeed an Englishman, and a rich one at that.

"All must be taught a trade, and the trade must be the one to which they are most drawn so they'll lend themselves to it fully." I had their attention at last.

"And what can we do that our fathers could not do?" Nicolas Udall asked, bringing his index finger to his temple.

"Don't spend your money furnishing your houses to impress the king," I said. "Help young men and women to read and to be made into apprentices. Fund healthy hospitals with your healthy rents, welcome the foreigner into your land, learn from the stranger." There was a murmur in the room and the guards at the door shuffled uneasily.

"Whoa! We'll be inviting Arabs and Jews to rule us," said Udall. "You've some lively ideas, sir!" He turned to his classmates for approval.

"But what benefit is there for the nation and for the king in relieving the condition of the poor and the mad?" Charles Durham asked.

"For one, there is great honour in living the true word of the one, the universal spirit, the place where we're all connected." I raised my foot onto my chair and leaned forward, an elbow on my knee, my head on my fist. I would not be afraid. "And there'd be fewer acts of violence and of theft because the poor wouldn't resent the rich. They would hold them in esteem as brothers. And you'd learn from the Jews about medicine, philosophy and from the Arabs about science."

Walsingham spoke up. "Every person would become more productive and hold the nation dearer in his heart."

"Exactly, dear boy."

Can we, with young men like this, create a utopia in this land? Can it be a place where all men and women, regardless of faith, live together? As Father says, the king of Spain may come to his senses, and the hermandad will have succeeded.

I was full of the future as I turned the iron key to my room that evening. There, thrust underneath my door, chewed at the edges, was a sealed letter whose handwriting I knew could only belong to Margaret Roper.

My Master Lewis,

The rooms of our home grow quieter without your presence.

A confession needs to be made: Your book, private writings—I needed to know what was in your heart, and though much of it I could not read, much of it I could. I wonder if you are truly the cuckoo in the nest or if you are still our true friend?

And yet the month since you have been departed seems like a month of dark days. If only I could call back the summer for just a day and you could tell me what those words mean, whether you are a Jew of practice.

Will you promise me that you will return for Christmas and take the goose stuffed with partridge and tell me? Will you accompany us to the Palace of Windsor on Christmas Day and bring your case before the king and queen? Or will you balk and pretend you know nothing about this secret to which I am alluding?

Yours in truthful curiosity, Meg

An hour passed. In my mind I was floating, taking my family to a safe place, perhaps as far away as the lands of India, where we could forget all of this. You, diary, have gotten me into trouble again, yet I cannot destroy you, for you are my only truth. You have told me that she wants me and that I want her.

There was a banging on the cedar floors. It was the messenger boy, and he thrust a folded letter, sealed, with a sense of urgency into my right hand and then ran away.

To my office, at once,
Claymond

In a state of panic, I flushed my face with water. With the dog that had to follow me, everywhere, I walked slowly to his room. "Today is an important day with special visitors." He could see I didn't understand, and he slumped back into the creaking chair. His focus was back on the glass. "Here to visit their special daughter."

"Special daughter?"

"Be ready. They're here to hear you and your views on the poor, the insane, and these hospitals you can't shut up about." He slumped forwards, lost in another world.

By dusk, I bumbled my way towards the great hall, and though voices buffeted me from obtuse angles, I registered nothing. I was in the lion's jaw, but here in the lion's jaw was my chance. The boys settled, the giant doors were closed, the front row was empty. The oak door swung open on its iron hinges and in walked Master Claymond. He walked straight to my lectern, ignoring me as he took the stand.

"My lords and noblemen, today finds us with the honour and privilege known to few. We are proud to welcome to our new college his Majesty King Henry of England and his good wife Queen Catherine."

There was a fanfare, a drum roll, and gasps and heavy breaths from the boys. Here was King Henry, like a visitor from the Book of Kings. He wore a purple coat with an ermine and velvet collar. He had a beard that was neatly trimmed. His face was like a wide-bowed ship. On closer inspection, he was thin-lipped but was twice the height and breadth of his Spanish wife, dressed in deep red and black. This was majesty and magic, a vision that emitted, without words, power.

Between them was their daughter, holding their hands. Before the royal trio, two young boys walked carrying silver crosses and behind them was my friend, Sir Thomas More. I looked eagerly, but there was no Margaret Roper. By Sir Thomas's side was a fat man in red, po-faced and grisled with a tuberous drinker's nose and an awkward gait. Who else could this be but the butcher's son, Cardinal Thomas Wolsey?

They walked to the front of the hall, and the king fixed me with his Zeus-like gaze. Then, like a thunderclap above my head, he exclaimed, "Well, talk, man. Talk!"

All I saw were expressionless faces. Where had Álvaro gone? In the front row was the woman about whom I had heard so much.

I spoke of education and lifelong learning, the rights of the common man, the responsibilities of the state in relation to the poor. I spoke about Venice, with its department of public health and its tolerance of Jews and others, about how it has prospered. I stopped, exhausted, my gaze resting on the woman in a bejewelled dress with an elegant Spanish hood, brown, grey-flecked hair peeping out from under it. Here was my fellow exile—but my sworn enemy.

There was silence as the king arose. The audience rose with him.

"Very good," the king said, but he had a flat expression. Had I talked myself into treason? They rose and left, the students followed them, and I was left standing at my lectern.

That night, my sleep was a chicken coop with a fox thrown in it. By dawn, I wanted to bury myself beneath the sheets and blankets and to hide away from the world. There was to be no hiding, for by the early light I was summoned.

Two officers with plumed feathers in their shining helmets were at the doors. They knocked thrice, and as the doors were opened from the inside, they announced my new name: "John Lewis of Oxford."

I walked forwards and saw the king and the queen, the princess standing between them once more. There was Wolsey and my friends, the two Thomases—More and Linacre—and John Claymond. I bowed low.

The king spoke with a voice like a hunter's horn. "Arise, John Lewis." The king was not adorned with jewels or gold. Instead, he sat quietly in white and black, as if toying with the idea of a new era of humility, or purity. His black hat seemed all the blacker against his auburn locks and his pale skin, his wet lips. His wife, though, was all gold and red and green, his daughter the same. What was he trying to convey?

"We trust you find yourself well situated here in Oxford."

I prepared to speak but was too slow. He asked his groom to bring him a small gold-painted writing desk, and he sat behind it and grabbed a quill and swilled the ink in the shape of a lion's head. "We have known of you now for some time. We acknowledge the dedication of your work to your king and you must relinquish all loyalties to any other kings."

I was happy to relinquish that, for here was what chance was left.

"I thank you, Your Majesty."

"We know the education of our daughter is of the upmost importance, although it is our sincere hope that God will deliver us a son—indeed many sons." He looked disparagingly at the queen. "Until that day comes, this is our sole heir, our future queen."

Could I align myself with him, this man who thinks himself the equal of God? Might I one day stand beside him as he turned his back on his Spanish wife and her family's decrees? My mind was a mess of Hebrew prayers, of uncertain loyalties and disloyalties.

"Sad it is," said King Henry, "but Thomas Linacre is now old and infirm. We need another to relieve him of his duties and become our sweet daughter's preceptor. You are a good man, señor. We are to become your patrons now, and Sir Thomas More can let you go, eh Tom?"

I looked at my friend, who had his arms crossed, one finger drawn to the mouth. He gave a flick of his wrist as if to say, "Go, Ludo."

The king went on. "She needs Latin first and foremost, and then Greek. Her Spanish is already good, so give her French and Italian."

"And Hebrew," I added, "to understand the bible without translation."

He lifted his torso from the chair, and the struts creaked with relief. He walked around the room, digesting the impact of my interjection. His wife and daughter looked at him, as if trying to read his mind.

"Hebrew. Yes, Hebrew, very good." There was a silence. "Well, man, speak up. Do you take the brief or nay?"

Master Claymond spoke up. "Lewis, remember that Fortuna audacis iuvat. Fortune favours the brave."

"If I can teach her toleration and the true message of Godly kingship, then I accept. I will do all I can to fill the role that Thomas Linacre so adeptly filled these last years." I saw quiet delight in the queen's face.

"Then it is a settled matter," said Henry.

I realised I was now risking my body in the flames. Could he see the terror and the impossibility of my position? He took Wolsey to one side as Sir Thomas walked up to me, beamed, and put his arm around my shoulder.

The queen turned to me and said in the Aragonese dialect, "Señor, welcome to our dearest friend and brother."

Would she have called me "brother" had she known that I, the secret Jew, had spent hours in Paris with her rival, Mary Boleyn, and her sister, Anne, teaching them of the need to question authority?

"Kate, Thomas, Wolsey—to Woodstock," the king said. "There is hunting to be done and the day grows old. Mr Claymond, Master Linacre—talk to the Spaniard about his brief and his pension, but do not be too generous."

The entire party departed, and I heard a voice in my left ear, a kind of whistle through missing teeth. "She is wilful. Oh yes, you will find her such," Thomas Linacre said. "I have not known a young mind so fixed on purpose and so strong in belief. She is already determined to stamp them as Lutherans at the age of seven."

"Where did she get such a fixed mind?" I asked.

Master Claymond took over. "You have to realise that her mother is a pious woman who quells any voice of dissent."

"And her father?" I inquired.

"Nay, not her father. The king listens to the people with their mistrust of the monasteries."

"Who else influences the princess's mind?" I sensed I was close to what I needed now to know.

"It is the rogue who stalks these corridors, whispering in her ear, pretending to be a man of modern thinking." Linacre looked up, worried.

"Rogue?"

"Reginald Pole, of course. The man who places the very fires of the holy office in her ear."

"And who is he?" I asked.

"He is the great nephew of King Edward IV and is versed in ancient lore and calls for our Hebrew and Greek library to be burnt to the ground."

"He would burn ancient knowledge and the future of learning?"

"He would light the fires of the Inquisition beneath your very feet, señor."

I took a sharp breath. There was a movement even here to stamp us out before we got a footing. For some, the prison of the Domus was not enough.

So where was the princess, my new charge? Clearly, I had no time to waste. Had she gone to Woodstock with the party?

I found her in the yellow-draped chamber, lying on cushions and looking out the window, surrounded by maids immersed in embroidering an epic scene.

"My lady, to dance?"

She got up and held my hands, twisting and turning. She repeated the steps a hundred times, working hard so that she could own the steps. Even her stony-faced maids clapped as she danced to the ancient song of nightingale voices that I sang by the riverbank: "Riu, riu, chiu."

"Why that song, señor?" the princess asked.

"It tells us that you must always protect the little ones, my lady."

23 December 1523

In those wintry days in Oxford, anticipating Christmas, I was with the princess every day, like a father. Sometimes we'd walk through the streets or gaze out the window. I wanted to play games and see her laugh, but I knew I had to emphasize the themes of tolerance, peace, and equality. She would come with me with something she wanted to know, a new word perhaps that she'd overheard, like "verisimilitude." And just when she was learning her steps, she'd say it out loud, over and over, until she had it, and not just the word, but the word with multiple translations. I wanted her to question everything, to argue. One day, it would be a solution to poverty or a way to provide schools for all.

All the while I worked by candlelight, deep into the night until my eyes could take it no more. My treatise, *The Education of a Young Woman*, though I was ordered to call it *The Education of a Christian Woman*, was now complete. I'd remember my love, my fair one in Bruges, and the little boy, Zeek, and my eyes would spark up again and I'd write something else down and hide it in the bibles I sent her: one in Latin, one in Greek, and one in Hebrew. She received them, for there were letters telling me that things had changed. The curfew had been lifted and the guards outside their door had been dismissed. Louis de Praet had even sent his best physician to tend to Señor Valldaura, and Zeek was speaking now.

Why didn't I go back there, at least for the season? Why didn't I write to persuade them to join me?

I don't know, but I do know there are thoughts of a woman in London, my diary, whom you know intimately. You promised me, with your carefully woven codes and dialects, that you did yield yourself entirely to her. However many times I've tried to put the thoughts of her out of my mind, they resurface. Perhaps the only way to put her out of my mind is to be close to her. Álvaro warns me against it. "You've been captured by the [kol ishah]," he says, "the voice of the woman."

I cannot help it though. I have to go.

Did you hear, diary, on the day we left Oxford, how Henry the hound yelped and howled when Claymond came to fetch him? Faster than fury we travelled back to London—faster than rainstorms. Perhaps what Álvaro said was true since something magical pulled me onward, and if I drank, ate, or slept, I have no memory of it.

Finally, my focus was sharp like an eagle's. We were at Bucklersbury House. I charged to the front door, forgetting all about Álvaro, drawn to the warmth of the house. But there was no Meg, no chorus of giggling sisters, only fifty strangers, an army of maids and boys. Everything went silent as we entered, and we stood like strangers in a strange land until blue-eyed Cicely came forward.

"Señores, you're here at last, but how you smell like a pack of road horses."

Lady Alice, bent in the middle with her trusted walking stick, emerged from the throng and announced us. I think most thought we were the entertainment because they clapped and cheered as she ushered us up the stairs. Where was Sir Thomas? What about Meg? There were no answers, just a ewer of water and soap that we might be ready for supper.

I saw her at supper, and I saw the bump in her stomach. She turned to me. Was there an ache in her eyes? Then there was nothing, and that nothing felt like a cleaver that had been driven through the middle of my heart. The sense of exile hit me like a seventh wave. I remembered my families in Bruges and Valencia and realised I'd rather be spending Chanukah with them.

To a fanfare, Master Roper appeared side-by-side with another man, tall and thin. His nose was high in the air, and he had a long blond beard and wore a badge on his black velvet cloak. Could it be in the shape of a diamond? It was Reginald Pole, the grandnephew of Richard III and Edward IV, bastions of Plantagenet England, friend of the pope. Everyone cheered. What treason was this in the home of a friend of the Tudor king? Reginald Pole nodded to Álvaro, as if he knew him, and I shivered.

I couldn't get a word to Álvaro, who was lost in chatter. I was overcome by the smell of blood and meat, horrified by whole cow heads placed on the table, cleft in the middle so that the guests could pick out the brains with their two-pronged forks. There were hams the size of a poor man's house, spiked with cloves from Africa. Above the highest one I saw her face again. She directed the servants to place the ham directly before me. Without smiling, she pointed at the ham and mimed, "Eat, man, eat!" Reginald Pole smiled vaguely as she identified me. A fool came between them, dressed in bright rags and bells. I shifted but found myself trapped in the tightness of strangers on either side, a row of serving men behind me.

A juggler arrived, and he became a fire-eater before producing a monkey dressed in ermine, like the king. I couldn't help but laugh, but how I cursed you, my diary, for the trust I'd put in you, trust that you'd surely betrayed.

The fool tapped me on the right shoulder with his false nose like a falcon's beak. "What are you about, Señor Academicus?" He rang his bells over my ears.

"I am about truth, freedom, clarity, and clear speech among academics."

"Oooh," he replied. "Go on, Señor Academicus. Perhaps not so Academicus after all?"

"I despise academic voices that alienate the people. I'm for plain speech that includes us all."

He laughed and offered me sugared fruit. As I ate, he found a pair of brass cymbals and brought the entire room to a standstill. In the silence, I saw Sir Thomas enter from the cold. He nodded to his guests and took his seat at the side of the table. I remembered he hated being at the head. He took power in going unnoticed. The fool began:

> I have a very nobleman,
> Philosopher from Spain,
> Who'd have the speech among us rendered
> very plain.
> No more will he have talk
> That only scholars know,
> For if that were the case
> His flowers wouldn't grow.

He twisted and turned and did a double back somersault.

> I spoke with him at length
> And this he did decree
> As clearly as the jingle bell that rings upon
> my knee.

Reginald Pole stared at me with no expression as the fool continued:

> For this is the truth of what he said to me:
> Any non-donkey of a man except Socrates,

And any other belonging to this same man,
Begins contingently to be black.

What did this mean? The energy of the room changed. He turned to Meg, to Pole, to William Roper, and they all turned to me. Could they see me for the alien I was, the enemy within? Was this the final unmasking? They say that fools could read minds and unmask villains. I turned to Meg and Álvaro. Nothing. The fool rang a bell over my head on the end of a curled green stick and finished:

See my point of view my friends—
He's a man who holds his nerve,
Says one thing to us perhaps,
Though it's another God he serves.

They laughed raucously while I laughed falsely. After supper, I caught her.

"Mistress Roper—Meg."

She shook her head, telling me that the name was not available to me anymore.

"They are random jottings. If you read them, you would know of the deep affection I have for—"

She cut me off. "Slow down, Juan Luis. What are you referring to?"

"My writings, my personal notes. You said you found them. Isn't that what the fool was referring to?"

"He's just a fool, señor, and as for your writings, I could hardly read them."

Could she see the relief in my face?

"Forgive me," she said. "I never should have looked. Is it Hebrew Spanish that you know, a family dialect?"

"Yes, an old family dialect handed down from many generations."

"Then don't worry about it." She paused. "But what, exactly, is your quest?"

"To finish my book, the one for the queen."

"So, Señor Vives, will you show us your book about the education of a Christian woman?" Reginald Pole interjected. He looked down at me from his great height, shoulders puffed.

"It is for the queen's eyes first," I told him.

"But am I not your queen?" Meg said with a chuckle. Pole chuckled, too, and began to murmur, "Show us, show us."

"In this house you are the queen, my lady. The book is for the most pious, the most goodly and Christian queen, ruler of all our hearts."

Meg turned and moved away. "Of course, señor. Of course."

The next morning, I saw her again, dressed in green and holding a pewter cup while leaning against the giant mantle as she engaged some gnarled aunt. I found myself between the two of them. I whispered in her ear, as Álvaro had once taught me, so that the small hairs within it would vibrate. "Why is it, Mistress Roper, that you are so quiet, so cool. Are you trying to break my heart?"

She quickly turned away from the ancient one and uttered, "Señor, my home is your English home, but I have many concerns. It will not be long." She patted her stomach and looked up, but her eyes did not shine. "If only I could break your heart."

Álvaro must have been watching from some nook, for he came between us, like a drawbridge slamming down. "My lady, he's the greatest challenge, this man Vives. His wife in Bruges is always saying it."

She bolted as if jabbed by a needle.

Álvaro grabbed me under the arm, humming, "Just walk away."

He took me to Sir Thomas, whom I'd not even spoken to the previous night. "Ensuring the conversos stay converted, Sir Thomas," Álvaro said.

I could have thrown him into the giant log fire.

"Vives. Yes, I remember him, but his real name is Hayim, no?"

It was the Hebrew name of my ancestors, meaning life, which they had translated into Vives. He slapped me on the back and pulled me towards him, kissing me on the top of the head and speaking, "Ad imo pectore."

"What do those words mean, Father?" asked a young boy, ruddy-faced and light-haired.

"From the heart, my dear son."

This was John, his only boy, with the face of an angel. Sir Thomas bent low and lifted him up in his arms. "My best boy, my only boy."

I was grieving the distance from my own father. Resentment reared up, and I bit my tongue. The rest of the day we ate, talked, and journeyed through the snow to St. Stephen's Church.

When I returned to the room at night, I found Álvaro asleep. I feigned sleep, and when I perfected my imitation of sleep-breath, he upped to depart as he had done the previous night. I lay there and whispered.

"Go carefully. Observe the ways of the ancestors."

"That is exactly what I am doing, Juanito."

Sometime in the silent stillness of the dawn, he stumbled back.

"Tell me, Álvaro, where have you been? The stews of Southwark?"

"No, my friend, I have not been to Southwark."

"Where, then?" I asked and sat up in bed. Although it was dark, I could tell that he was looking at me. "Come, Álvaro, tell me. You know me well enough. Have you ever met a more tolerant man?"

"Have I ever met a more conflicted man?" he replied. "I am entrusting you with my life and the lives of others, but I still believe in you, Juanito. I still believe that we cannot fulfil our quest without you'.

"Please, Álvaro, tell me."

"Yes, you must now know, for this is the moment when everything changes. I have been in two places. First to the Domus."

"The Domus? Why?"

"Because I won't leave them there to rot! I sit outside and sing a song for tuppence. Then I change an English word for a Spanish word or a Hebrew one that they might feel less alone. I've also been to a place they call Creechurch Lane, to the house of a spice man, Jorge Añes."

"Who is this Añes?" I knew the name was to be found among my own people. "And why visit him at night, brother?" My heartbeat was in my throat, loud as a mighty drum.

"This Portuguese merchant, this Añes—he understands the commandment 'welcome the stranger.' Do you remember that one, Juanito?"

"Of course I do."

"He welcomes strangers, some from our own land, some from elsewhere, who have been hiding for generations. He welcomes them into his home every Friday night." I'd completely forgotten it was Friday night, lost as I was in this new world.

"Who has been hiding for generations?"

"The children of the English Jews, the ones who they thought they'd got rid of two hundred years ago. There in the attic, with you here, obsessing about a married woman, we've been celebrating the festival of lights, Chanukah, this very night."

"Good God! This is not safe. You have placed my quest in jeopardy."

"Your quest, Juanito? You underestimate me if you think I'd spend every night in Southwark. I'm working for our people and their place here in this land, which will be a safe home for us in its proper time. Until that great day, it's not my task to visit whores in Southwark but to keep the flame alive."

A smidgeon of grey light emerged through the middle of the heavy drapes.

"No! I am the one. It's I who has been chosen for this work. Of course you go to Southwark. You've told me all about it."

"You are the one distracted by love and lust, but now's the time to bring you back. Things are about to change for you." He took in a sharp breath. "There were no nights in Southwark last summer. I was preparing, watching—seeing if you were with us or if you were leaving us."

"Then I, too, must come to the Domus. I can play the lute and you can sing to them."

"You're too clumsy, too noticeable."

"But what of the tortoiseshell penis or the husband baying for your blood?"

"A good trick, no? If I was to get caught and questioned, I needed evidence. The husband who wanted my blood is named Abrahams. The flame has never gone out here and never will."

"Why did you come to me then, Álvaro de Castro? Why not just do it all yourself?"

"I came to you because I had been told to by the voice of the silence. Some call it the Kabbalah. Believe me, I was told."

"The Kabbalah?" To my own embarrassment, I knew little about it. This was the man who the gypsy told me saw more than I saw. I looked into his dark Sephardic eyes. "Álvaro, practitioner of the Kabbalah, what do you prophesy for me?"

"I'm no fortune-teller—you must know that much—but I know you are a part of this, and when you ask for me, I will be here for you. Do you not remember the Book of Ruth? 'Wherever you go, I will go. Wherever you lodge, I will lodge. Your people shall be my people, and your God my God.'"

"Of course, but do I know you, Álvaro?"

* * *

Is this why he sleeps so soundly? Safe in the embrace of the God his secret community shares together? And now, my diary, what do I want you to be? A witness, perhaps, to the tide of feelings that surge through me this morning, for I know that I have been distracted by the kol ishah, the voice of the woman. Yes, the old fears surge through my bones, and my fear grows fast like a flame reaching up the timber of the stake, but I am back now. I am inside. I am ready for the greatest challenge of all.

25 December 1523

On Christmas Day, with a new dedication since I had missed Chanukah, which means "dedication," we made our way to the Palace of Windsor. We climbed the wide but worn stone steps to the great east door, and there at the door were a group of thin young ladies in green and red singing, "Gaudete! Gaudete! Christ est natus ex Marie virgine Gaudete!" "Rejoice, rejoice, Christ is born to the Virgin Mary. Rejoice!" I wasn't seduced by it, for I was there on a mission. I listen to higher orders.

My heart went out to them, though, those thin ladies standing in the cold with just a brazier burning nearby, for soon we'd be in the warm inside, but these ladies—who knew how long they'd be there? Did they sing just for a blanket for a child or for a loaf of bread for the Christmas table? I gave them all the groats and pennies that I had, and so entering the palace with empty pockets I had a clear conscience.

Once inside, a cup of spiced mulled wine was thrust into my hands, but I found it hard to hold because my fingers seemed frozen, like claws. We were then taken up to our rooms. This was like a military campaign, and we were just one more company that had been mustered for it. Our meagre room looked out across the green towards the river in the distance, rolling towards the ocean, that, pray God, would one day take me home to Marguerite. Álvaro made his home at the foot of my bed. I said a prayer for my Henry and Marguerite, for the little boy, Zeek, and I said another for my father and sisters, that they would soon be here, safe and well.

Sir Thomas arrived in my room, looking as eager as a child going out to play in the snow. "It is time, young brother. Bring your book, quickly."

We hurried through the vast array of rooms—the sheriff's chamber, the ladies' chamber, the presence chamber. Each was hung with tapestries: Jesus and Mary, the Three Wise Men, shepherds tending flocks, and more. Each chamber was a sea of candlelight and seemed grander and more elaborate until we arrived at the privy chamber. The doors swung open and the king and queen sat before us on small thrones raised on a dais covered in crimson damask. Grooms and pretty ladies surrounded them, and I could see that the prettiest, with a sunset-coloured hood, was Mary Boleyn. She looked at me with recognition and then turned away. I pray God that she will say nothing or let the queen know that she once knew me.

"Sir Thomas More and Master John Lewis of Oxford," the herald announced.

"Thomas, Thomas, Thomas," the king said, beaming. "And our daughter's preceptor, the champion of the poor and advocate of clear speech. What have you two brought for us?"

"Sovereign, here is my reply to Luther's tract," Sir Thomas said. "It is simply called *Responsio ad Lutherum*." He presented his book, and the king grabbed it and his face became a storm cloud. He thumbed through the pages and muttered into his beard.

"Order, Thomas. This is good. Mine is the way of order, and Luther's is disorder. I see you champion your pope above your king. A brave fool, eh? Let a thousand be printed, and let it be translated and sent abroad. Let it reach the eyes and ears of the heretic himself."

"And you, Spaniard, what have you brought us?" the king asked.

"My king and my queen, Your Majesties, I have brought you the work over which I have laboured since I first arrived in this blessed realm. It is called *The Education of a Christian Woman*. I presented it to the queen, who read the dedication.

"I dedicate this book to you, noble queen, like a painter who designed your portrait. In the canvas you would find an image of your body, but in my book, you will encounter a likeness of your soul. As a young girl, a spouse, a widow, and now a wife, you have left to all women in every way of life a magnificent example. And the Princess Mary, through your work, will be the greatest and kindest queen our realm has known."

The king's face soured. He looked to us and then to Mary Boleyn. "We still hope God will bless us with a son." He turned to both Sir Thomas and me, and with a renewed jolly countenance said, "This is a season of giving and receiving. First, for Thomas, we have something, here, Kate." She handed him a box, inside of which was a small golden cup gleaming with a Latin inscription around the rim that I could not read. Sir Thomas was effusive in his gratitude.

The king turned and handed me a small box covered in blue velvet. "Of these there have only been four made."

I opened it and saw a gold ring with a blue enamel Star of David. I closed it again with a reflex jerk.

"Thank you, Your Majesties."

"Now go, the pair of you, and enjoy the festivities," the king said.

"One last thing, Your Majesties," I said. "I made a promise. Master Owen of Chatham begs to make an apology."

The king looked puzzled. "Who? Owen of Chatham?"

The queen sat upright, her face red despite the white nightshade make-up.

"Oh, Owen, and his buxom daughter Abigail of the horse stables, wriggling like a snake on my lap when she came in," the king said.

Mary Boleyn sniggered, and the queen snapped her fingers for her to shut up.

The king, who was still laughing, leaned towards me, elbow on his knee. "Time for you to go, methinks. We will see you tonight at the masque."

What had I done this time?

"Sorry," I said to Sir Thomas, who had seen the ring.

"Shut up, you fucking fool. You're the one who should be covered in shit now, and as for that," he said, pointing to the ring, "keep it hidden."

Had I alienated myself to the one I was trying to win over? I was deaf to the Christmas court. Did the king know me for a Jew? I hurried back to my room.

"Álvaro!" I called. "Look at this! The king presented me with this as a gift and said there were only four in the realm. For whom are the other three?"

Even the implacable Álvaro de Castro looked shocked. "It is as I thought," he said. "He knows. This is a message, Juanito. Stay low. Listen rather than speak and all will be revealed."

"What does he want? What will be revealed?"

In the early evening, we made our way to the great hall, the hearth itself the size of a small room. On it sat the Yule log. Singing and music filled the space, along with the smells of the banquet to come: venison, lamb, and game birds. Long tables were arranged in the shape of a U, and the seats were neatly covered in red velvet. There were cloths of pressed and starched damask— from Florence, I guessed—and the heavy silver cutlery came from Venice. I found my name on a vellum card and looked at the card to my left: "Reginald Pole." It wasn't long before he arrived.

"Agh," he said. "It is Señor Hayim."

My Hebrew name. How did he know that? He took off the cloak to reveal a black silk shirt.

"I didn't get the chance to explain at Bucklersbury. The first bit you'll be pleased to hear. I've returned, for the season only, from

Padua. The second bit, I fear, señor, you'll not like so much. I've returned on the command of the Holy Order of the Inquisition, señor."

His words were like a sudden jab in the ribs, but I'd not let it show. "I am delighted. Let's talk of Rome, of the pope."

"You're a scholar, señor. That I know. What I'm not certain of, however, is why you won't stay in your own kingdom."

"I'm sure that if you're working for the Holy Order, that you know the difficulties faced by a Nuevo in Spain. Thankfully we have a warm welcome here."

He turned his entire body and looked at me with eyes that yearned for power. "Why the king trusts you I'll never know. We have a word for your sort in Italy, much easier on the ear. *Marrano*, which means pig."

Trembling, I grabbed the heavy tablecloth and clung to it like a drowning man clinging to a single wooden oar in the ocean. In the distance, like a rescue vessel, I saw Meg, and the very sight of her gave me strength.

On my right were Lord and Lady Lisle, the governors of Calais. He was about sixty, and she was half his age. Lady Lisle said, "Sir, call me Honor."

I felt a hand between my thighs, and I felt its stroke. This was the hand of Honor Lisle. I turned and whispered, "Don't."

She had something to squeeze on to now and laughed. Finally, she let go, whispering, "More later."

I scanned the face of her husband, who looked at me, smiling and nodding.

The queen waved at me before turning away. Was I forgiven?

Lady Lisle pointed at the bulge in my pants and then turned and thrust her bosom into the chest of her corpulent husband. Acrobats came in running, tossing each other ever higher into the air. Two men, tanned and painted, held green-winged parrots with crimson neckbands that flew from their arms and circled the rooms in opposite directions before landing on the hands of their masters. The audience shrieked and cheered for more.

With a crack like thunder, a wooden castle was dragged into the room and was placed in front of the fire. Children in bright blues and yellows ran in, chased by a red-clothed dragon that somehow breathed fire and exterminated the children one by one. Next, a young woman with a mask and pointed hat entered the room, followed by the midget minions of the dragon, who chased her onto the floor and tied her to a post. Just as it seemed as if the dragon would burn the woman alive, in came a tall man in shining armour with a sword and mask. He lunged at the dragon, which replied with more flames. Would the whole palace be set ablaze, with the country's nobility cremated en masse? I looked for an escape route.

The knight pierced the shoulder of the dragon, which groaned with a final crash of the cymbal before slumping to the floor. The knight removed his mask, revealing the king himself. He bowed and moved towards the young lady, untying her, kissing her hand, and removing her mask. There was a gasp followed by more applause. This was not Mary Boleyn, but another young lady whom I'd once known in Paris. This one was raven-haired and dark-eyed, with a cut-glass figure and a proud, defiant look.

I turned to Lady Lisle. "Who is it?" I asked.

"La petite Boleyn," she replied. "Anne."

She took his arm and they bowed to the audience. They took their seats next to one another and the banquet began. The queen, dignified as ever, greeted the king with a kiss and smiled sweetly at Anne Boleyn, although it must have given her pain to do so. Mary Boleyn also appeared, taking a seat at the top table. I noticed she didn't look at her sister. Would he pluck two cherries from the same tree? Would he do it before his own wife and the entire court?

A great cooked bird, a thing from the New World called a turkey, with peacock feathers thrust into it, was wheeled before the king. He seemed to take great pleasure in carving it, as if he was the high priest performing a sacrifice at a holy temple. He told us that within the great bird were smaller birds: peacock, swan, goose, chicken, duck, woodcock, and quail. They all cheered at every new bird he announced. Was there anything he could do for which they wouldn't cheer?

We sat down to eat as four musicians, dark and handsome, began playing.

"What is this new kind of fiddle?" I asked Lady Lisle.

"They call it a viol."

"And who are the players?"

"They're Italian musicians, the king's new favourites. Very exotic-looking, no?"

The dancing started after dinner. I used my crooked back as an excuse not to join Lady Lisle in the energetic galliard. I got up from my seat and hid by a garlanded pillar. I glanced at where Meg had been sitting to find her gazing straight back at me. William Roper was in the dance, now a pavan, intricate like a knot garden. He was strutting like the peacock the king had just carved. I took his seat.

"Why is one season so warm and the next so cold?" I asked her.

"My dear friend," she said, "you want everything, but what of your wife in Bruges? At least my husband, although imperfect, is here."

"You expose me, my lady." She looked at me, expressionless.

"Things move very quickly for us. Today we have the king's favour, but forces are at work that may change the status quo." She nodded towards the Boleyn sisters. "You're not secretly part of those forces, are you, señor?"

"No, my mistress, Meg. Listen, why don't we run away from here and visit Bedlam—continue our work there?"

"You'd take me to Bedlam, but you wouldn't truly take me to heart, would you? If you relinquish for me that which is in your blood, then I'll be your secret companion for all time."

"My lady, where is the fresh smile that you tendered in the summer months? I long for those summer days, my mistress."

'Señor Vives, my dear, I can be no Israelite's slave any more than you can be an Egyptian's." She quickly joined her husband and left.

I retreated to my room, where I found Álvaro deep in meditation.

"You stink," he said. "The Italian viol players—they played well."

"Beautifully. Is it significant?"

"Did the king look pleased at their playing?"

"Very pleased. Why do you ask, brother? Are they known to you?"

"Good. It is as it should be."

6 January 1524

Álvaro de Castro headed into the purlieus of the city. I waited there, at the Palace of Windsor for the king, but I wouldn't join the hunt for stags or otters, so I found myself with an impossible wait. I found solace as my father found solace, in the books of the ancient library. Patience, diary, was my friend. Let me tell you why.

Among the musty smell of the centuries-old gospels was a purple vine scroll hidden among a series of Greek bibles, a part of the Talmud. It wasn't complete, of course, but it had a German stamp on each of the four volumes, and the ink was still shiny, surely less than a year old. Who'd brought it there? What other Jew resides in the court of Henry VIII? Does he or she have one of the other rings? Would Álvaro tell me if he knew? Our hand strengthens.

I was alone in the library when the queen's guard found me. An audience at last! I must have been pardoned for asking William Owen to be forgiven. She was wearing pale blue, talking with her

Spanish lady-in-waiting, Maria de Salinas. I have seen her before, this Maria, a thin, fragile, high-pitched creature who goes by her married name, Lady Willoughby. She looked uncertain as I approached them, floating as they were on a sea of candles that reflected gold from the rosewood panels. Here was the daughter of the enemy, the architects of the Inquisition. She told me to get a great coat and make for the jetty, for we were to take a barge upstream to a nunnery known as Syon.

Waiting with the ladies that included the Boleyn sisters, I seized my chance. "Mary, Anne, happy is the day, but you must entirely forget that you know me."

They huddled together in the cold, waiting for the queen, like a pair of young witches. Anne, dressed in black, whispered back, "Voy a mantener nuestro pequeno secreto, al menos por ahora, por cuanto tiempo se shebe nuestra Reina?" *I will keep our little secret, for now at least, for how much longer will she be our Queen?* I remembered how sharp and gifted she was. She went on in low tones. "Para mi amigo, Vives, el secreto Judio, podemos ayudamos unos a otros, no?" *My friend, Vives, the secret Jew, we can help one another, no?*

The queen arrived and we boarded. She called me inside the red cabin. We set out on the wintery morning, a gentle mist rising from the withered rushes on the banks of the river. A watery sun, just beginning to pierce the bank-side willows, shone through the panes of the cabin and lit her rounded face.

"Señor, you are a good man. Tell me—can a man's mind, infected by lies, ever heal?" She was focussed intently on the wading birds, stock-still in the cold mists.

"With patience and reason, of course, Your Majesty."

"And with good counsel from wise men?" she asked.

Lady Willoughby was fussing around her like a wasp at the honey pot. Anne Boleyn had crept into the cabin and was trying to give the queen a glass of something warm. I asked them both to leave.

"My lady, if you're asking me to counsel the king, then I accept, but how can I counsel him unless I'm allowed an audience with him."

"I can barely get an audience myself," she said, touching my limp shoulder. "Who did this to you?"

"There was a peasant revolt in Flanders and scuffles in the streets. It was hard not to get caught up in it." She sighed as Anne Boleyn, who hadn't left, leaned forwards, thrusting mead under the queen's nose. Was she trying to poison her?

"This is precisely what will happen here if he is persuaded by the new factions," the queen said. "There will be a civil war and brother will fight brother." She fixed her swollen eyes to the floor. "Señor, I am nothing if not for my daughter, Mary, and my father Ferdinand's faith, which is the king's faith in his own heart. Surely, with good counsel you can show him that the only way is to remain united?"

"And what of Prince Arthur?"

"Señor, why do you ask? It's long resolved and between God and me."

Maria, who had been observing from farther down the cabin, walked quickly towards us and tried to wrest the carafe from Anne Boleyn's hands. As the wine flew around the cabin, she yelled, "Su Majestad, su Majestad," but the queen would not be stopped.

"Go from here," the queen replied.

Maria, muttering to herself, walked to the back of the cabin, taking Anne Boleyn with her.

"What passes between you and me will remain between you and me," I said. "Confide in your Spanish brother. Were there intimate relations between you and Prince Arthur? If you tell me, I can perhaps help you with the king."

"There were indeed relations that, save from Maria, I have not spoken of to another living soul. There were nights of passion, and there was something else in Durham House. No one but the old king, the brutes of his Star Chamber, and a dead maid know."

"I am your brother and also like a loving uncle, not merely a schoolteacher to your daughter. To help you, I have to know."

"When they saw the bump, they laid me down and thumped on my stomach. There was a miscarried boy, perhaps six months, that the old king's men forced from my belly after Arthur died."

My chest felt like a lead weight had been placed on top of it, making it impossible to draw breath. I had not anticipated this.

"The king's men launched an attack on you? Men took your dead son? Why should they do so when that boy may have been king?"

"They said it was not a son, but a bleeding. The old king, the tyrant—his queen had died, and he had wanted me first for his own bride so as to get his own sons on me."

I sighed in disbelief. "Why launch an attack if he wanted you?"

The queen slumped and chewed on a fingernail. "He wanted me intact, a virgin to the world." She seemed tenser now. "My father utterly rejected the match, so the old king, a horrible man, took his revenge."

"You could have left, no? Gone back to Spain?"

"Yes, had they not kept me prisoner in Durham House for seven months without a window on to the world. My Henry wanted me, and I wanted him. So, my secret son, my firstborn, whom I'm sure I heard cry, was given, they said, to the gods of the river. I thought God would give me six or seven sons from Henry and that I should forget the little one, but I never forgot."

Whatever I had previously heard or witnessed, this seemed far worse. It jarred my soul, but why was I coercing her to confess? I remembered the little boy, Zeek. If it weren't for Spanish brutality, his parents would still be there to love him and raise him.

I glanced at the bank. The horses had gone, and the sun had broken through. Everything seemed clearer. Anne emerged from behind the small table where a carafe had been placed. She was filling glasses with it.

"Go away," I said. But she was like a leech that would not budge.

"That girl, does she understand Spanish?" I asked the queen.

'No," the queen answered. "She reads and speaks French, not Spanish."

I did not correct her ignorance. I knew, though, that everything had changed, for though we were speaking the queen's dialect, it was close enough to the Castilian I had taught Anne Boleyn in Paris that she would have understood every word. The secret was out. One day it would get to the king, and it was my doing. Things would change, and it was my task to ensure that the lot of my people would change with it. Alhough I had cajoled the queen into revelation, I wanted to be the one with the weapon, not Anne Boleyn. I beckoned Maria de Salinas from the back of the cabin to take Anne away once and for all. Happy with having overheard us, she went. I sat down again close to the queen.

"Your Majestad, I will counsel the king, but there is a great favour I must ask."

'Señor, anything. Just ask." She was all mine now. This was the moment.

"There is an old man in Valencia who lives in La Juderia. He has three daughters—Eva, Beatriz, and Leonora."

"His name is Vives?" she asked, alert like a deer in the open fields.

"There is an issue—Limpieza de Sangre-the impurity of the blood. Unfounded, but it persists, and they are to this day heckled and harassed."

"I am sorry for your father and for these women—your sisters, no?"

"There is no truth in the rumours. We are Nuevos for many generations. Just look at my writings. There is no doubt."

"I know this, señor. Why do you think we've had the cardinal's groom in your room?"

"Yes—Álvaro, the cleverest one of all. My lady, I beg you, speak for them. Get them safe passage and have them here soon."

"Stop, brother. Don't tremble so. It's done. Leave it with your queen, your other sister and Master Pole. Speak no more of it, for by the end of January, they'll be here."

"My lady, Master Pole is another agent perhaps? He does not seem friendly to my cause."

"All right then, the new ambassador, Louis de Praet. He'll be in London soon. He can arrange it."

"Louis de Praet is the new Spanish ambassador to England? Surely, this cannot be true?"

"It is, and very soon, brother."

Pole or de Praet? Did relief or horror spread over my face? I moved away, shaking, and then returned, not thinking my words through. "Perhaps we should have Reginald Pole, after all."

"All right then. Pole it is. Don't ask me to change my mind again, though. Have faith."

The barge eddied upstream with the oarsmen silent.

Later, the queen, outside the cabin with her hands in a fur muffle, seemingly caught in meditation, called me back. "Señor, out of the two, adversity or success, which would you choose?"

"Success, Your Majesty. And yourself?"

"I would prefer an equal share of both. If I still had to choose, I would prefer the former because those with only success frequently lose their minds."

She let me contemplate her words in a silence, broken only by the sound of the oars breaking the surface of the gentle river. Anne Boleyn had crept back again. Did she know no fear? The queen turned to her and said, this time in English, "Or their heads."

Anne drew the back of her hand across her neck as if slicing it off and then threw her head back.

We toured the nunnery, with its elaborate cloisters, garlanded pillars, and roaring fires. Before we turned into the abbess's private chapel, I caught Anne Boleyn by the shoulder.

"Do not grab me, señor. Only Lord Percy or the king can grab me." Rumours in court said that she had bewitched Lord Percy, the future Earl of Northumberland. She went on. "Señor, don't worry about what I know. Just remember that we can work together—that we have common goals. One day you'll see the sense in my words."

As our tour of the nunnery drew to a close, and after the abbess had been given a small chest of silver coins, I caught up to the queen.

"Your Majesty, let us talk about the princess's education. She's wise beyond her years. But for her own good, she needs more exposure to the world and its peoples, the rich *and* the poor, traditionalists *and* reformists."

"Reformists, never. It is out of the question."

"Shouldn't she be taught about the love of God, of being, and the Universe itself rather than the Holy Order?"

"Señor, I will do for you what I can, but she is a true crusader of our faith."

"We have to bring her out of the darkness of the past. To keep her Catholic, yes, but let it be Catholicism that celebrates the unity of creation, not its difference."

She shook her finger and put it to her lips. "Basta! Enough!"

I retreated, but back in the palace, as darkness lay all around, I prayed to the God of creation, of oneness. I prayed that there might soon be a time where I could experience that oneness with my father, my sisters, and the woman I would make my wife. I prayed for Zeek, who I would treat as a son. How could I be one if these were not here. I would only experience God when I experienced the true love of family.

The king would not see me, and I had to get back to Oxford. By February my family would be here. Then I could work on the king for the grand plan. In the end, it would make this land a new world of concord, peace, and harmony.

15 January 1524, Oxford

"A misfit. Nothing I like more than a misfit," said Thomas Linacre, still clinging to life when I told him of my solitary days in the library at Windsor while the others hunted. "I'm still earthbound," he said as we ate beef and drank sweet wine. Later that day, we walked slowly to the Oxford players' revival of Aristophanes's comedy *The Frogs*. He fell about in laughter, and I was sure that he would fracture his frail ribs, and Henry barked when the players became frogs. What privilege to be with him on the final part of his earthly journey. Perhaps he'll hold out until Father is here.

I wait impatiently for a letter, any news of their journey. They must be on their way by now. I hope they don't waste time packing old things or saying goodbye to old friends. I pray that when the men deliver my letter signed by the queen and Reginald Pole that they will just come.

There was a surprise last week, a gift of money from the queen and a letter offering me a royal privilege of importing Gascony wine. When Father gets here, he'll find a house big enough for the families Vives and Valldaura.

There is work to be done. The princess is back on the morrow, and my father will be here soon. So, diary, I've got plans to make. You'll have to go now. I'll get you again when they're here and you can meet them. For now, it's adios.

2 April 1524

No. Dear God, a thousand times no.

I rip my shirt. Shema koli Adonai. Lord, hear my voice. Tell me it is not so.

6 April 1524

This letter, get into the flames. Burn, burn, burn!

An hour passes and though the letter has been burnt, its news has not died.

An hour more and I dig my head out from my hands, only to find that the nails have scoured my scalp with lines. I ignored the whimpering hound and was deaf to Álvaro's words, "Let us say the mourner's Kaddish."

I was right. I was too slow, too clumsy.

Was this the price I paid for my self-love, for my cowardice, for procrastination? As January passed and February turned into March, I made no move to go there.

Father, can you hear me? Why did they do it? Was it Reginald Pole or was it Louis de Praet? Did the new neighbours who took de Pinto's silver workshop vilify you? As you packed to leave, did you by mistake reveal the Torah scrolls hidden within the wall cavity by the fireplace? And what of my Eva, Beatriz, and Leonora, who dispersed into the night with the clothes on their backs?

The letter from the Lady Willoughby made no attempt to save me from my suffering. It said that they chained you to a post, shaved your head and beard, and painted a Star of David on your forehead. What was that moment like, Papa, who used to hold me so tight and laugh as Eva sidestepped and high-kicked?

She said that, as the flames started, you chanted loudly and rhythmically: "You shall love the Lord your God with all your heart and with all your soul." And you called my name and the name of my mother, Blanquina, and of my lost brother, Jaime, and my own name with that of my sisters again and again.

Did you hear the crying and wailing in the streets from the men and women who had always known you? Did it seem to you, as she said in the letter, that there would be a riot, that you would be rescued even as the flames licked at your feet? I pray God that you were gone before the hour on that windless day, that the report of your slow death was not true.

"I shouldn't have meddled," I muttered over and over. "I must get my sisters out and rescue them. I must make amends. It's not too late."

*　*　*

I left a princess and a dying Thomas Linacre. All credit to him, though, who refused to go to the next world once he'd heard the news, as if trying to be my father, to spare me another grief.

We rode that night and gave him his leave of this tortured world. Álvaro was ever by my side, like an archangel, but wearing black from head to foot except for a tzitzit-tassel that flowed from beneath his jacket.

First, I would get to the queen and tell her what her meddling had done. Then I'd be in Spain to find my sisters. When they were safe, if anywhere in this world is now safe, I'd go to Padua for Pole. Crows of death seemed to be laughing at me: *Turn back, Jews.*

Álvaro said over and over, "We'll be safer in Oxford. We mustn't go to the queen. Things will be worse."

Eventually, the lights and the smoke of the city appeared in the distance. Through Ludgate and over the River Fleet we rode, past St Paul's, which was battered like a ship after a long storm far out at sea. In darkness, we came to the Barge. I felt that Margaret Roper would help me. I had to be with her for comfort and warmth before going to the queen.

The guards recognised us and fetched Dorothy, the housekeeper, who came to the gate.

"Gentlemen," she exclaimed. "We were not expecting you. Master is away at court."

"And Meg?" I asked.

"Mistress Margaret is at home, sir, along with Mistresses Cicely and Agnes."

"Dorothy, show us to her." I walked through the front door.

"Meg!" I shouted. "Meg!"

Chattering from the drawing room ceased, and she came out. Could she see the grief in my road-weary face?

"Juanito, what on earth…"

Her sisters parted like the Red Sea and out strode William Roper, prouder and taller than I remembered. He pushed Meg to the back of the group, and I saw that he carried a bundle.

"You called for Mrs. Roper, señor?" he asked.

"Yes. I have things I must discuss with Meg."

"There is a Margaret Roper in this house whom you will address as Mrs. Roper, not Meg, and whose company you will obtain only on my own warrant." The bundle cried. "Tonight, that warrant is not granted."

I staggered and found myself in the arms of Álvaro, as strong as my lost brother. "Ande va la piedra, en el ojo de la ciega," I said.

"What did he say?" William Roper asked.

Meg came forward, holding an arm out to me, and translated. "Where does the rock go but into the eye of the blind person?" She gestured to speak again, but he raised his left hand, the right still clutching the baby. He wore thick gold rings on two of his fingers. One had a large stone, and he thrust it at the top of her head until she fell to the floor with a shriek. Cicely and Anne rushed to pick her up. I tried to help but found myself surrounded by a wall of guards.

"Thank you, but we cannot stay tonight," Álvaro said. "We simply meant to extend greetings. My friend has received bad news."

"Oh, but you must stay here," piped up sparkly, blue-eyed Cicely.

Roper lifted his left hand again, and she backed away with a whimper.

Álvaro spoke up, sounding like a biblical prophet. Was he one of the great rabbis of legend? "Be among the students of Aaron. Love the Lord your God. Pursue peace in your own house."

I stumbled out of the entrance hall, Alvarao supporting me at the waist as we made our way into the biting cold wind.

'Álvaro, we must help Meg. We have to go back in."

"No! There's nothing more we can do."

"Then we must get to the queen. Take me there, Álvaro."

"Yes, I'll take you there. Come."

We trudged through dark streets lit only by the night-guard's torches and faint glimmers from tiny windows. We walked through archways and past churches that I neither knew nor recognised. It seemed we were walking away from the river, not towards it, which is where we needed to go in order to get a barge to the palace. Finally, we reached a tavern outside the eastern city wall. Álvaro took to the back entrance to stable the horses.

We walked through a horse yard and into the back of the smoky tavern. There were a couple of men there, one drinking and the other snoring, his arm over the back of a chair to stop him sliding onto the stony floor. Álvaro spoke to the landlord, but I was beyond pleasantries. I simply followed. We walked down wooden stairs into a brick-lined, vaulted cellar. A thick door was shut and bolted behind us. I thought to myself, "Let it be over and make it quick," for I was convinced that this was the secret home of the Inquisition in England. There were vats of beer, bottles of wine, and river sand strewn on the floor, the space lit by a pair of candles.

In that moment of great despair, clarity reappeared. There was a tall, thin man with a dark beard, older than I, and he had a long neck. He and Álvaro talked Portuguese. I was given a yarmulke, soft and silky, and though there were only three of us present, the tall man led me in the mourner's Kaddish.

He looked me in the eye and said, "May his memory be for a blessing." Then silence filled the dank room.

Álvaro touched my forehead with his first two fingers and closed his eyes. "I," he murmured. He traced a line to my left hip and said, "Malkuth." He moved his hand to my right shoulder. "Ve geburah." He traced the line to my left shoulder. "Ve gedulah." He then traced the line to my right hip and concluded with, "Le olam. Amen." He took a dagger from beneath a silken sheet. My heart stopped. Was this the final act of his play? A pagan sacrifice? But he simply put my hand on the dagger and traced the same pattern.

He said, "Thrust and speak with me, YHVH. I was not supposed to say the name of God, for no one is. He turned me a quarter of a circle and said, "Thrust again and say with me, Adonai. He turned me another quarter-circle. More words were spoken, and I followed him blindly. "Feel the breath that is your soul," he said.

Above me was a bright blue sky and the sound of nightingales. I focussed on their song. It was one of joy, of survival, of courage. There was the breeze, and a warm wind drifted into the evening of my childhood. I saw my parents standing together as one and in the peace of their courtyard in the shade of a lemon tree. Their suffering was behind them.

That night we stayed in the ramshackle tavern known as The Flying Horse in the street known as Houndsditch. It was close to Bishopsgate, the main road north out of the city. The tall man of fatherly wisdoms, a specialist in Portuguese wines and ceramics, was introduced as Benjamin Elisha of Lisbon.

"May the Lord bless you and guard you," he said. "May he lift up his face to you and give you peace."

There was calmness about him, a sense of knowing. Of what, I was not sure. He was simply a sage man.

"Your family?" I said. "How do you live here?"

"Señor, it's important that we are here in some form, however we do it and regardless of whomever. Our time will come again in this land, and in all the new lands in which these funny English folk settle."

"The *b'yi-to*, the proper time, but when is the proper time?"

"When? None of our business, my friend, but it will happen. For now, you have done all you can."

"It would have been better to do nothing," I said. Releasing those words seemed to release me from my burden.

"Not so! This is all part of our story, part of the great journey of our people, and you're part of that journey, my son."

Was my father talking through him?

By the break of dawn, we trudged to St Katherine's dock, for what was the point of demanding justice from a queen whose loyalties had become crystal-clear? The ship went only as far as Calais, but it went there peacefully, and the next morning we left that boat. We acquired two old nags and rode into the rising sun to Bruges. After two days of silent riding, we entered the city at evening. Saddle-weary and shoulder-sore, we found the Verversdijk. It was there still, three stories high and unguarded. We knocked and waited. A kind-eyed Spanish girl opened the door, and Álvaro said something quick, as if in code. She fell back and opened the door wide.

From the hall, we could smell the freshly baked challah bread. There was a familiar scraping of chairs from the kitchen that sounded as if someone was rushing to hide something. Who would be inside?

The Spanish girl opened the door to the kitchen an inch at a time and whispered something. It was dark and hard to see, but the first to emerge was Nicolas—taller now—dressed like his father, with a dark jacket, kerchief, and tufts of beard. Behind him was Maria, unable to hide her amazement. I was all eyes for whom was behind her. She emerged, holding the hand of a little boy, blond and awkward. It was Zeek. Her hair was cut shorter now, her face a little thinner, but she still had beautiful eyes that glimmered like diamonds struck by the sunlight.

"It's over," Marguerite said.

"What's over?" I asked.

"The waiting."

Maria, bolder now, grabbed us both by the hands and led us into a circle with the maid between her and Álvaro. "This is Susa. Who knows how she got here from Girona? Let's say it was a miracle."

There weren't enough of us for a minyan, but there never was these days. Nonetheless, Nicolas led us in a prayer of thanksgiving, the *ha gomel*. Then there was a slow and muffled rumble from the back room and a stumbling of weary steps.

"What is happening here?" asked Señora Valldaura, emerging from a chair that was hidden in the alcove at the back of the room. Stooped and bent over like a willow branch, grey hair peeping through a black scarf, she touched my cheek with her cool, motherly hand and nodded her head.

"And Señor Valldaura, where is he?" I asked, looking up the stairs.

"Father is no longer with us," Marguerite answered. "He passed but a month ago."

"May his memory be for a blessing," I said.

All I could feel was the second that led to another second. And if there were to be no more of these seconds, if Louis de Praet was here and was to break down the doors and drag us all to a prison cell, then at least I would have these seconds. The little boy looked into my eyes, and I remembered the day I saw his father, the peasant rebel, being marched through the streets of Bruges. I remembered the day that I saw his mother, distraught, in the small town of Eelko that had since been razed to the ground in a war between Catholics and Protestants. I went up to him, knelt down, and put my arms around him.

"Zeek, little man, you're safe here. You've a home here. There are people here who love you very much."

I blessed that day when, dressed as a monk, I spied on Marguerite and became embroiled in the judicious murder of the little boy's father. I couldn't have changed that. His mother and father are gone now, but we are here, a family, a hermandad. Here is a chance for all of us, a chance in this troubled world.

He looked up at me, but all that he said was, "I remember you."

With my hand on his shoulders, we slowly moved towards the long table in the back room. A meal appeared as if from nowhere.

There was spicy fish, pickled beetroot, and fresh challah. Once we had eaten, my words flowed.

I skirted the subject of how my meddling led to Papa's death and the breaking of Bernardo Valldaura. To my surprise, no one seemed to bring it up. Marguerite, with her hand on mine, led me down the path I needed to tread. "Juanito, we know you tried, my love."

Then it all came out: my foolish pleading with the queen, my plan to manipulate her position with the king, and the terrible day that the letter from Lady Willoughby arrived. I put my other hand on top of hers and said, "I've tried so hard for so long to be—"

Before I could utter the word "strong," a storm of tears and shaking came, a quivering from head to foot. But this was not an apoplexy. They let me have my moment, for this was love, this was family, this was home. With the sweet sound of the blackbirds outside, Marguerite opened the window to the daylight and drew the curtains.

"Look," she said. "The same family of blackbirds bringing food to the nest. There in the eaves. Look!" What business did I have with joy? Álvaro took me to the windowsill, for we were safe with de Praet en route to England. And before he left, he'd granted this family its full liberty, for he had what he wanted: a ruby rosary from Toledo, a dedication in my book, and the ultimate prize, his new role as Ambassador of Charles V to England.

I leaned my head out the window and took a breath of freedom. In that glorious moment I was wholly in the now, and in that now, I was free at last from the horrors of the past, from the fears of the morrow.

27 July 1524

I've reunited these ripped-out pages with their leather-bound jacket… the other half of the diary. But even these pages are coming to an end, and I must put them away or burn them, perhaps? But there are a few lines left, so let's fill them first.

With the promise of summer and the site of shirtless tanned men bringing fruit into the marketplace, Álvaro and I began to laugh again, for like Father said, "What you can laugh at, you can rise above." We laughed for Henry the hound, and we laughed as we sang songs for the Jews of the Domus and for the secret Jews of Houndsditch.

Letters arrived from the queen. There was an apology. The messages had been confused. Reginald Pole had issued the right instruction, but it got to the wrong person. It wasn't her fault or Pole's. It was all a dreadful mistake. Had I heard yet from my sisters?

I had not yet heard from them. Thomas Linacre had finally gone celestial, and Corpus Christi wanted me back. Both she and the princess were expecting me. But I could not go, for the warmth of the home and the bonds of family were too strong. And there, in that home, love happened. You couldn't see it with the eye or touch it with a finger, but it was real, nonetheless.

"Juanito," Marguerite said as we walked into the backyard two days after my arrival. "You seem warmer now, more real."

I put a finger to her lips, which felt cool and yet warm, more precious than gold.

"Why is it so hard for you?" she asked.

"My mother said to never love a woman too well in case you lose her and see her suffer. But I can't help this love. I can't."

"So, the sonnet—it was easier to write as you left than to say when you were here?"

"I didn't get the chance to say it."

"You did write it then?" she said.

"Of course, my sweet."

"Not Álvaro?" I denied it, but she had a window into my innermost thoughts.

"Álvaro wrote it, but I told him what to write."

She laughed and kissed me gently on the lips.

*   *   *

Then, the great thing happened, or should I say the great *things*. For the first celebration, some came from Paris. Others, like Erasmus, came from Louvain. There was an unknown man from London making copious notes, an emissary of the pope, ensuring that all was done properly. That was in the church of St. Donation, strewn with summer flowers and with a choir of young boys. Zeek, in a black jacket with a white ruff-collar, was our page. The dancing and the singing and the drinking went on for two days.

Then there was the silent wedding beneath the canopy in the dead of the night with sand strewn on the floor. There was hushed singing in Hebrew-Spanish and visitors from Antwerp whose names I will never mention. It was over quickly and quietly, as was our wish. Our rampant passion did not begin until then, but since it began, it hasn't stopped.

No more nights in the lonely, terrible torment of the soul. Instead, I wake to the warmth of Marguerite, the love of all the loves. She lies next to me, breasts rising and falling. In her breath I feel her soul. I am not alone now, for love has met with love and found peace and, dare I say it, found an expression of God. This is why I cannot go back to the queen and the princess.

After we made love, by night—I am sorry, diary. What did you say? Why did you laugh? You expect me to talk of that? The skin, soft as butter, the hair under my hands, and the joy—no, I can't. Well, perhaps. Writhing and listening to the sounds she makes, with my tongue deep in her mouth, and my... After I pretend to fall asleep, I know she lies there, next to me, watching. Then we laugh, pull the sheets up, and start all over again.

When I can't sleep, I climb into the attic for silent meditation. Mama and Papa come back to me. They tell me not to live in guilt. But what of Beatriz, Eva, and Leonora? Where are they? And how do I get to them when my meddling only leads to suffering? That is for another day. But you, diary, you have to go once and for all because I've got a family to protect, people who need me. Down you go, beneath the walls, beneath the floor. *Adios!*

PART THREE

FOR HENRY THE KING OR FOR CATHERINE THE QUEEN?

"It is not your duty to complete the work, neither are you free to desist from it."

Mishnah Avot 2:16, The Talmud

24 September 1528, Bruges

I t was a time of healing, of putting broken bits together, of floating and of being rather than of doing. Five years passed. Our little boy is ten, and our family of three lives here in peace.

She could sense a change as the spring turned into summer and the swallows left their nests.

"Don't go cold on me, Juanito," my wife begged. "As you get stronger, stay close."

I did stay close. I let it go, at least for a while. Although we were not blessed with a child of our own—not through any lack of passion, you understand—our home was blessed with love. The little boy who we'd adopted, though he had his own name and head full of blond hair, was our boy in every other way.

It was the words from Valencia that disrupted that peace. I couldn't ignore them. Even though she insisted I burn them, for they are of my own flesh and blood, how can I possibly do so? The letter was sealed with blood-red wax in the shape of a diamond. My heart sank. What new hell was this? What bad news?

It commended me for my daily observance of Mass. Clearly, the far-seeing eyes and ever-open ears of the Spanish king were still working in this town. The letter said I must help find my youngest sister, Beatriz, "still abroad in the land of Judah." Eva was safe in the arms of the convent of Carmen, and though she wouldn't say a word to anyone, she had turned to Christ. Her husband's wailing could be heard from the vents of a prison cell, but Eva was safe. She had turned her back on him. Leonora married into one of the very best Valencian families, one with many names and several titles. tried to lull her with the promises of salvation, a large home, an amnesty. At the meeting place, though, on the first night of Passover, one of Beatriz's warriors put a knife to her throat and threatened to use it if she didn't keep her mouth shut.

What did they want of me? It's true Beatriz was devoted to studying Father's Talmud in secret, that her eyes squinted by the age of fourteen. It's true that her own betrothed—well, no one can write of the medical dissection of a living man. But would she have threatened her own sister under any circumstances? And would she galvanise a band of warriors hell-bent on revenge? I don't wish to know the answer to that because the answer is yes.

I turned the page of the letter.

> Señor Vives, the warrior Jewess known as Beatriz Vives rallies Nuevos, burns houses, plunders churches and is the enemy of us all. We must save her soul. Any knowledge you have, you must at once report it, for if she would kill her

own sister as the Jews killed their own brother, Jesus Christ, where will she stop?"

Although I had not written a diary for five years, something about that letter compelled me. It fired my will, not just to save Eva and Beatriz, but to right the wrong done to my people, for this is not how we act. This is not how we have ever acted in the Sepharad. I have to re-enter the fight to rescue my people from the abyss. Was that their secret aim, though? To flush me and the others out?

I sit here in the attic, night after night, writing by the light of a single flame. How do I tell Marguerite of my decision? Shall I chase her around the four-poster bed before tying her down until she finally submits and then tell her? Or shall I just leave like a coward?

Earlier tonight, sleep, that transitory guest, left me in the early hours. I crawled out of the bed and watched her. She seemed encased in the scent of the lavender pomanders that she has placed all around the room to help me sleep. The peonies by her bedside seemed to be watching her. In the end, I didn't have to worry. The words took care of themselves.

As I crawled back into bed after watching her, we were both awakened by a shout. Neither one of us could catch its words. All was dark and cold, though my body was bathed in a wine-scented sweat. She kissed me on the forehead and patted my soaking head while uttering the words, "Puh, puh, puh."

They did not calm me. Last night, when sleep welcomed me once again, it happened. There was a kick of the left leg. I sat bolt upright.

"What am I? Who am I?"

I was on my feet, banging my body around the room, rubbing my eyes, wiping away the cold sweat.

"What's happening to me?" I shouted.

"Sweetness," Marguerite cried.

"If I am only for myself, then what am I?"

"Come back to bed, darling. This is too much. Everything is going to be all right."

But I could not stop it. Words were coming out of my mouth from the great rabbis.

"If I am not for myself, then who will be for me? And if not now, then when?"

"No, Juanito. Please." She grabbed the sheets around her in the cold night as I left the bedroom and chased me down the creaking stairs. Dawn had just begun to slither through the heavy green drapes, and I arrived exhausted at my kitchen table, sweeping away crumbs with the back of my hand. She was behind me. It was as if she knew what was at stake. She came up behind me as I slumped there, my head in my hands like a hideous gargoyle. I realised in that moment that I had no choice. Zeek, from the top of the stairs, cried "Papa," and Marguerite groaned, "Hijo, back to bed."

With a throbbing head, like a man inside was randomly wielding the sharp end of a pick, I remembered what I had tried to forget. The gypsy's words at Bartholomew Fair had come true again: "Your dead mother will be killed." Yes, my dead mother was killed. The letter before this one told me all about it. A trial was held for a dead woman. Her crime was to give to the poor on Purim and to light the candles on Sabbath as the first three stars appeared in the night sky. And though she had met a hard hard-enough rest, coughing blood and covered in pustules, this was nothing compared to the second death. They exhumed her peaceful corpse and piled her bones and rotting flesh against a stake. They burned her remains not just once, but three times and ploughed the ash into the soil.

I was in madness then. "As a girl, she used to sweep the bimah of the old synagogue. She always said the mourner's Kaddish for her father."

"Juanito, there's nothing we can do. Don't upset the little man. Come back to bed."

I heard him slam his bedroom door shut and felt certain that I could hear the sound of crying. It was terrible, but I could not stop. "She liked a drink and had a temper that rendered me weak to women, so surely she deserved it."

Marguerite slapped me, I stopped for a minute and said. "Well, let's say a prayer now, for the men who dug her up. Those poor men developed the buboes that my mother died from, and they died an agonising death."

Marguerite was past the tipping point now. She retreated, dragging the sheet behind her back up the stairs, looking to me like a sorceress. As she left, I sat at the kitchen table and drifted off once again. The dream came back. We were walking along the Calle del Barco, Father and me. There were no words, just the warmth of the Spanish sun and the gulls arguing over scraps. We turned into the Paseo Caro and went along the quay. When we could walk no further, he turned to me and said, "Son, you are ready now."

"Father, my wife, my little boy... the peace I have known here..."

He looked at me and said, "You're no longer free to desist. Now go!"

*   *   *

Later that day, I walked on Groenestreet. Who should I find there but Johannes Van der Poel, Although he had lost some of the pudginess of youth, he was a fine, strong man, with flowing blond locks.

"Brother," he called with the confidence of a young bull. "Your latest work, *On Assistance to the Poor*, is it not the most revolutionary book ever written?"

"No, the Hebrew bible was, my friend."

"How so, señor?" he asked.

I still feared his loose tongue, for he nearly got me to unmask myself with that diary. He was a clever lad—there was no doubt of that. I put my arm around his shoulder.

"Because men wrestle with God and challenge kings. God himself challenges kings."

"Señor, what's the message?" he asked as I moved away, for I had to get back home to tell Marguerite my plan.

"Tikkun olam, Johannes—a most Hebrew message. Repair of the world, if it risks death and danger. That's the message!"

I ran even though the joints on my swaying back creaked like the rusty hinges of an old gatepost.

Marguerite was inconsolable. Crash went the oak door, kick went the washroom bucket, bang went the window shutters. Her mother and the little man hid.

"Traitor! Coward!" She stormed through the house, her long green dress rustling down the hallway, hair flowing back like the hair of Lilith. She picked up a manuscript and threw it into the fire. I stood there, stunned, in the acrid smell of vellum and ink. She lunged at me with her fists and turned to leave but couldn't. "Use the queen's influence to defend Beatriz, who already has a price on her head? Have you forgotten what happened last time with your meddling?" She threw a plate at my head. It smashed against the wall, scattering into a thousand pieces. I tried to pick them up but sliced my thumb. "Leave it!" she said.

"I have to persuade her, my love, to give us an armed guard. With me and Álvaro, I can do it." She looked at me with desperation, for here was someone who had lost so much and about to lose something more.

"Cardinal Wolsey hates you. He's banned you. It's impossible."

"He banned me from Oxford for preaching dissent. He can't ban me from the queen. If the queen can't help our cause, then perhaps the Boleyns can." I dodged a fine Venetian wine glass. "With this change, there is a chance, not just for us, but for our whole people."

"You're mad to believe you can do that," she screamed. Her jaw was rigid, and she struggled to get the words out. "It will be the end of you to try, the end of us, and this boy we've been entrusted to bring up. Don't be so selfish. Think of the little boy."

"My fair one, I have to try." I had to quiet her, for Louis de Praet had fallen out of favour with the cardinal, too. "I also have the royal privilege to consider, the fruits of which keep us in this beautiful home." It was queen's guilt that paid for the plates and the glasses that Marguerite was liberally tossing around the house.

"It is my father's legacy and my brother's hard work that keeps us in this house," she said. "In fact, some say that's the reason you married me."

I tried to placate her all the way to the bedroom.

"That's not true. You know it."

"Why not wait for Margaret Roper's bedroom?" she said with pain in her Sephardic eyes.

"Never," I replied. "Without the Mores and Ropers, I'd be peddling old rags and pieces of cloth in the backstreets."

"Were you peddling before you knew her?" Then she smiled, something I was not expecting. "I shall come with you."

I shook my head furiously.

"It's not safe. The king can turn against his friends in the blink of an eye and will use their families as blackmail. Never."

"You write about the equality of the woman, that she is the equal of her husband." She sighed and looked at the broken glass and ceramics and finally at me, knowing she had lost. "You write that she should always stand by her husband, yet you prevent me from doing so."

I grabbed her, whisked her to the bedroom, and made love to her madly until the day was gone and she slept, believing she had changed my mind. But as she slept, clarity came upon me. Long ago I committed to making England a safe homeland for the Jews so that my people might follow in the footsteps of the explorer, Sebastian Cabot, and settle peacefully in the so-called New World.

After the commotion of the previous night, I didn't have to tell Zeek much the next morning, for he'd heard everything.

"Papa, I don't understand. Don't you love Mama anymore?" He sat on my knee as I wiped his tears away and stroked his fine hair with my fingers. I hummed to him, holding him close, for who knew if this would be the last time?

"Zeek, my special boy, it's hard, but no, I haven't stopped loving Mama or you. Nothing would make me stop loving you."

"Then why?" he asked again.

I could hear Marguerite outside the door. Her heavy breathing gave her away. I almost changed my mind there and then, but as I opened my mouth, someone else's words came out.

"Son, when I was a little boy, I was lucky. I had three sisters, just like the first three stars that appear in the night sky. They were pretty and dazzling."

"I know, Papa, but they're in Spain and you're going to England."

My wife, in her emerald skirt and brown jacket, entered and looked as if she were about to say "exactly." I shushed her with a finger to my lips.

"Mama is going to take good care of you while I'm away."

Marguerite put her arms around us, and we huddled in the silence. How I wish that moment could have lasted forever. I tried to seal it into my very being, so I'd have it beside me on my difficult journey.

"I'm going to ask the queen to bring my sisters back from Spain. But don't worry. I'll be back."

"My first papa said that." The remark hit me like a cleaver.

"But I am the clever fish, and I am the brave bull, El Torro Bravo."

And then I left them.

30 September 1528, London

Álvaro was dressed in black and towered over the scurrying dockers. He stood out like a shining beacon. Beside him was a mass of black fur that was Henry the hound. Could the dog recognise me after all these years? As I made my way off the boat, he stood on his hind legs, pink tongue lolling out the left side of his mouth. Álvaro let him go and he was on me, all four legs! Álvaro and I hugged like long separated brothers and walked up out of the muddy chaos of St. Katherine's dock. Henry ran into the market stalls, barking at a woman in a great white hat, cocking his leg on a crate of country apples.

We walked to Bishopsgate and made our way out of the city into Houndsditch, where the king's kennels had once stood. Amid this community, foreigners were able to trade, and this is why they made their home here. Here were Lutherans, who smuggled in bible tracts; here were the Blackamoors and Portuguese merchants, who attended Mass by day, but did things I won't mention by night. Here also were women dressed as men, and men secretly married to other men.

We entered The Flying Horse, the stench of stale ale assailing us. A few drinkers, unaware this was a truly sacred site, sat at the worn oak bar. A couple more slumped around the blackened fireplace beside a rusty iron candelabra. One woman woke as we entered. She was unable to push Henry away. "Oh, darlin', 'ere he is again. Ain't he bootiful."

With a hint of Lisbon in his voice, thin-faced Benjamin Elisha, whom I'd met years before, greeted me with open arms and a warm hug. With greying hair hidden in a woollen cap, and the fringes of his tzitzit just visible, he had the calm magic of a great sage. He stored my kegs of Gascon wine and took ten shillings for the privilege. No wonder he was pleased to see me! But it is he who sold it, not me, the soft-fingered academic. He stored the kegs in a cellar where once I found comfort in a Kabbalistic ritual, a dark place that no knew was now the chief synagogue of England.

Álvaro de Castro had the bronze vestiges of summer on his face. His wife, Sarah Elisha, daughter of the innkeeper, was by his side. A grin was on his face, for the years had been kind to Álvaro. Stories were exchanged like coins in the marketplace until we were breathless and dry-mouthed. The queen is under siege, the Boleyns were on the rise, and Sir Thomas was battered and worn.

"Now is our time," Álvaro whispered.

"And what of Meg?" I asked.

"Steer clear," he replied.

As sunset cast a ruddy light across the dung-ridden yard, we put Álvaro's young boys, Gasper and Eduardo, to bed with a kiss and a blessing.

> May the Lord bless you and guard you.
> May the Lord shine his light upon you and
> be gracious to you.
> May the Lord lift up his face to you and give
> you peace.

Night fell. Some entered through the inn and waited there until the last drunk was bundled out. Others entered through the back door. Some had been waiting in the cellar all along, patient as lace-workers. There were the Isaacs and Harts from Southwark, ancient English survivors, and Spanish families named the Añes and Lópezes from Creechurch Lane. There was one, a wizened scrawny thing with no name, slumped in the corner. There were the Portuguese Elishas, de Castro of Burgos and one Vives from Valencia a man whose real name was Hayim, meaning life.

Once we had the finest synagogues in Burgos and Seville, the homes of learning. Those places, they tell me, let shafts of light through stained windows, lit up the proud faces of our fathers and mothers, free to practice their old ways. But here was a brick-lined cellar with the dank smell of kegs, barrels of ale, and spilled wine. There were once ceilings of gold leaf turning our thoughts towards the heavens, with tiles, mosaics, and the colours of the Sepharad, but now there were blackened bricks, a trickle of water, and the droppings of rats.

The stomach churning began. Here was fear, but here also was hope. The service began with psalms, a call to prayer, and then the dialogue.

Álvaro: Alas, our father, is this the recompense we have sought?

> Who is the father who raises children
> Just to take vengeance on them?
> To pour anger on them
> With great and fuming wrath?
> We have sat on the ground.
> We have wept.

Benjamin: Why do you all cry out against me?

> Your murmurings have reached me.
> In my kindness, I have daily saved you from sufferings:
> You yourselves are my witnesses.
> But alas you have not kept my ways.

Álvaro: But even if we have sinned, where are your mercies?

> If in anger you expelled us, tell us how your children can make recompense?

Benjamin: You, my people, will be redeemed by justice,

> For you have prevailed in your suit with God.
> No more will you be ploughed like a field.
> The eyes of my congregation will see
> The moment of your salvation,
> A home, here, in its proper time.

A collective sigh seemed to unite all, and the pale man from the corner came forward. He recited the sh'ma as if he hardly knew it, as if each word were spoken through coarse fabric in his mouth. Who was this strange and bent man? When the others had departed into the night, breezy and full of fallen leaves, I asked Álvaro.

"Edward, Master Scales. There's a story!"

"And?" I asked. Nothing much had changed after all these years. I still had to push him to include me in his inner world.

"We just got him out of the Domus."

"How? When?"

"Ropes and smoke, Juanito. Coded messages and the love of God."

"How long had he been there? Where does he live now?"

"Twenty-four years he was there, whisked off by the old king under the orders of Ferdinand to purge the Jews of London. That was a condition if he wanted his daughter for Prince Arthur. And he is a tenth-generation hidden one, living here in the attic, taking care of the synagogue."

No wonder he struggled to speak Hebrew or that his face was like that of a ghost. I sat back in awe and wonder, and then went over to Master Scales and hugged him.

"You can share my sleeping space, sir," he said. He pointed to a straw mattress in the corner and offered me a blanket. I almost agreed out of solidarity, but I had work to do and plans to make, for we had to get a party to Spain and get at least two out of there.

4 October 1528

I sent a letter to the queen, for she had to know I was back.

No sooner was it sent than I was called upon. I boarded a skiff on the grey river downstream to Greenwich. In the cold, grey English light I pulled up the fur collar of my dark tunic. I tried with all my strength to walk tall and straight, though my spine was more bent than ever, and my shoulder wanted to hang loosely to one side and pull me with it. At the steps of the palace, a man at arms greeted me. He sounded desperate.

"We have been waiting for you."

The queen sat in a sea of candlelight. This was majesty. She was dressed in blue, the faultless illusion of virtue in human form.

"At last, Señor Vives, my brother, you are here where we need you," she said, embracing me. Her face was pale, the wrinkles around her eyes more deeply etched, the chin fallen. "And your wife, whom I begged you to bring, is outside now. Let me meet her. Bring her in."

She searched deep into my eyes as I lied about morning sickness and a child in her womb. Sadly, since the last miscarriage and the bleeding, there have been no more kicks and screams from the womb.

We sat and talked, Maria de Salinas warbling beside her, high-pitched as ever, like a starling. She tried to sing a cantata.

"Sing up! Play louder!" I told her.

She jumped and squealed at that as if I'd slapped her on the arse, but the queen cried. As for my poor father, she said, it was a miscommunication. It was not Reginald Pole's fault. The problem lay in Valencia, the inquisitors misreading the message. "But the royal privilege of Gascon wine, it recompenses, no?" How could a payment from wine compensate for a father burned slowly at the stake?

"It keeps me in fur collars and leather coats, my wife in silks, Your Majesty."

"The king calls me sister, not wife. He is convinced of my relations with Arthur. Promise me, señor, that you have told no one of our secret on the barge those many years ago."

"No one," I replied, reminding her that Anne Boleyn had been listening to every word.

"She knows no Spanish."

"She arose, but was bent in the middle now, walking as if dragging a cart behind her. "Majesty, you once pleaded with the king for the lives of the apprentices who'd rioted in London."

Maria Salinas must have been listening despite her warbling. She switched languages, as if on cue.

> For which kind queen, with joyful heart
> She heard their mother's thanks and praise
> And lived beloved all her days.

"Señor, this is true, but why bring it to my attention now?" She leaned on the window frame.

I joined her and watched the young men below riding out with leather-masked falcons. She sighed.

"Madam, there is a sister of mine. She is in the hills above Valencia, accused of terrible things, untrue things. We need a letter and a small band of men. Then I can go to Spain and find her."

She turned with a sudden fire in her eye, walked to the table like a young woman, and banged her fist. "No!"

"But Majesty, you do not understand."

"I need you here as my brother, as uncle and tutor to the princess. You cannot go to Spain."

I'd almost forgotten about her, now twelve years of age.

"She needs you. We need you."

"But the cardinal has banned me from Oxford for subversive teachings."

"He cannot ban you from court or from my daughter. I still have the say here."

I needed this queen five years ago to help someone in my family, but my sisters needed her now. I was in the midst of a violent internal conflict.

"But Your Majesty, I can be all of that for you in time, but first there is a grave matter."

"We do not have time, and your grief is now done, señor. We must stand firm—Pole, you, and I."

What irony was this? Stand with Reginald Pole? My grief was now done?

"Very well. How does Pole fare with the princess. I hear he's been in charge of her education?"

"Exceedingly well, and stricter than you. Wouldn't leave a bible translator standing, that's for certain."

"Or a Jew, I dare say."

"Much less a Jew," she said. Funny how the woman who calls me brother and studies the bible does not protest while my true brothers and sisters are hunted down.

She looked tired, but I had to keep pushing. Sir Thomas, you'd think, would be her ally, but she hadn't mentioned him. Other questions flew out of my mouth.

"And Margaret Roper?" I asked. "She must come here often? Is she as pretty as ever? As sharp and clever? Will she be visiting soon? How often do you see her?"

The queen sat down again. Her maids rushed over with cushions and a cold compress.

"They're trying to poison me," she croaked. I could see that Meg Roper's whereabouts and concerns were not high on her list of priorities.

"Where is the king?"

"Where else but Hever."

"Where's that?" I asked as if I didn't already know everything about the Boleyns of Hever.

"Be quiet. Don't make yourself look foolish."

"Sister Catherine," I said, "I'll stand in your corner. I'll defend the princess with my dying breath. When she is ready, I'll lead her into the light. But when the time comes, you must help me and my sisters. You owe me that."

I didn't wait for the reply. I bade her farewell and said that I'd be in Houndsditch when she was ready.

*   *   *

Álvaro was sitting at the back door when I got home. He was throwing a soggy leather ball over and over to Henry the hound, who would retrieve it and then wrestle with him for it. Sarah was breastfeeding, and I turned away, but not before smelling the baby breath that I had once longed for myself.

"I can't get a band of men from her yet, but in time, I think I can."

"Then you can't go."

Who was he to dictate? My years of cowardice were behind me. "No one will know me there now save my sisters. I know where she'll be hiding." I didn't believe a word I was saying.

"With a crooked back and soft writer's fingers, who else could you be but Juan Luis Vives?"

"But look what happened to my father from waiting for the right time."

He got up and put a hand on my shoulder. "Don't get yourself killed. The queen may yield in time. Just be patient."

I trudged up to the Biett Tefilah, our secret House of Prayer within the attic of Jorge Añes in Creechurch Lane. It seemed the heart of the city, with its penny-bakers and ragmen, pipe-players and potioners, beat loudly enough for all of France to hear. My heart, as ever, beat loudly enough for the spies of Reginald Pole to hear. Once inside the dusty attic, as Álvaro, the chief rabbi of London spoke, I let go an involuntary, ancestral sigh. I was in the moment. For once, I was at peace.

"Friends, when we gather to pray, we do not pray as one," Álvaro said. "And when all the congregations have finished their prayers, the angel takes them all and makes them crowns to place upon the head of the Holy One."

Then it happened. There was the sound of footsteps on a staircase. Our moment of deep contemplation was shattered. There was a crack like a horsewhip, a rap on the attic door.

I looked to the others for comfort but found none.

The door swung open and a strong light shone behind a single tall figure. Was it an emissary of the king, a henchman of the pope? The tall figure was silhouetted against the attic steps and became monstrous as it made its way into the room.

There was something familiar in his swagger.

"Ambrosius Moyses?" Álvaro asked. There was a collective sigh.

I realised this was the king's musician, the Italian who played viol. What was he doing here? His eyes went slightly in opposite directions. His skin was very dark, like the darkest of Arabs. Against the lime-wash of the wall, his blue cloak was lit by the giant candle. He showed me his fist. Was he planning on punching me? Then I saw the gold ring, the kind I also own. It was the same one that the king had given me years ago, of which he told me, "There are but four in the realm."

I was nearly sick. Was it that I did not want to know the depth of the Jewish underworld in this land? I avoided his intent gaze, and we resumed our prayer. Afterwards, we descended to a meal of heart-warming puchero.

"How do you survive in the king's court?" I asked. I noticed that my hands were suddenly animated, like they were being moved by a celestial puppeteer.

"By stealth," he replied. He nodded, clasping his musician's fingers as if in prayer.

"And the younger Boleyn, Anne—I hear she's around the king these days like a playful puppy."

"More like a mosquito," he said. "The mosquito's bitten him and he can't stop scratching."

"Does he love her?"

"Perhaps," he said, placing a hand on my thigh. "She's a cunning puss."

"So, she's a puppy, a mosquito, and a puss?"

"A bit like you, eh? Like you, she won't give herself fully." He threw his head back and laughed.

"Can she help our cause? Is she well-disposed towards us?"

In the court of the French queen, she'd sat on my knee and questioned me on the wealth of the monasteries and the abbeys. She'd talked about rich men, camels, and the eyes of needles.

"If you offer her something, she'd be well-disposed, but what would you give her? Remember that she is the cleverest puss in the land."

"Cleverest puss maybe, but cleverest woman, no. That is Margaret Roper."

"Si, señor." He grabbed the finger with my wedding ring and said I should be wearing the ring that he was wearing, that by doing so we'd be brothers forever. "What'd you give her then?"

"What do you know of precious metals," I asked him. I released my finger from his pinch.

"Gold, señor?"

"There is one far more precious, and not platinum."

"You're talking in riddles," he said.

"Yes, the most prized metal of all. What is it?"

"Power, señor, but how do you propose to get it?"

"Try the metal known as knowledge," I countered.

"Won't he grow tired of Anne, as he did with her sister?"

"Is this knowledge?" I asked.

"I don't think he'll grow tired so long as she keeps this game up."

"She will for sure," I said. "Think of the titles, the furs, the jewels."

"The only title she wants is queen," he said. "But he may grow tired of her, so she'd better give him sons."

This was the grand plan. Although the queen first rebutted me, she could be blackmailed if necessary, to help my sisters. When the royal game was played more fully down the line, we could work with Anne and the reformers to give us a safe homeland. Was I mad to think it could work? I could then bring Marguerite and Zeek to London. We could build our synagogue on the edge of the city. By stealth and with God's love, we could make it happen. England could take the refugees and become a greater nation for it. It could export them across the world. It could be done.

"And the king acknowledges you?"

He laughed, turned, showing his proud jaw and strong nose. "Ha ha, my friend. It is not really the king who is the problem. Have you ever heard of him torching a Jew, or even criticising a Jew? No, it's Reginald Pole who's the problem. It is he who fuels the flames of the pope."

"Enough, my friend. Who are the owners of the other two rings?"

He shrugged his shoulders.

"Good night, my friend," I said.

He closed his eyes, feigning sadness. Surely this was a game he had played a hundred times over, one that would one day get him in trouble.

10 October 1528

There was a plan, and I had to petition the queen like the mothers of the London apprentices once petitioned her. She saved their sons, and she could save the lives of my sisters. And she owed me a life. But my arrival in London had not gone unnoticed, and as the autumn rains pelted like arrows and we put sandbags at the front door, a boy thrust a letter into my hand. It came from Chelsea. And who, in my absence, had moved to Chelsea but Sir Thomas More and his daughters. Assuming it was from Meg, I opened it with the energy of a starving man who'd been taken to a banquet.

I scanned the page rather than read it. And yes, there was an invitation to Chelsea. I wiped my brow with the handkerchief given to me by my wife. To Chelsea, then, although Álvaro counselled against it.

"But I owe this family something," I said.

"You're your own person, Juanito. You don't have to justify yourself."

I left the ale-stained inn two days later, and the sunshine broke through as if the divine presence was shining to guide me on my journey. I left the city at Ludgate, with its familiar London scenes that I found so endearing. There was a street brawl, a mangy cat being chased by five hungry street hounds, and a toothless whore lifting up her dirty skirt. I made for Kings Road and arrived in Chelsea in the early afternoon. There could be only one house new enough and grand enough to belong to the Mores, so it wasn't hard to find it.

I gazed from the gate and was struck by the weak scent of late roses and freshly turned soil. The formal gardens were laid out with ponds and fountains. Each one of its five wings pointed like a long finger to the sacred river. There was the barking of dogs, the chattering of young women, and what sounded like an angel singing, "Love me brought."

The doors swung open and all was golden, with the shafts of light on the wood panels and polished floors. Cicely was the first to embrace me, now fully grown with a massive bosom and rosy cheeks. There was young Elizabeth, slim and elegant, dressed in white. "Do you remember me, sir?" she said, giggling with the preciousness of the youngest child of the household.

"How could I not?"

Alice More looked more stooped and aged but greeted me with a friendly "Welcome home, son." Then in strode Marguerita Charism, Meg Roper. Had she dressed for me with a Spanish hood and an autumn-coloured gown? The younger girls were silent.

"Mistress Roper, the season becomes you," I said.

She blushed. "Señor Vives, did you not notice that the autumn sun shone today for the first time?" She paused. "Because you're here, where you should be!" My heart leapt; my cheeks flushed. Elizabeth giggled. I wanted, in that moment, to be with her forever. Then she turned sideways, and I could see a bump in her stomach.

"Master Roper, he is well?" I asked with the sincerity of a gutter whore.

"Yes, but away at court on business of state."

I sighed with relief. "And your father—when do I see the great statesman?" I asked, hoping that he, too, hadn't been called away on matters of state.

"Soon," she said and took me by the arm to the drawing room.

I could smell something on her. Was it rose, geranium, bergamot? Perhaps it was the scent of all three, but it took me back, to a summer's night, lying on cushions in Bucklersbury, when I nearly gave up everything for her. As we entered the room, with its diamond stucco ceiling, the autumn sunshine poured in.

"It's been too many years," she said, and brushed away a tear. She then said, "Señor, forgive me please."

"Forgive you for what, Meg?" I asked.

"For my whispers."

"I don't understand."

"Whispers to Reginald Pole of a found text that I didn't understand, that I had no right to find, whispers that grew a life of their own."

The diary. She had discussed it and understood bits of it.

"You understand where those whispers went then?" I said. How was it that I could forgive her? What did that say about my weakness?

Sir Thomas's man, a short, stocky fellow known as Will, barged in.

"He's ready for you, Señor Hayim."

"Don't call him that, Will," Meg said. "His name is Señor Vives, or Master Lewis. Anything but Hayim."

I was led up a great oak staircase and taken to his private room, where Will told me, "Go on, knock." I placed an ear to the door that still smelled of the workroom of a carpenter. There was nothing but silence from within. Still nervous around him after all these years, I knocked anxiously.

"Enter." And so, I did.

His back was turned to me. He was gazing out of the lead-panelled window towards the river. "I must get rid of these clothes."

"Sir Thomas, do I not get an embrace after all this time?"

He looked up. "I will expose you for the secret Lutheran you really are, pretending to be a Catholic. Come on down to the cells."

"But, but Your Majesty, I am not. Haven't you read what I've written about them? Is that not proof enough?"

"The net's closed in. A washerwoman testified against you. That's good enough for us."

I was struck by the creases of his eyes, which seemed much deeper. His mouth was sunken at the edges. He grabbed me by both shoulders and drew me towards him before throwing me off like a ball in a game.

"Don't make jokes about it, Vives."

"What we can laugh at we can rise above," I replied.

"I'll remember that when they take me up the scaffold!" He walked back towards the window and then started. "It wasn't Pole's fault—or Meg's or the queen's. It was a miscommunication."

"It can be made right. I've sisters there still. I need you to intercede, to talk with the queen, to get an army of—"

"Enough! I will do what I can. You have my word."

He removed his chain, his jacket, and his shirt. I tried to avoid my glance. As he stripped away these layers, there was a coat of grey, matted sheep's hair between his white shirt and the skin. It was his penitential hair shirt.

"Why on earth do you wear that?"

"To remind me of my sinful mind and that my pain is nothing to his."

I could not hold back. "So, Jesus wishes you to wear that?"

"I can't say yes to that, but I wish to wear it to bring me closer to him."

I thanked the heavens that I was born a Jew.

After dressing, he took me downstairs and through the gardens and wrought-iron gates to the riverbank. Many of the leaves had fallen, and we kicked them away, the smell of the English autumn enveloping us. I noticed that the golden beeches were still clinging to their oval russet leaves. The wind swished through them, and I tried to catch its words. Was it telling me to take strength and to be like these clever beeches, to hold on to the very end? We sat down on a fallen tree trunk.

He spoke to me softly, like a brother. There were rumours of a schism with Rome and Spain. There were rumours of an invasion that may follow, a second War of the Roses. "I will not forsake the queen," he said.

"Won't you bend just a little? You wrote it in *Utopia* that toleration is the very thing we should strive for. Can't we find a place amid the changes that no man can stop?" But he did not respond to that.

"Just be a brother to her and forget your unrealistic dreams," he said.

I contemplated a future with the queen as her honorary brother. Then I remembered what her family had done to mine.

I remembered what I had always stood for: justice, concord, and toleration. No, I wouldn't sell my ideals for the privileges that being her brother would bring. But I wouldn't tell him that.

"Of course, Sir Thomas."

At supper, above a small mountain of quail, I glanced towards the woman who, like a magnet, had drawn me there. She was still magnificent. She looked elevated, buoyed by the love that motherhood had given her. I sighed, like the slow drawing out of the tide on a sandy beach. I felt both entranced and wounded by her, for she had what I craved: parents, brothers, sisters, and a daughter of her very own. Could she feel that?

When our plates were cleared, she looked across the table and spoke. "I had a letter from your wife."

"Why did she write to you?" I stammered. The old paralysis hit my lips. What new torture was this?

"She tells me many things, señor. She tells me to feed you and keep you warm in Chelsea, away from grimy Houndsditch and away from meddling in the court."

I sat frozen. My wife would rather I was with another woman than with the queen or my secret community. That was sacrifice, was love. I couldn't hide the tears in my eyes.

"Am I deserving of such a love?"

Meg looked at me. "I don't know, señor."

Elizabeth changed the tone, suddenly imploring her father. "Daddy, this is just like the old days, before you got so serious. Can you recite us some poetry or some Greek?"

Sir Thomas, sparking at the thought of performing, replied, "Plato it is. The Spaniard will like that! This one makes me think of our queen."

For Hekabe and the women of Troy
Tears were fated from the day of their birth

"Stop, husband!" Lady Alice interrupted him. "It's too sad. We want joy in this house again."

He thought for a moment. "All right. Jolly Plato it is."

> My star, stargazing? If only I could be
> The sky, with all those eyes to stare at thee!

Meg looked at me from the other side of the table, still piled high with bones and plates. "And from you, señor—you must have something Greek that you can share."

I acquiesced:

> Asclepius cured the body: to make men whole
> But Apollo sent Plato, healer of the soul.

"And Mistress Roper, I know you, too, study the Greek poets," I said. "Do you have anything for us?"

"Yes, I do. Have you heard of Kleoboulos?"

> I am the maiden in bronze set over the tomb
> of Midas
> As long as water runs from wellsprings, and
> tall trees burgeon,
> And the sun goes up the sky to shine, and the
> moon is brilliant,
> As long as rivers shall flow and the wash of
> sea's breakers,
> So long remaining in my place on this tomb
> where the tears fall
> I shall tell those who pass that Midas lies here
> buried.

"That's beautiful, Meg," I said, and then cursed myself for letting the name out. "Is it a metaphor for someone or something?"

"I wronged someone a while ago by invading his private space, and something terrible came of it. Was it my fault? I don't know, but I'll be forever trying to make amends for my part in it."

I could see why Álvaro had counselled me against coming here. Heavy and slow with red wine, we sauntered to the drawing room. I hoped to catch her again, but as I walked with Sir Thomas and looked over my shoulder, she was gone.

After Madeira wine and heavy port, I sat in my room, the light autumn fire dying a slow death. I did not stir it. I sat with my scraps of paper and thoughts of this imperfect world. Is repair really possible, tikkun olam? And what if I love two women. What does that make me? But I must not commit adultery.

We congregated at breakfast the next morning with fresh eggs and kippers. William Roper, who had taken a barge from Hampton Court, greeted me with all the enthusiasm with which one greets a plague victim.

"And what has the great scholar been working on this last year?"

"I published *De Subventione Pauperum*," I replied.

"What did he say?" he asked his wife.

"Señor has published a treatise concerning the relief of the poor," she replied.

He smiled. "Another indecipherable work in Latin, no doubt. My father-in-law now writes in English. Is English not good enough for you, señor?"

Sir Thomas looked embarrassed.

"It seems it's not good enough for the bible," I said, looking at everyone at the table except for him. "Strange, isn't it, that the Greeks, the Germans, and even the French have bibles in their own tongues, but not the English."

I realised I was walking a dangerous path here. I asked Sir Thomas what this new work consisted of.

"It is a dialogue concerning heresies and heretics and what we do with them."

That old feeling returned. The ceiling lowering and the walls closed in. I began to speak in short, stuttered sentences. "Master... Roper... feel free... to translate my book... if you can... if the subject moves you. I'm all for English translations, you see. But for now, at least, Latin is the universal tongue, eh, Sir Tom? And I need German counts and French kings, Holy Roman emperors, and even Sultans to read it."

William Roper threw me a cold dark stare. I was glad I was not alone with him on a hunting trip, deep in the forest. "And for the secret rabbis of London and Bruges, perhaps?" he said.

"I know of no rabbis in this land, sir, but toleration, in my view, is necessary for any civilised society and nation."

Sir Thomas interceded. "After all I've done for you, you'd rather ally with the reformers who have bewitched the king?"

"I am your friend until the last moment," I said. "But I'm for a world where no one has to live in fear of being wrenched from their bed in the middle of the night just for the way they celebrate God."

"Piss and shit on you," he said. "The punishment for a Lutheran is to give him a faggot and march him around Smithfield for an hour."

"Would you rather put faggots underneath them, as in Spain?" I asked.

"My sweet brother," he laughed. "You have taken the bait once again. I will stay fixed to the one true order of the Catholic Church, whatever it takes."

I rose from the table. "Even if that means an Inquisition in this land and the burning of heretics and friends?"

"Whatever it takes," he repeated. Sir Thomas got up and walked towards me.

Meg broke the silence. "Father, please listen to him. Save yourself if no one else. The world is changing."

Her husband raised his scratchy voice. "Don't you dare speak to your father like that in this house. And you, Vives, had better watch your back in your smoky purlieu in Houndsditch."

Sir Thomas walked over to me, linked his arm into mine, and led me into the library.

There were no words that I could find. It was clear our paths were going in different directions. I couldn't stay in this house, whatever my wife or I wanted. I requested one thing: a memento. He went upstairs and returned with a sketch in chalk and ink by the artist Holbein. He was sitting in an ermine collar with his great chain of office around the neck. The sketch was full of holes. The artist had blown charcoal through them to outline his painting. I rolled it up and placed it in my case.

I kept my goodbyes quiet. As I mounted the horse, I glanced over my left shoulder and saw Meg looking out an upstairs window, taking her hood off, throwing it on the floor. I saw her husband go towards her as he raised his left arm. I couldn't bear to see what was about to happen.

I arrived at The Flying Horse by late afternoon, fighting my way through barrow boys, ragmen, and carts stuck in ruts.

"Are they with us?" Álvaro asked as I dismounted.

"No. I should have stayed away."

"And, how is she?" he asked.

"She cares for me, but that husband—what a brute!"

"He's obsessed with us and puts his men in the street to watch. Luckily, no one takes any notice of him. Look, Juanito, you love her. It's not your fault. And her father is a great man. He saved us once, but times change."

"This country is divided."

"Yes, and we must be on the winning side."

How could I walk away from them and leave Meg to deal with that horrible man?

Álvaro put his arm around my shoulder and spoke quietly. "He's living in fear. He's lashing out and we can't be in his way. There's too much at stake."

What could I do but agree with him?

12 November 1528

I almost went back to Bruges, for the pain of separation from Marguerite and Zeek was sharp. The finality of my final separation from Meg made the pain even greater. And though the queen called me, I stalled.

She wrote to me again, this time in desperation. The king had changed. Where he once treated her like a sister, he now treated her like a leper. Princess Mary was coming back to court soon, and the queen needed me there to reason with the king on their behalf.

"Perhaps the princess gives us a chance?" Álvaro said over a breakfast of herby-lentils and nettle tea. "As a bargaining tool, I mean."

Reginald Pole was in Italy on papal matters, and I realised that I couldn't go home yet; nothing had been achieved. The princess was coming, and the king would go to see his daughter in court—more quickly if Anne Boleyn found a reason to be there, too. I had to exploit this, and so we hatched a plan.

*　　*　　*

"Tutor!" The princess shouted down the long gallery of Greenwich Palace. She raced towards me with wide-open arms, bigger and ruddier than before.

"You've been in Wales," I said. "My goodness, how did you find it?"

"I think you'd love it because it's full of trees and birds, and you always talk about trees and birds."

"And what do they sing of, these birds in the trees?"

"They sing of Christ and his passion."

"Do they also sing of freedom, liberty, of the joy of the forest? Of how foolish men are??"

"No," she replied, scrunching her eyes.

If she couldn't see the true beauty of creation and how it resonated with God, she would be a dangerous monarch. I had work to do.

We made our way down the gallery with its portraits of the kings long gone. Here was the Lionheart, there the Conqueror. Of course, we had maids and guards listening to every word, but I wasn't frightened. "We can learn from them, mostly how not to do things," I said, pointing at the portraits.

Her lady-in-waiting, Agnes, with soft cheeks and a sweet smile, moved forwards. I was enveloped in the scent of rose water. My pulse raced for a minute and I found myself wiping my brow.

She said with her soft, whispery voice, "Gently, sir."

I talked with the princess, loud enough for all to hear. Reginald Pole had kept her in isolation in Ludlow, and I couldn't have that.

"I'll be your tutor again, at least over the winter months in court, my lady. I've been thinking that learning is always better shared, so we're going to bring in other young ladies to our classes."

She stopped still. Was she frightened by that prospect?

"Yes," she said at last. "I think it would be good. I would enjoy that."

I worked hard over the next few weeks finding her the companions who'd help her, but also finding companions who'd draw in the king and Anne. I got plump Frances Brandon, her ten-year-old cousin, who bustled into the room with little thought of learning and was concerned with her next pastry. There was Margaret Douglas, slightly older, a cousin for whom I held out more hope. She was stern, yet open to new ideas. Red-haired and ruddy-faced, she and the princess could well have been twins. There was pretty Mary Shelton, who wore perfumes from Paris and threw her hair back with a toss as if she was doing magic with it. And there was eight-year-old Mary Howard, the bemused daughter of the Duke of Norfolk, who brought out the princess's early mothering spirit. Both Marys, Shelton and Howard, were cousins to Anne Boleyn.

These minds, though, were a long way from my challenging boy-scholars. To get some fire going, I persuaded Álvaro to take me to his printing press in Holborn one Sunday morning. We slipped through the streets, covered in snow and ice, sometimes clinging only to window ledges. Then we unlocked the heavy oak door and set about our work in his magical cave. We kept the shutters fixed to the windows so as not to arouse suspicions. We worked by candlelight so that our eyes strained and ached. We made out a poem for each of the girls and put their own names on each one. It was from the hand of the king himself.

As the holly groweth green
And never changeth hue,
So I am, and ever hath been,
Unto my lady true.

As the holly groweth green,
With ivy all alone,
When flowers cannot be seen
And green-wood leaves be gone,

Now unto my lady
Promise to her I make:
From all other only
To her I me betake.

With the fruits of our labour scrolled tightly in my leather satchel, we slid back to The Flying Horse as innocuously as if we'd just emerged from Sunday Mass. As we entered the inn, Benjamin Elisha rushed to me with a worried smile on his rabbinic face: "There is a letter from overseas in your room."

Who could it be from but my wife?

I climbed the stairs and there it was. As I opened it, another fell out. There were no secret codes, and there was no book with notes hidden in it. It was a simple message, clear and desperate.

Brother,

My world descends into the darkness. The others have abandoned me. I am accused of witchcraft and Judaism.

Will you come for me, speak for me, get someone to speak for me?

You know where I am. I wait for you.

I live in hope.

Beatriz

What new torture was this? I guessed the others were safe, even if they had abandoned everything.

The other letter was from my wife.

Juanito,

The house grows cold and lonely without you. Why will you not forget the struggle? We need you, here. You are our guiding light. This is your home. Can you see your letter from your sister? I could have burned it, but Juanito, you can't go. We need you in the land of the living.

Tell me, O thou whom my soul loves, where you feed, where you make your flock to rest at noon: for why should I be as one turned aside by the flocks of thy companions?

Come home, Juanito. Forget about your
grand plans. We can pray that God brings your
sister home. There is nothing more you can do.

Your Loving Wife,
Marguerite

She and Zeek needed me. But I was so close. I was soon to
be with the king. If I pushed a little farther, surely, I could save
them all.

30 December 1528

Back at court, in the stateroom hung with tapestries of David
and Goliath, I gave the girls their printed sheets. With gasps that
sounded like they were coming from angels, they noticed their
names on the poem from King Henry.
"Look! My name!"
"Mine, too."
"It's magic!"
"My young ladies! Enough of the wonder. Let's read."
We read aloud. Then I felt a vibration, and then another
thump. Heavy footsteps were stamping down the long gallery. The
pretty little faces looked up as if scanning each other for comfort.
What terror was this? What invasion? There was a rap on the door,
and before we had a chance to respond, the doors were flung open.
In strode the royal party. My trap had sprung, for I'd printed
another sheet, put the name of Anne Boleyn on it, and sent it to
her with a date and a time. There was the king, the queen, and
the Lady Willoughby, frail, gaunt and fiddling incessantly with a
Psalter. Between the lady and the queen, with her swan-like neck,
was Anne Boleyn. Holding Anne's hand beside the king was a man
who I guessed was her brother.

"Master Lewis, we are here to inspect these ladies' lessons," boomed the king, who strode forward, codpiece underneath a golden tunic.

I caught the thick smell of red wine on his ginger beard. He gave no regard to his own daughter. She could have been a flower girl from Spitalfields.

"Well, man," he said with eyes almost crossed, "what's the lesson of the day?" I showed him the pamphlets I had made for the girls.

"Ha, my own work! You are good! Lessons in English. We will have no more bloody Spanish, for we know what they do! All lessons are to be in English, Latin, or Greek. Or Hebrew even. Anything but Spanish."

The queen, carrying rosary beads in her hands, was dressed in layers of black. It was as if the demon of exclusion had entered the room and made her its target—and Anne its champion. Anne was dressed in gold and white, with ermine that must have come from Milan or Florence. She stood between her brother and the king as if she had always belonged there.

Suddenly, with a stammer at first, a voice welled from within the throat of the queen. "But Castilian Spanish—it is the tongue of our daughter's heritage."

"Curse heritage," the king snapped, pointing at me. "Look what it did to this man's family."

Anne Boleyn's eyes sparkled even more brilliantly.

The princess ran to her mother, sniffing. The queen held her with the love that only a mother could muster. The king reacted with a string of curses, and in the confusion, Anne sidled over and fixed me with her raven eyes, chuckled and said, "Interesting how she leans upon a Jew in her hour of need."

I stammered, "I am a Nuevo Cristiano, señorita, not a Jew."

She laughed like a harpy and added, "The Nuevo Cristianos need the king, not the queen."

The king turned to her and said, "Anne, enough meddling. Now, what would you have these daughters of England sing?"

"Something English, something romantic," she said. "How about 'Love me Brought'?"

The king nodded and stormed around the room, taking the princess's hand and guiding her away from the queen. He told her to sit on his knee while he played on the lute. "Sing for Mistress Anne."

This was too much for the princess. She leapt off her father's knee, turned to Anne Boleyn, and shouted, "I will never sing for you."

The king threw down the lute, and it smashed with a horrible noise. I thought for a moment that he might strike his young daughter dead. George Boleyn sniggered like a girl. Anne looked at the princess, tossed her head back, and laughed like a sorceress.

The king raised his hand high above his daughter's head. At the last moment, when all seemed lost, the queen shouted, "Enrique, no!"

"Go to your room, child," he said. "And Kate, sister, do not follow her."

The princess left weeping, her lady, Agnes beside her. Though I wanted to comfort her, I needed to stay. Maria Salinas rushed to the queen with a lace kerchief, but she pushed her aside, looked directly, at the king and said, "I am your true wife, not your sister."

In that moment, I think he believed her. He must have remembered the good times, the passion, and the babies who never lived.

"It's God's punishment," he muttered. "You were my brother's wife. Vives knows that. And Lady Anne, who understands a few words of Spanish, knows it as well."

The king walked over to the young ladies. "I see you belong to my family or to Lady Anne's. The daughters of the realm don't whine. Sing for me and for your mistress, Anne!"

They tried. There was a murmur here, a crackle there, and finally a throaty melody from Shelton, but without Princess Mary to lead them, they were like lost lambs.

This is what I had wanted, what I had planned. I turned to Anne Boleyn, and said, "Esta claro, no descansaras hasta que destroces esta familia." *Clearly, you will rest at nothing until you have destroyed this family.*

She turned and said in the very Spanish I had once taught her: "Si Señor, y darle la voz de reforma." *Yes, sir, and shown it the voice of reform.*

She rolled her head back and laughed. It was a shrill laugh, a venomous laugh. She seemed like a viper about to feast.

I realised her power and heard a voice in my head. *She will change this nation forever.* If this voice is true, I must change it with her.

When the girls stopped singing, we all clapped our hands, except the queen. She looked at me like I was a traitor.

The king looked at me. "Master Lewis, I have matters to discuss with you this season. I need to pick at your ancestral memories." Anne nodded to him and smiled at me. The party turned around and left.

*   *   *

The next day was bitterly cold, though it didn't snow. It hung in the clouds, waiting, as everything in the realm was waiting. I expected the king to call me, but nothing happened. I also expected the queen to dismiss me for bringing the princess together with Anne Boleyn's cousins, for I know she would have preferred to keep her in isolation. In the meantime, I stayed close by the princess.

"She's a witch sent by Luther," she said the next morning.

And after that, there was no further talk of social justice or toleration. My plans to take her to visit Bedlam and walk among the craftsmen of London were abandoned. The princess was on fire. "I will have them burnt. As Reginald Pole told me, 'Don't suffer them. Burn them.' " She said it like a chant.

"Your Highness, we must teach, not burn," I replied, clenching my fist inside the long arm of my velvet jacket.

"When I'm queen, I'll burn their heresies and lies."

"No, no, no. Do you want to be remembered for that?"

She was silent for a minute, but I could already smell crackling human flesh. I tried closing my ears to the terrible groans of my childhood, but, how could I? I wondered in that moment if she saw the truth in me—saw in me the enemy and not the friend.

"Then so be it" was the last thing I remember hearing. It was my own voice, but it felt distant, like woodsmen chattering deep in the forest.

An hour later, I found myself alone in my chamber save for the little man with the pick trying to break out of my skull. Shivers travelled up and down my spine like lightning flashes. A river of sweat drained down the lines that framed my wizened jowl.

I was paralysed in my own bed, cold compresses all around. There was a green jacket and a note from the queen, who must have visited me. Was this good? I stared out the window to the distant river, alive with wherries and skiffs carrying families home for Christmas. Would they ever carry Jews home for Chanukah? Am I a fool to even dream it? Though I knew that I was of no use to my poor sister hiding in a cave outside of Valencia or to my wife in Bruges, there was absolutely nothing I could do. It wasn't until the third day that I got out of bed.

Clarity re-entered, although her visit would be brief. Christmas was here. Everyone would act as if there was no trouble in this world. One by one, the great and the good arrived at Greenwich. I watched as the king's butchers came in three barges laden with carcasses and caged birds. I watched the special delivery of oranges from the king of Spain, his men carrying their flags. I guessed there were also dates and spices in the sealed crates. Perhaps there were gifts from the New World.

I made my way down as the palace filled up. There was a gathering of statesmen in the great hall. I dragged myself upright and tried to put a sparkle in my eye. Here was the new Spanish ambassador, the tall, blue-eyed Iñigo López de Mendoza who replaced one-eyed Louis de Praet, now back in Flanders. I wasted no time and introduced myself.

He bowed low to me. "Your reasoning is ahead of its day, señor, and for your sadness, I am truly sorry. Spain still lags," he said with a saddened look in his eyes. He beckoned a girl to give us mulled wine and sugared fruit. "Please, eat. You look so thin. I was expecting a bear of a man."

"Spain lags," I said, "but is she still beautiful to the eye?" I remembered fiestas and cartwheels off the quay. I recalled leading a girl named Ana into the hayloft.

He nodded and it was if he could see into my soul and was not displeased with what he found there. But this man, I knew, was once Isabella's page. He was now late in years and must have seen many Jewish families. I'd heard that he was not a man of the sword or the torch. But the ways of the Spanish king were clever! One day they gave you sugared fruit; the next, they took you away with a sanbenito on your head.

"Tell me, don Zuniga, you must know of the queen's position," I said, hoping to get a notion of the progression of affairs, for three days was a long time in court.

"You know that the pope is now a captive of the queen's nephew and of the awful massacre in Rome?"

I did not know. It was a Spanish massacre executed at the command of the Spanish king, her nephew Charles V. The pope's hands were tied, and he would have to side with the queen.

"And poor Reginald Pole. He survived?"

"Thankfully. He was by the pope's side throughout."

"It's a bloody world, no?" I said, trying not to let my disappointment show. "But this is good news for Her Majesty."

"Perhaps. Anyway, Cardinal Campeggio is on his way to London to hear her case and the king's."

"If he sides with the queen, will she be safe?" I asked. The log fire was roaring, and all around the room bright eyes were watching us. Perhaps the way forward for the king and Anne Boleyn was not so clear.

"Unless the king breaks with Rome. What then for our faith, our future?" Before I could comment, he held out his left hand and touched mine. "I know the fate of your father and mother. May their memory be for a blessing." Was this the cleverest inquisitor of all?

"Señor, there is a favour I must ask you," I said. Before I mentioned the name Beatriz Vives, there was a clash of an almighty bell, the playing of pipes. Dinner was served. I said something else entirely. "Can you get me an audience with the king of England?"

"I would if I could," he replied.

Though I wanted to run, though I was aching to get my Jewish bones out of there, I knew I had to stay, for who else had a chance with the king? We moved into the hall, and Sir Thomas and Alice were surrounded by their children. Were we still friends? I counted them: Elizabeth, Cicely, Anne, and John. I caught a glimpse of William Roper, and there was Meg Giggs, his adopted ward, but where was my Meg? I excused myself and crossed the floor, brushing past jugglers and fire-eaters.

"Brother," Sir Thomas said, his countenance flat. "It is too sad."

"Where is Mistress Roper?"

William Roper had gotten close enough to hear us. "Mrs Roper is at home in bed. She has lost my child."

Why was he not there with her? Why were her parents and her sisters at court? Why was it *his* child, not *their* child? Sir Thomas seemed to catch my thoughts.

"We have no choice but to be here. The king demands it."

The music grew louder, and the acrobats entered, leading a performing bear that would normally have struck fear in my bones. Cicely turned white and one poor woman collapsed in a heap. But there were stranger animals here, too: the king as King Arthur defending Guinevere, who could be no one else but Anne Boleyn. As all this transpired, the queen, unannounced, took her seat at the top table. I was tired of this charade, and all I could think about was Meg, alone in Chelsea.

It was a commandment to visit the sick, so I had to go.

I rushed back up the staircase to my room, grabbed my satchel, climbed out the window, and slid down a lead pipe. Dogs barked, but I bribed them with veal bones from the banquet. I showed papers to the groomsmen, knowing they couldn't read them, and stole out through the side gate. I rode through the night, the ground quickly turning white with snow.

There were guards at her gatehouse, almost asleep, huddled together like lambs. They recognised me and said, "The house is empty, sir."

"Not entirely. I've brought gifts from my wife to the Lady Roper. Please call for Dorothy. She knows me well."

Five minutes passed. Dorothy arrived in dressing gowns and a long coat. Older than she looked, she saw and heard everything that happened in the household. She knew of our bond, knew that Meg needed love. She let me through, though she would not disturb Meg tonight. But I had not come this far to wait. I crept from my room, shoeless, walked softly down the corridor, opened the door, and made my way to her bedside. She did not stir; her nurse was asleep on a couch.

I stood and watched her for a while, the pale skin and highbrow. She sensed my presence before opening her eyes.

"I knew you would come."

The nurse stirred, and Meg asked her to leave. Reluctantly, she did. We sat quietly with snow piling up outside her window, and the bedroom fire casting a reddish light.

Finally, words came from some place deep within me. "How can it be? So together and yet so divided?"

She reached out for my hand and pulled it to her cheek. My face was next to hers and I got in bed and lay next to her. She fell asleep again, and I lay there, just watching.

The nurse returned in the morning with a tray of hot bread, a kettle of hot water, a pot of honey, and lemon. She shrieked when she saw me lying there. I jumped off the bed, grabbed my boots, and ran back down the corridor to my room.

Later, Meg came and got me. She was weak but managed to walk through the corridors and empty rooms of her father's house. At one point, our fingertips brushed past each other and our hands clasped tight, like a newborn baby's around a finger. We talked about the summer at Bucklersbury, of angels and redemption, of an evening long ago when we fell half-asleep on the cushions in the courtyard.

"Do you remember what the gypsy told me?" she asked.

How could I have forgotten that she predicted that my dead mother would be killed?

"I do."

"She said that the new queen would hate you, that new queen won't be called Mary. Will she?"

"Anne," I said. "If not by Rome's way, then by Henry's. He'll find a way to make her the new queen."

"Why will she hate me?" Meg asked.

"Because you are cleverer than her and because the king will admire you, always."

Later, she spoke of the words of my books that had persuaded her that a free woman could affect change, that the voice of the woman must be heard. She apologised once again for speaking to Reginald Pole. I put a finger to her lips.

"Will my father keep away as it all unfolds?" she asked. "Will he meet the same fate?"

"I do not think so."

"But you, señor, will benefit from the changes?"

I remained silent.

"My husband will come. I don't know when, but he can't find you here."

I kissed her on the forehead and said my goodbyes. I wondered if this would be the last time. Although I had no stomach for the court and was tired of its intrigues and masquerades, I had to get back. That is where I am now, scribbling this down, for he has called for me at last, this very night, and soon I must go.

3 January 1529

I was passed from one group of guards to another like a confused little mouse being toyed with by alley cats. I was taken through passages and up stairways into the heart of the palace. His Majesty the King of England, in the dead of night, sat on a purple cloth chair and held a gold cup. He was writing something on a timber lectern balanced between the arms of his chair. There was a minute of enforced silence before he spoke, sighing heavily.

"I did not give you leave from court, but I knew by the minute where you were. Do you think I do not know my own realm?"

"Your Majesty, I visited Mistress Roper with gifts from my wife, for they've shown me such tender hospitality over the years."

"Shut up!" he bellowed. "There are more spies in court than you realise. And don't pretend to be having another bloody fit. You think I don't know about your fellow Jews and the grimy hole in Houndsditch? This is my realm. Mine! I know very well about your synagogue and the rescue from the Domus, and I know all about Señor Hayim known as Vives known as Lewis."

I knew this might be my only chance. I had to stay strong. "Majesty, I am your loyal friend and your supporter, and together—"

"I have need of you, Lewis," he said.

"Indeed, you do, sir."

"You know about my great matter?"

I nodded.

"Then you know that the Book of Leviticus does not allow a man to marry the wife of his dead brother. You know the marriage was consummated and productive. But Deuteronomy says I should marry my dead brother's wife and take care of her."

He wanted a Jew's opinion, a rabbinical mind to make sense of this.

I looked at him in the eye. "The bible is the word of man, not the literal word of God, though God's intent is there if you search for it."

His countenance softened. "You are agreed that the annulment is legal before God?"

"I'd need time to consult the Talmud and to interview you to see what's in your intent."

"A Jew to interview the King of England? What treason is this?"

An overwhelming sense of joy engulfed me, a freedom I'd not previously known.

"So, you want your freedom here. The king of Spain won't like it. Very well, Lewis. It is too late tonight. Tomorrow the Jew will interview the king." He nodded to his guard. "Show the Jew his chamber."

In my father's house, we were once told that sleep is one sixtieth of death, when a small part of the soul visits the other side. I think it's true because that night a ghost spoke to me.

"Stay true to your heart," my father said. "Love your very being, the thing that was, that thing that is, and the thing that will be." He then vanished behind the shutters of our whitewashed house in La Juderia.

Dawn broke like a whisper. A pale light shone briefly through the grey sky of the English winter. As I peered through the windows, I saw a riding party return, the king at the head. He brought his horse onto the cobbles below and was soon back in the palace. Soon after that the men arrived. I was strip-searched and even had my buttocks parted, as if I could hide a knife there! When I got to his chamber, the men, bar one, were sent away. He was hot from the hunt and had the remnant of pickled fish on his breath.

"Talk! That's what this is, is it not?"

I asked him of his boyhood, his favourite pet, his mother and father, of the forests he ran through with his brother and sisters. His very being relaxed as he slumped into the purple-backed chair raised on the dais. I walked as I talked.

"And what was your relationship with Arthur like?" I asked.

"I could match him in archery or fencing, but his knowledge of Greek, of Latin—he was brighter, better."

"No, that only describes him. How were your relations?"

"Cold, remote. Father's boy. Arthur, the king's best boy. And then he was gone. I was sad for mother, but it served Father right."

"You were glad for your brother's death. How did the gladness of personal tragedy make you feel?"

He looked at me as if I were mad. "I felt, felt like a cunt-ass. Does that make you a happy Jew?"

"Cunt-ass, Your Majesty, is not a feeling. I asked you how you felt." Had I stepped too far?

"Good Jew, indeed." The king could not help but chuckle. "So good that you're bloody useless with women but easily distracted by them, or so I am told."

We were here to talk of him, not me. I waved my hand as if to say, "Come on."

"I felt pain and guilt for a while, but I vowed I'd never ever feel either again."

"But you feel them, don't you—pain and guilt?"

"Never! I knew God would raise me up above father and brother."

"Raise you up to be a great king?"

'Yes, I still want to be a good king, not a pawn of the old guard or the pope, to show them what a king can do and to be a proud son for Mother."

"Your mother died before your father?" I asked.

"That was the saddest day for this kingdom," he replied.

"Don't you mean the saddest day for you? Then understand how the kingdom will feel if Queen Catherine is put aside."

"This is not why I have brought you here." He banged his fist on the arm of the chair. "I have brought you to decipher scripture and obtain your support."

Here was my chance. This is what the brotherhood had been waiting for during the last six years. I had to make the King of England want something from us.

"Campeggio is on his way from Rome to give you advice, is he not?" I asked.

"What if I said Rome's jurisdiction in this land is waning, that I'm after an older interpretation of scripture?"

"I'd say you were very a wise, enlightened prince, that this realm could be a new utopia, a beacon, a model."

"Yes, yes, yes. But what do your books say?"

I had to think hard, for how could I be a true Hebrew scholar when those texts were banned in my own home?

"I can advise you with my head and my heart, but those two may give you quite separate answers."

"What does your head say, Jew?"

"The Torah and Talmud tell me that the divorce can proceed, but only in a nation where Jews can freely live." I was lying.

"I knew it. But your heart, what does it tell you?"

"My heart tells me that the people love the queen like a mother. It also tells me you'll have to go carefully, or Princess Mary may one day exact a terrible revenge."

That fired him up. "She is my bastard daughter, one of many. She will not be queen, and Anne will give me plenty of sons. That much she has promised."

"No one can promise you that," I remarked.

"It is God's will!" he said, rising in pitch. "And I know very well what the queen told you on the barge that day—that Arthur had her not just the once, but many times over."

My face fell. Anne Boleyn had heard and understood the words between the queen and me. I wanted to run.

The king shouted at his one guard. "Bring in Raphael."

A door in the panelled wall opened and in came an old, tall man with a long grey beard and spectacles on a single eyepiece. This was a rabbi.

"Look at his ring!" the king exclaimed. "And there it was, the third gold ring with the enamelled Star of David. I had kept mine hidden with my wife in Bruges. "This is Raphael, the great German rabbi."

I looked from the rabbi to king and king to rabbi. Their faces were empty, expressionless. This game had not gone as expected. What about our rights to live in this land? A small army to rescue my sister?

"Shalom, rabbi… shalom," I said. Was this the one who had brought the Talmud from Germany, the one I had seen in the king's library? The king told me that he had called for him secretly and had not let him down once. I wondered how much the king had paid him. Why would he ask for my opinion if he had the rabbi's?

The rabbi stood there, looking like a wizard with his long beard and dark coat all the way to the floor. With a wry grin, he blessed me in Hebrew and asked in broken English, "How is your secret shule?"

"Shule?" I asked.

"Yes, your secret synagogue." Caught as I was like a hare in a wolf's den, I could not answer except in vague terms. "The family of Nuevos are well. Thank you for your concern."

"Spaniard, my spies are everywhere," the king said.

So, there was one among us in league with the king and his henchmen? Was it Ambrosius Moyses, the flirtatious musician? Benjamin Elisha? William Roper?

"As long as you support your king, you will be safe. In time you will get what you want. You support your king, don't you?"

I remembered the queen and the princess. My head was a storm of conflicting thoughts and misplaced loyalties. Clarity deserted me, and I played for time.

"You are my host, my king, and my friend. But why do you crave my support if you have the rabbi's?"

"They take you seriously—all of them. Erasmus, More, Wolsey, the queen. Look at de Praet. You turned him from lion to lamb, which is why Wolsey booted him out. I need men like you. You're good, Jew. I always said it, and so I have your support, yes?"

"I will always support my king in a realm where Jews may safely live," I said.

"Charles V—can you imagine his response?" the king asked. "And Sir Thomas and the bishops—they won't like it either. Wolsey I can lose, but Thomas, no."

"But think of the gain—three thousand years of wisdom, the best scientists, physicians, and financiers. Sir Thomas must bend."

"Bend at the neck before he'd agree to it," replied the King. After a moment's contemplation, he said, "Then you will declare for me when I ask for it?"

"On the condition that Jews may be allowed to return by a lawful means to find refuge in this land and in all the lands which the English settle," I replied. "And I need a small army to take me to Valencia where—"

"Good," he interrupted. "The two great Jews agree. Vives, you will speak for me when asked. Be assured that no Jew will be burnt here so long as I am king."

"That's a promise?" I asked.

'Yes. None is to be burnt."

A guard ushered Raphael and me out of the room. We were in one of the antechambers with a small fire and giant candles. The king's man stayed with us.

"It has been many generations since our two branches were one," I said to Raphael.

"Perhaps forty generations," he replied, blank-faced. Was he my friend or not?

"May I call you brother?" I asked sheepishly.

"Yes." He smiled at last. "One day we'll sound the great shofar for our freedom. We will all be brothers again."

"In this land?"

"It will happen, and when it does it will be a most precious moment."

What I most wanted to know was when this would happen, but I knew I'd be told, "B'yi-to," in its proper time. He had to be secreted away, back to German lands. His barge was waiting.

The king knew of our meetings and gave his word that there would be no burnings. But was he frightened of the Spanish king or of upsetting Sir Thomas? Have I got any farther at all? With my sister still in the same danger, where can I turn for help?

30 January 1529

The king was friendly though his hands were tied. That's the message I gave to Álvaro, to Benjamin, and to Señores Isaacs and Añes. They sat in a circle in the dingy cellar. Edward Scales studied an ancient fragment of a Torah scroll by candlelight. They listened with eager ears and bright eyes, like little children on the first night of Chanukah. No one reacted when I spoke of Rafael, the German rabbi. What did they know that I didn't? Why did they need me?

"I've got no army to take to Spain," I said.

"Don't stop trying," Álvaro said. "Go back to the queen. It's my guess that she's feeling it."

"Feeling what exactly?" I asked.

"Guilt, desperation, fear. She doesn't want to lose you. Use it. Work with it."

Álvaro handed me two letters, one from Bruges, one from Chelsea.

Husband,

It broke me that you would not be coming home for the season, that you would prefer to light candles elsewhere than here with your wife and family.

If Mother weren't so frail, I would board the next ship and find you somehow in that city I've never visited. I would cross the ocean for you, Juanito.

Will you not give up the fight and bring me fruit and flowers on a Friday? Will you not be content with your writings and your plans, your hospitals and your schools? And the little one, he pines for his father. He prays that you'll return. He prays so hard that he cries.

Come home,
Marguerite

My mind returned to Bruges, to life in a slower city. I was building hospitals, writing prose, and teaching youth. I cast my eyes towards the other letter, the one from Chelsea. I pried open the seal, looked at the writing, and sank into my frame. It was not written in the hand of Meg.

Señor Vives,

You invaded the chamber of a miscarried woman, the private sanctuary of a wife. A warning: make your way overseas and quickly. If you value anything you have, then go.

William Roper

Who had reported me? The nurse? I threw the letter in the fire and banged my fist against the plaster wall of the small kitchen. What new dangers would I be facing now?

I planned my escape. I would take a barge downstream to St. Katherine's, board a merchant vessel, and pay my way to safety. I would be in Bruges in four days

* * *

On the first night at the palace, I heard something strange outside my door. It sounded a bit like a simpering dog, and my first thought was that Henry, the smart hound, had somehow followed me here. I put my ear to the door that was arched into a rounded apex. I barely heard the words. What was I to do? I slowly opened the door as if opening Pandora's box.

It was Maria Salinas, the queen's lady, clutching her psalter. All I could gather was that I was needed immediately. Looking back, perhaps I should have tied her up and fled down the drainpipe, but I was moved by the distress in her face, her gentle "Por favor, señor."

I followed her down the gallery to the queen's privy chamber, where I found her surrounded by a sea of candles. She looked smaller than ever, a face of frowns and lines that formed sharp angles.

"Ludovicus Vives," she called. "Is Spain not your homeland? Is the Lord Jesus Christ not your saviour? Am I not your queen?"

"Yes, all of these things," I replied.

She was on fire. "Then promise me that you are still my brother."

"I will always be your brother," I replied.

"I know you've met with the king. He says you support him, that you sway to the teachings of Leviticus and Jewish law."

"Your Majesty, I support him only as far as the scripture is ambiguous. He does not know of any secret conversations."

"You have not told him about my relations with Prince Arthur? About the lost baby?"

"No, Your Majesty. He knows nothing of it." I lied. Her face lightened.

She still believed my lie. She clasped her hands together and smiled vaguely. "Then there is still time and hope. I knew you would never betray us."

She walked to the window and pulled the curtains apart. She looked across the gardens with their ice-sculpted bushes and frozen fountains. I held the curtain back and felt very brotherly to her. "I knew your love for me was deep."

What was I to do? I had one foot in each camp.

"Sign this," she said as she threw me a scroll of paper.

It was a sheet written by Sir Thomas and Wolsey proclaiming that, with the Spanish ambassador of England, I supported the queen's case as it was to be put before Cardinal Campeggio of Rome. It proclaimed my belief in the legitimacy of the marriage and my allegiance to the queen and princess.

I tried to make excuses. I said that I must leave court immediately. My wife would soon be in labour. The queen would not be dissuaded.

"Sign, my brother, if you love the princess and me," she cried frantically. "If you love your country, then sign." Involuntarily, my hands working independently of my spirit, I signed. Was I signing my own death warrant? Was I betraying my own father?

"No, Lady, I cannot." I threw the quill down and made for the door. She could not help my people. My allegiance was to the king, who could.

"Señor, you have sisters in Valencia, no?"

"Yes. Eva and Leonora, good Christian women."

"And another I think, known as Beatriz, the warrior Jewess, who hides in a cave above Valencia."

"What do you know of Beatriz?" I asked.

'Señor, if you are my brother, then she is my sister. What wouldn't I do for my sister? The other two are safe, but Beatriz Vives—her life hangs in the balance."

I sat and held my head in my hands.

"I'll not send you there because there is a price on your head in Spain."

This was news. I'd been right to avoid going home all these years.

"But I can smuggle her out safely to Bruges, Antwerp, Salonika—anywhere you ask if you just sign."

"You promised me that with my father," I said.

"I knew nothing of the gravity of his situation or of Pole's treachery."

The king had promised me no Jew would be torched in his realm, but if I allied with the queen, there was a chance that my fractured family would be whole again. I signed that sheet of parchment and was out.

I made it here, to Houndsditch by nightfall. I would be on my way to Bruges, to the loving arms of Marguerite, the following day.

Álvaro asked, "Which way did you bend. For Henry the King or Catherine the Queen?"

"Perhaps we should close this synagogue, for a while. The king gives me his word, but that was before I signed for the queen."

"You signed to save your sister at the cost of our future?" he replied. He sat me down at the beer-stained table.

"No. I have the word of the king, his promise. He sees our position and supports us as far as he can."

Benjamin Elisha looked on as he put the Bellarmine jars away.

"She is my own sister. Have I not suffered enough? The queen knows where she is… in the cave. Forgive me, but—"

"There is nothing to forgive, Juanito." He stood up and hugged my shaking body. "You did what you had to do."

"We are done for," I said suddenly. "We will never know peace in the land."

"That is not the truth," he said. "We must keep the flame alive until the proper time."

I didn't share his resolve, for surely this could only end one way for the secret Jews of London now that I had double-crossed the king.

"Álvaro, we can board up the inn and take everyone to Bruges or Antwerp. Louis de Praet is a changed man. We can create our new homeland there and leave this fight for other people, for other days."

He got up and turned for the stairs. "Good night, Juanito."

I followed him, but he shut his bedroom door and turned the key.

I hastily packed my chest with my clothes, books, and papers, and put what little coin I had in a silk purse. I would creep down to the cellar and leave them behind a loose brick. Tomorrow I'd be gone.

3 February 1529

We made for St. Katherine's at dawn. It seemed as if the chorus of merchants and mariners had kept rolling through the night like an endless performance on a giant stage. By my side were Álvaro, Sarah, and Henry the hound, who I was taking with me, for Zeek needed a friend. Álvaro put his hand on my shoulder and Sarah smiled, gently. Though I feared that their days here were numbered, they had a calming peace about them.

"You know, Juan," said Sarah, "the greatest commandment of all is you shall not be alone."

There was a trio of Arabs—blackamoors they're called—who greeted us at the bottom of the steps.

"Españoles con su perro," they shouted, meaning "Spaniards with their dog." They tried to sell us raisins and dates in wicker baskets, and when that failed, they tried to sell us brass mirrors. At the far end of the dock, low in the water against a grey sky, was my boat, laden and ready. I could taste the freedom.

Each stride brought me closer to the promise of home, a warm bed, loving arms, and sweet kisses. I was a few steps ahead of the others, and when I turned around, I saw them. I froze, numb. Surely this could not be real, not now, when I was so close. Six guards of the king, with pikes and shining helmets, stood upright like bell towers, watching everything. Were they here to check for smugglers or to make sure customs were paid? The leader pointed at me with a silver dagger. "Vives, known as John Lewis, there is a warrant on your head."

Sarah rushed up to Álvaro. "Do something!" she yelled, kicking and screaming her way through the guards.

They formed a tight wall around me. All I could feel were heavy hands all around me. I smelled a leather gag and wristbands. My hands were dragged behind my back, and my shoulder popped. A gag was forced into my open mouth as they lifted me up the steps. They put me in a cage on wheels that screeched through the streets, horses whinnying like ambassadors of the yetzer hara.

All was dark when I heard a portcullis lifted. Where else could this be but the very home of the axe: The Tower of London. If the noblest and bravest had lost their heads here, what hope would there be for me, a coward, a liar, a Jew?

I was dragged up stony stairways and thrown into a whitewashed cell. I heard someone say it was called the Lion Tower. How appropriate, I thought. They took off the gag and wristbands, and my left shoulder throbbed. There was a narrow slit for a window, but I sat huddled in a corner, not daring to peer out of it. Eventually I looked up and saw men with hammers and nails on Tower Green, bringing in pieces of timber and erecting a shabby scaffold and a gibbet. I sat in the frozen desolation of the nothingness.

My gaoler brought me cooked mutton and water, but I did not eat, preferring to simply pray. My gaoler was the famous Master Kingston, and though he smelled like an old unwashed scarf, he had a strange peace about him. He tried to comfort me, but I found no solace in his words.

Would I say the Hebrew prayers my father taught me for this moment? Would I swear my allegiance to the Christ in the hope of saving others? Would I be dignified, or would I struggle and have to be carried up? What would my wife know of my last moments? Would Zeek ever forgive me?

The cries of a young man brought me out of introspection.

"No. In God's name, no!" a man screamed in the cold late afternoon air. "I am innocent. I have not wronged. Help me, Mother!"

I stood on my stool and peeped through the window, dreading what I might see. There was a young man in the flower of his beautiful youth on Tower Green, perhaps not more than seventeen, a little older than the boys I taught at court. He had a shock of red hair and a piercing scream that hit every one of the hundred or so onlookers.

They dragged him up the ladder, beneath the gibbet. And then there was calm. He looked to be praying. His hands were tied about his back, and he started kicking, but his head was already in the noose. The ladder began to topple, and another redhead, a woman of thirty years screamed loudly. "Not my boy! Have mercy!"

They pulled the ladder away with a thick, hard chop, like the slap of a wave against a vessel in the ocean. Had his neck been broken? It was quick, and I slumped to the floor.

I taught young men the beauty of the philosophers, and I taught young women the art of the poets, but this is how it ended for those not blessed by wealth and comfort. What kind of barbarous world was it that we lived in? I was, in that moment, quite happy to be leaving it.

Master Kingston came to my cell later. It was dark and cold. He brought me two blankets and a Latin bible.

"You will not be here long, sir," he said.

So, I thought I would be next. I thought of my wife, of all the things we should have done, of all the kisses I would not have, of all the closeness missed. I wouldn't feel her breath, wouldn't see her breast rise and fall, and wouldn't hear her laughter ever again. I thought of all the women I had ever loved and the trouble it had caused, and I laughed. I thought of Ana in the hayloft, of Adeline in Montmartre, of Meg, but it was totally clear that it was Marguerite whom I really loved. Would she ever know it?

"Tell me, Master Kingston," I said, "who was that young man?' I asked.

"Ah, yes, the redhead. Better not to remember their names," he said, his voice calm like the low tide on the muddy bank of the river.

"What was his crime? Was it a heinous murder?"

"He stole lead from the roof of St. Katherine's Hospital. He was caught in the dead of night, claiming he and his widowed mother needed money to feed his young brothers."

These are the consequences of poverty, left to the charity of the church to mend? A young man steals from the church to feed his family and ends up with his head in the noose. I blessed the day I spoke out about poverty and thanked God that my words had met with the black ink of the press.

"Pack your things," he said. "The king's men will be here within the hour."

What use was there in packing? Would it save Master Kingston the job after my execution? I looked to Tower Green and could see the gibbet and the empty noose swaying in the breeze. It was dark. Would they kill me secretly so it wouldn't look bad for the king?

On the hour, they arrived, a small army with pikes and swords. My breathing grew shorter yet louder, my chest constricted as if in a harness. There could be no escape. The certainty of my fate hit me. I had no powers of persuasion. "How is it to be done?"

Kingston looked at me kindly. "They will take you by barge to an undisclosed location. It will be done there."

Who would be there? Would it be the new Spanish ambassador? Reginald Pole? Would there be an auto-da-fé and a bonfire?

The men rushed in, put a black sackcloth over my face, and drew a rope across it, forcing my mouth open so I couldn't speak. My hands were tied behind my back again, and the pop from my left shoulder made everyone laugh. I tried hard not to trip, to do this with grace, to make Mother proud as I marched past the cells of other men and out into the courtyard. It was then that the searing pain from my shoulder burned and travelled up my neck and down to my fingers. I guessed I was being taken through the traitor's gate, for I could hear the lapping of water. My feet were shaking as they bundled me onto the barge.

What reason did they have for not simply tipping me over the edge and letting me slowly sink to the bottom—for saying it was all a terrible accident? Again and again, I repeated what my father had told me to say if ever this should happen: "Sh'ma Israel, Adonai Eloheinu, Adonai Echad - *Listen Israel, the Lord is your God, the Lord is one.*"

We travelled upstream slowly against the tide. That was all I could tell. The oarsmen worked hard against the tug of the tide. We must have passed by Chelsea, and I wondered if anyone was watching from the great house of Thomas More—and if any there cared? Perhaps it was Roper and his spies who had orchestrated this for invading the chamber of Meg?

The boat came to a halt. When I was lifted up and thrown onto a timber jetty, the pain from my jaw and my shoulder felt like it belonged to someone else. This person was jostled on rough cobbled paths, and I hoped he wouldn't trip. His wretched shoulder hung limp, like a dead man's arm. Every bone in his poor body was bruised. He heard a gate being opened and then women's voices, gasps as he was taken out of the wagon and marched through a maze of chambers until he was dumped in a cold, damp cell.

It was only then that I came back into my body. There was a simple rush light in the wall, a stone floor, cold as ice, a black cloth that I could barely lie under, a pile of straw, a pitcher of water, and a barrel for a piss pot. After all my time in the English court and the nights of passion on a four-posted bed in Bruges—after all the letters to Erasmus and the conversations with Sir Thomas More—this was what I had left. What futility lay in possessions. What greater a possession than liberty.

Time passed. I looked out from a small window the size of a hand and saw a winter garden with one man working the frost-hard mud, smashing through it like he was carving granite. In the distance was a flimsy village with timber-framed buildings and a small church. Smoke billowed from the chimneys. I could make out figures walking hurriedly, jumping on horses, and riding into the distance, into freedom.

It started raining the next day and thankfully warmed a bit. Occasionally, one of the sisters, with a wide-brimmed white hat she'd hold onto with one hand, would dart out. She gave orders to the young man digging the rose beds in the rain. I spent hours imagining their conversation. That scene was all I had, and it played over and again in those first few days.

When the rains ceased and the frost returned, sculpting the gardens into a kind of mythical scene from a Norse saga, the young girls emerged. They were wringing sheets and linen and hanging it on a line that the young man had put up. He stood in the distance and looked at them. It seemed as if his every sinew ached to approach them, but there was obviously a line that he could not cross. They looked to him occasionally, and when he saw them, he looked down, consumed by his digging. Each day there were a few hours of pale English sun that dried the sheets. From this distance I couldn't see their hands, but they must have been red-raw, like my body. I called to them, but my weak words were lost on the wind.

After three days of solitary starvation I became delirious and sweaty. Three burly young men entered my cell. One pinned me to the back wall with a gardening fork, one placed some items on the floor, and the other took my things away. The one with the pitchfork backed off, still facing me. I couldn't help but laugh, for what could I, the soft-fingered academic, the peace-loving Jew, do against them?

But what bliss that visitation was! They brought me fresh straw, a new barrel, and a new pitcher of water. Best of all, they brought bread, milk, and mutton bones with fat and gristle. I knew I must eat slowly and make the bread last, for I'd been told in moments like this that it can swell up and stick in your throat and kill you quickly. I had to choose life, however hard that was in my early days.

Time passed, but how much time, I do not know. How many days had I left? Was this the glorious finale of the Jews in England? Surely Álvaro and Sarah could not have survived? I sat with my knees drawn up until they seemed to fuse to my chest. The silent men came and went, and one day I finally heard voices.

"Vives, Vives, Vives."

"Yes, that is my name."

"You let the king down. Why? He promised you everything. You're a treacherous Jew."

This went on for days, the words drummed into my head, an unending verbal torture. Was I an experiment in sanity? Were they trying to weaken me so that I would say the things they wanted to hear? If so, it was working, for the voices brought me out of prayer and meditation. The questions took me back to the torture of self-reproach. I'd turned my back on my family at seventeen for fear of the dungeon but look where I had ended up! I'd turned away from my wife and our adopted son to fight someone else's hopeless cause. I'd caused the death of my father and been no help to my sisters. I had worked to get the king's support and then lost it within a day. And what of the secret Jews of Houndsditch? Where were they now? In a worse prison cell than this? On their way to the stake? On their way back to Spain?

I was mired in turmoil, a contorted ball of self-loathing and self-pity.

On the day I decided to answer these voices, something happened. A shiny male blackbird landed on the bar of my window. He sang, "Aren't I just like Álvaro?" I gave him what was left of the gristle on my lamb shank, and he took it in his beak. But he didn't fly off afterwards, although I had nothing else for him. He didn't speak any other words or phrases. He came and went over the next few days with the rhythm of my faceless interrogators. As they arrived, he departed; as they departed, he arrived. I listened to both his voice and his silence. "Just like Álvaro?" He had searching, beady eyes and perfect feathers, a blackness that was unearthly. In song, he gave me a riddle, just as Álvaro had. What was it? After a number of days working on it, catching the rhythm and the pitch of the chirrup, it was revealed.

It was a song of forgiveness. A bright sun emerged from behind the clouds, and I realised that my struggle had not been in vain, that others would continue my work, that I had done my very best. And I realised that I must not crack.

*   *   *

After the fourth week, when they realised I would not talk, something even stranger happened. I was visited by the Spanish ambassador, Mendoza di Zuniga. Though the years were turning against him, he was still as sturdy as a Spanish pine. He helped me to stand, although I must have smelled worse than the floor of an unclean kennel. He said that I looked like a newborn calf, shiny in the eye, ready for the world, just a little unsteady on my knees. He wouldn't tolerate my apologies for the sorry state of my clothes, my beard, and my tattered clothes.

Had he been sent to prepare me for the final day? Was he here to take me, the exposed Jew, to his own king?

He said it was the end of March and that he had heard of arrests in Houndsditch. This was the Priory of Sheen. No sooner were the words out than three young men took him away. Instead of marching him down the corridor, there was the unlocking of the empty cell next to mine and the sound of a door slamming and a turning of the key.

The Spanish ambassador, the former page of Queen Isabella, was imprisoned alongside the Jew from Valencia. Although the doors were solid, he, too, must have had an unglazed window in his cell. We could hear one another by talking through the window. He had been arrested for speaking for the queen and thrown into Durham House, but the king had decided that his two Spanish prisoners might reveal more if they were overheard talking to one another.

"What jurisdiction has he?" I asked in Aragonese, which the guards would not understand. I choked out words from a dry throat and a tongue that had lost the strength of speech. "They cannot execute the ambassador of Charles V."

"No Spaniard will be executed," he replied.

"I have stepped too far and have been found in the wrong places," I said. "I have served too many masters."

We talked sideways out of the tiny windows in our prison cells for two days. He compared the king to the Roman Emperors Nero and Caligula.

"Señor, you are a good man," he said. "If I ever see the emperor again, I will support the cause of your people."

"You really will?"

"Yes, I will speak for the Jews of Spain."

"But I am not a Jew."

"You are a fine Jew, my friend. You must always be proud of that."

I felt complimented, strangely liberated. "And if we ever get out of here, will you vouch me safe in Spanish lands?"

"For your loyalty to the queen, of course," he replied.

"And my sisters in Valencia?"

"I will do whatever I can."

The next day, I heard him storming around his cell, banging fists against the wall. I was going to call to him and offer words of comfort when the door to the long chamber of cells swung open. I heard the heavy steps of several guards.

"Which cell holds Vives?" The voice was piercing.

My cell door was unlocked, and they entered, silencing me with a rough hand to my mouth. My hands were tied behind my back, and I was marched past Zuniga's cell. The hand over my mouth was momentarily loosened

"I will watch out for you, my friend, from the other side," I shouted.

"In the name of the kingdoms of Castile and Aragon, do no harm to this man," he replied.

We travelled through a myriad of tiny, damp passageways that must have been underneath the main church and ascended to a small chamber. They hurled me inside into semi-darkness. My eyes gradually focussed. There was a large tub of water and a bar of London soap, clean clothes, sheets of paper and ink, all the things I had requested. A tiny candle burnt on a long bench. There was a bed and warm woollen blankets.

What could I do but write? That is where these pages were written, though I may be sentencing myself and others to an early grave. Perhaps it is a trick, now that they know I will not buckle from interrogation. By virtue of the fact that I am writing, it shows me that the angel of hope is still with me. As I finish it, my eyes strained, I hear in the faint spit of the candle flame the words from my boyhood.

"Shalom al-Israel, aleinu ve-al-banenu."

"Father, what does it mean?"

"Peace over Israel, over us and over our children."

8 April 1529

What happened next was like an earthquake that struck without warning—the guards, the unlocking of the door, the grabbing. I didn't have time to set the papers afire as I'd planned. Instead, I dropped them and kicked my piss pot onto them so no man would pick them up.

I was led blindfolded through more passages, past gasping nuns to the corner of a darkened room. The men took my blindfold off and left me there. As my sight gradually returned, I could see a figure, crouched and covered with a dark veil. I could see the eyes, the nose, the parted lips, and the teeth. She turned to me, removed the veil, and said in soft, monastic tones, "My dearest friend, what have they done to you?"

I was ashamed at my appearance, a beard down to my chest and a stench of urine, sweat, and gruel.

"Mistress Roper, I must smell worse than a dead cat. I am so sorry."

"Shhhh," she said. "It's your Meg. Your poor arm. You are so thin—the ribs, the pelvis."

I apologised again. "Are they to finish me here?" I asked.

"Juanito, you are not finished," she sighed, her brown hair showing now, long and wavy.

As my vision focussed, I could see the apple green of her dress. I jolted as she put her hand on my left arm, held lifeless on my lap like that of a dead child.

"How so?"

I reached for her with my right hand and found that she, too, was all bone and hanging flesh.

"Meg, my sweetest one, what happened to you?"

"What use is food in this world?" she answered.

I didn't like this talk, for I had seen the starvation sickness even among the rich.

"You must eat, my love, but first tell me what happened out there?"

She began picking at the cuff of her green dress incessantly. This was a different Meg. After a time of gibbering, she told me of her long journey to the king's chambers. She had waited there for three days before he would see her. She had not been able to eat or sleep since my arrest. Her guilt had become a monster, slowly killing her, and she had to act.

"No guilt, no guilt," I said.

She shook her head. "Mea culpa," she said and then continued. When the king emerged from his chamber, she threw herself at his feet, begging for clemency. He kicked her off, but he caught her eye, her desperation, and against Anne Boleyn's pleading, he gave Meg a private audience. Anne was at his side throughout, scoffing at the pleas for mercy, telling the king they no longer needed the support of the Chelsea Mores or the Spanish Jews. After an hour of pleading for my life, the king looked at Meg. "I will do this for you, Margaret Roper, and nothing else. You will not grace my court again. I declare that no one will ever ask me for clemency again." He pointed to Anne and said, "Not even her."

The king and Anne Boleyn fought like brother and sister.

"You will do this for her but do nothing for me!" she screeched. Her frantic brother was at her side, egging her on.

"No one talks to me like this," the king roared. He then softened and turned to Anne. "I would change my kingdom for you, my little duckee. And the price you will pay is sons."

"And if I only give you daughters?" she asked.

"It won't happen, it is against God's will."

Anne turned and kissed the king on the cheek, inspecting Meg from head to toe before shouting at the king's guards. "Get her out, now!"

It was true what the gypsy told Meg all those years ago: "The next queen will hate you."

My legs began shaking at that thought.

"Meg, I would not be shy after all this. You risked everything for me, and yet your husband said I invaded your chamber. Why?"

She sighed, looked at me, and a tear welled in her eye. "Because I have not loved a man but you, señor. I loved you before I found your secret diary, and I loved you again after, even though I had it decoded. I know code when I see it, so I asked Álvaro to work on it and then had it checked by William Grocyn, the preacher, who told Reginald Pole."

"What did Álvaro tell you my words meant?"

"The truth you are trying so hard to forget—your Jewish heart. That you loved another with all your heart and soul but that you cared for me and loved me as well."

I breathed a sigh of relief. Álvaro was my brother. He had shielded her from the truth though it had not helped my father.

"Then why break my heart with that letter from your husband?" I asked, lifting her chin and looking into her brown eyes.

"My husband is a powerful man. He has spies everywhere." She broke away from my touch but looked at me in the eyes until hers glazed over. "You see, he has me in his grip. He can be violent, even to my sisters."

"Why tolerate this nonsense?"

"Because he has threatened to turn against Father and give evidence to the king of Father's campaigns against—" She broke off in shame.

I knew well that her father, once my great friend, had launched a vicious attack against the heretics and that he had privately declared against the Boleyn faction. If William Roper told the king everything he knew, then Sir Thomas would be guilty of treason.

Meg had risked her life for mine.

"This sacrifice might hurt you, my sweet. How can I express my gratitude?"

"You don't need to, for what else could I do when I owed you a life?" she said.

"The king of Spain took that life, not you."

There was a knock on the door. Our time was almost up.

"If I hadn't raided your trunk, if I hadn't spoken to Grocyn," she said. "If Pole..."

"It's all right. Justice will be done in the Lord's own way, and there is still a life that I will yet save."

"Your sisters, you mean?"

"Well, one of them."

"The warrior Jewess?" she asked.

"That's the one."

Goosebumps spread over my face and cheek, and I shuddered with pride to know that Beatriz Vives, whose very existence dangled by a thread, was indeed a warrior Jewess, perhaps a present-day Lilith.

But I remembered with whom I was sitting. I touched her soft, cool cheek and kissed her on the lips.

The guards entered the chamber to separate us.

"You are not to leave with her," the tall one said flatly.

"But she has come for me," I pleaded.

"It is the order of the king. She is to go, and you are to be taken tomorrow to the city. You are not to see her again, nor are you to set foot in the royal palace. You have a day to leave England or you will be brought back here."

"No, sir. This is my Meg. We must visit the sick in Bedlam and work together for my hospitals. This is not right!" I shouted louder with every word, knowing this was probably the last time Meg would hear my words.

She turned to me and said, "It is as it must be. It was the bargain. Farewell, Juanito." With that, she was gone.

When I returned to my chamber, I found Zuniga picking through my piss-stained papers, drying them on a rack in front of a set of candles. He had been allowed in specifically to read what I had left there.

"It is as I thought. There is a secret world that lives among us."

"A secret world that does no harm and that is true to the word of God."

I offered to give him anything for his silence—a book, the gold my wife had in the cellar of our house—but he would have none of it.

"We have taken enough from you, señor."

He handed me the papers. The guards came for him next, and he said to the tall one, "It's nothing but Spanish love songs to his Spanish wife." Without a struggle, he was gone.

As he left, I shouted, "She lives in the caves. She's a good woman. Her name is Beatriz. The others' names are Eva and Leonora." But he was gone.

*   *   *

There was no ceremony as I was kicked out of the barge at Billingsgate, with its skiffs and nets, its smell of shore-crabs and street soil. "Fuck off and sward with your own," said the young man who'd held me to the back wall of my cell with a garden fork. Struggling through crowds at the market, the half-mile to Houndsditch seemed like ten, and I staggered through the throng, slipping on discarded piles of fish guts. I pushed through the hawkers and coney-catchers of Thames, fuelled only by spring's light and the sparrow's rapid chattering. I was near The Flying Horse. Would I find there a torched ruin? A new family who had made it their own?

I opened the back gate from Camomile Street, and there, like the calm mystic he was, I found Álvaro de Castro. He was sitting on the back step reading from a book. Sarah Elisha was hanging out washing, and Gasper was teasing Eduardo. Henry the hound looked up, his pink tongue hanging from the corner of his mouth. He yelped for joy, jumped at my frail chest, and knocked me over. They were safe; they had survived.

"Hermano," said Álvaro, picking me up from the cobbles while looking into my ravaged face.

"Juanito," said Sarah. "We have been expecting you."

I fell to my knees, exhausted. "Expecting me? The next world is the only place that's been expecting me!"

"That is not true," said Álvaro. "We knew it was not your time."

Had my incarceration meant so little to him?

"How did you know this when even the king did not know?" I asked him.

"God speaks."

They gave me food and clean clothes. They also gave me warm water in a wooden tub, soap and perfume, and a sharp razor to trim my beard. There was a letter, too, that he gave me, embossed with the royal seal of the queen. I was to leave England as soon as I was able lest the king change his mind. If there had been a boat, I would have been on it that night, but I needed to talk with Álvaro. When all had left the inn, and Sarah and Benjamin had gone to bed, I cornered him.

"Álvaro, help me."

"Juanito, you must delve deeply within your soul. Take the path your conscience dictates."

"But I can't see my own conscience. I am tortured."

He knew that I was asking him to open the door once more to the celestial path, to the mystical world, as he had done once before. He looked at me for a minute and took me by the arm, saying, "Come."

Into the cellar we went, the chief synagogue of England, lighting candles and drawing a Magen David across my body. He gave me the dagger to pierce the cellar's dank air. "Visualise the four archangels."

Michael was before me, Gabriel behind. Raphael was on my right, Uriel on my left.

"Now the shechinah, the light of God above your head," he said.

It was a golden light, and then it happened. Once more the cellar's brick-vaulted ceiling disappeared, and I could see a beautiful blue sky. This was not the sky of Valencia or of England, but the sky of Flanders. There were children laughing and running in the street. One of them was Zeek. There were burghers walking past, arm in arm. There was my home on Verversdijk. I noticed an open door, and inside there was not my wife but my father, looking up at me with outstretched palms. "Son, you have done well. You have worked and toiled, and you have paid the price. Your great work will be done one day. Now come home."

I looked into Father's dark eyes, rushing for his outstretched palms, but before I could get there he was gone. Instead, I saw my wife cooking, laughing, and talking to Henry the giant poodle.

The scene then shifted, and I saw Princess Mary sitting at her studies, bereft and abandoned. I saw the queen in her chamber, also abandoned. I saw Mistress Roper sitting alone at her studies, thin and sick-looking, translating a text from Latin into English. Then I saw my father again, and he walked past the princess, the queen, and Margaret Roper. He looked at me and spoke without compromise. "Son, there is nothing more you can do. The only life you can save is your own. You must leave. Pain is the way of the world, and the world wants you, at least for now. Your greater work is not yet done."

The sky rolled back and there was the warmth of a Valencian sky, the sound of the nightingales seeking out Persian roses. There was the running of children in the streets and the smells of the kitchens of La Juderia, the lavender of my mother. I could hear the tinkering of brass on silver from the home of our neighbour, Eduardo de Pinto, and squeals from indoors as my brother, Jaime, was chased by my sisters. My focus shifted from Jaime to Beatriz and would not leave her.

"Your work will be done in its proper time," Álvaro declared. "B'yi-to. You can do no more here. You will not be safe. Go to Flanders. There you will know peace."

"But what of my great plan? What safe home for the Jews will there ever be? We will all be destroyed."

"It is not *your* great plan. We must make our own way for now and keep the flame burning. When it is ready, it will happen in England and in all the lands in which she settles. In this is our salvation.

"But who will sing to the old ladies of the Domus when you're gone? Who'll be here to welcome our brethren who wash up on these shores?"

"It's not for you or me to answer all these questions, brother. There are others here in this house and others will come after us. What we put down here will guide them along the path."

Álvaro made to leave, but before he reached the creaky stairs, I asked questions. Why had the king not come for him? Why did he tolerate the Jews of Houndsditch if he himself was a fervent Christian?"

"There is more to King Henry than history will remember."

"But why tolerate the Jews if he won't even allow a bible in English?" I asked.

"He knows he can call on us when he needs to, and he knows we are no threat to him, just to the old bastards around him. And we control the spice and wine trade from Portugal."

"But you're not brave enough to force him to open his doors to us," I added.

"Toro Bravo, you dared where others would not and were prepared to pay for it with your life."

I had always considered myself a clever and cunning little fish. El Toro Bravo was an act. Perhaps I had been wrong about myself all along?

"Still, Álvaro, I do not understand why he allows us to continue."

"Can you not see the turmoil and unrest if he opened the doors now? He knows that we have secrets that we will take to our grave. The queen's miscarried son, for example."

"How do you know about Catherine of Aragon's first son?" I asked.

He walked to the back of the cellar, removed a loose brick from the wall, and uncovered a silken bag. He reached in and produced my papers. "These, I think, belong to you." He then put his scrivener's nimble hand inside the silk bag and pulled out a ring—the fourth ring. He held it up to the light of the candle, and it glistened as if it were a message from God.

"Dear brother, it is a matter on the one hand of finance, on the other of God. Henry knows that one day we will bring great wealth into this country. He knows that he pleases God by having us here."

"So why will he not accept us and defy the pope and emperor?"

Álvaro looked at me and smiled again. "Because unlike you, dear brother, he knows that this is not the proper time."

"But that time will one day come?" I asked.

"Indeed, it will come."

*   *   *

The next day, Álvaro and Sarah took me to the dock and said, "God be with you."

This time the hound would not be drawn from my side, knowing as only a hound can know that this was really goodbye. I thanked them for all they had done and hugged them, forcing my left arm up with my right. I didn't care who saw or if my brittle bones might break.

"We are family, a brotherhood," Álvaro said.

"And evermore will be so?" I asked.

"Evermore."

Ghastlier than ever, though, that crossing! I shored myself up between Henry the hound and chests of English wool that smelled of the lanolin, the ocean roaring and rolling the beginnings of the apocalypse. I envied the gulls looking down at our frail boat. What an injustice it would be to have survived the king's prison only to meet a watery grave! But we battled down the side of one final sheet of water and were jettisoned safely into the harbour.

Henry bounced off the gangplank as if he knew just where he was going. The first night was spent in a tavern, recounting stories of the horrific storm. The next morning, I joined a group of wool merchants, and paying for my share of their armed guard since these were lawless times. An occasional squall sought us out, and although the rain was like arrows with the ice of the north in its quills, I didn't care. I'd soon be home.

I spotted the spires and towers of Bruges and yelled a "Hallelujah." I jumped from the wagon, and Henry followed me. I kissed the very ground. I had survived.

I made the Verversdijk by early evening. There was no guard. Everything was as it should be. I turned the handle and found that the front door was not locked. How things have changed. I let the dog go forward into the kitchen, the cooking smells proving too much for him.

"Oh," I heard, then "oooh" and "Pero—Enrique?" This was followed by a hopeful singsong of "Juanito, Juanito?"

I waited by the door as Marguerite made her way to the hall with tiny steps. Were there tears on her cheeks? I stood there with a smile, body twisted as always, and waited. This was my home, and she was my true love. She ran towards me, black hair flying back. She threw her arms around me and placed her lovely forehead on my weary shoulder.

Then there were other footsteps, tinier than hers. A smile broke out on Zeek's face. "Papa, you are home. I didn't think you'd come."

"Zeek, I promised you and Mama."

"But so too did my first Papa," he said.

"He did his best, Zeek, and I promised him that I would keep his promise for him."

We moved to the kitchen and sat at the table, its scratches and stains as familiar to me as the lines on my own hand. I told them I would never go back. What of the others though? The house seemed so quiet. Maria had married a good Christian burgher and led the double life. And so it was with Marguerite and Zeek, along with Nicolas, who was practising medicine at the new hospital.

"New hospital?" I jumped in my seat.

"The one that Louis de Praet built," Marguerite said.

I sighed. "Is it really true that he's a changed man?" I found it hard to believe that the man who'd demanded a book in his name would actually have read that book, let alone act on it.

"People change when they meet you, Juanito, and they see the good in you," she said.

"And señora?" I asked, but I knew in my heart that she had gone. It had happened in March. "May her memory be for a blessing," I said.

The bed saw lovemaking for three days and nights. We were drunk on love, and it was only because we had a boy and a dog that I got up and ate. How I needed this human touch, this warmth, this love. Nicolas came back from the new hospital and laughed at the two lovebirds in his own home.

On the fourth day, Marguerite and I walked, arm in arm, along the riverbank. Zeek and Henry, best friends now, trundled beside us. As we made our way home, I pulled her tight and kissed her, telling her that I'd never let her go.

"I received a letter from Margaret Roper," she said.

"What did she say?"

"It's all right. You can call her Meg."

"Why would I call her Meg?" I asked, my voice high-pitched.

"She loved you very much," Marguerite said without a breath of bitterness. We stopped dead on the cobbled path. There was no point in denying it, and the liberty of the truth was overwhelmingly good.

"To save my life she has exiled herself from court," I said, transfixed by the symmetry and tones of the cobbles.

"Then she is my dearest sister," my wife proclaimed. "I owe her a life."

"What did she say in her letter?" I needed to know.

"To fatten you up and to keep you fat and warm because you've still great work to do."

We made our way home in silence. Henry and Zeek played with a ball in the backyard while my wife and I sat where the brotherhood had once sat, at the table that had become an anchor.

"Are you feeling stronger now that I mentioned her name?" Marguerite asked.

I cast the net wide in my soul for an answer. "In the proper time, I'll be strong through your love and no one else's if you are patient with me."

"I promise you that, Juanito."

Later we nestled before the fire in the drawing room, with Henry's head on my lap, Zeek's on hers. These were like the babies she was never able to have.

"Day by day, you will get stronger," she said, "and time will show that you have not failed."

She leaned into my body as I played with her hair. This was no dream. This was real, was heaven on earth. And so, we put them to bed, the dog and the boy. We made our way up to bed and became lost in the honesty of pure being. I was home. I was safe. This gentle woman was mine, and I was hers.

PART FOUR

END OF DAYS

9 August 1529

Thin-faced Louis de Praet was at the door, banging hard even as I opened it. He thrust me a book of blank vellum pages.

"This gets you talking, I'm told." He pushed past into my house. As he pushed, I noticed there was flesh on my body where there had been just bone. I also noticed that there was the old bounce in my step as I stumbled backwards. But where was he going with such ease, and why?

"Señor, please. My wife is—"

De Praet sat calmly at the kitchen table, the sacred space of the brotherhood. Marguerite, who was pickling herrings, became ashen-faced and fell back in her seat.

"Stay out there," she shouted to Zeek.

She offered de Praet white-fleshed herring with dark rye bread. He looked at it with his one eye and grabbed it with his dirty fingers, munching on it like a dog.

"To what do we owe this pleasure, Señor de Praet?' I asked, smiling as best I could.

"Let's be frank. We are exiles, you and I. Wolsey kicked me into the ocean just as the king kicked you. Louis de Praet is thinking that he and this man Vives… can be of help to one another. Agreed, yes?"

"But how?" I asked.

I recalled the diamond seal of the Inquisition that had been stitched to his cloak and blazer, the prison cell in Bruges, the twisted, dislocated shoulder. The seals were gone, but my shoulder was still useless. What could this man want of me?

"Something in your words reached me. You might not believe that because you think I'm a brute and a pig. I have been, and at times I still am. But you keep dedicating your works in this direction, and you're safe to light your Shabbat candles and eat your challah bread."

This man was ever a man of deals, bargains, and negotiations. He had a pricing system for everything. It had once been a ruby rosary and a diamond crucifix for an old and battered Jew's life. Now it was the printed word in exchange for freedom. Could I not bargain with him to improve the lot of my people? He must have seen the machinations in my head and intercepted my thoughts.

"We can work together," he said. "Look at our new hospital. Perhaps your poor-boy school will be next."

This was the deal, then: he would take credit for change, and I would be the silent voice that steered that change.

"Of course, Señor de Praet," I said with gritted teeth.

"I must see to Zeek," Marguerite said, stepping outside the back door.

"I am very sorry," I said. "She's feeling faint, it's her monthly course."

"Shut up, Vives. I killed her father. Is it any wonder she can't bear the sight of me?" He laughed and shoved my left shoulder. I thought it would fall out of its socket again, but the shove seemed to push it back in.

"Juanito, if I may use that name, exile has hardened me to the church, softened me to you. I can't be remembered as a butcher."

With a sudden twist of his black hat that had a yellow peacock feather, he got up to leave. This was a man of action and deals. At the front door, I managed to squeeze in front of him.

"We live as good Catholics, sir. You know that, don't you? Remember the wedding at St. Donatian?"

"Of course. Very good Catholics. By the way, her parents died of syphilis, if anyone should ask. The father gave it to the mother. Put it in writing or there'll be trouble." He kissed two fingers and placed them on the doorpost as if putting them on an invisible mezuzah. Then he was gone.

So, I am to bargain with the souls and reputations of the dead in order that we may live. I cannot. Against my will, I find myself writing in this book he left me, although I have no stomach now for secrets or codes or magnifying glasses. If they find this, they find it. Let us all be damned.

3 October 1529

But they didn't find it, and we were not damned. Nobody came knocking on the door in the small hours, turned us out of our beds, or searched beneath our floorboards. In fact, the early sound of the swallows calling in the nest outside the back portico is the only sound that disturbs our sleep.

Some days ago, a letter arrived, crisp and addressed in a hand I knew as well as my own, with fine black letters slanting medial to lateral and imbued with extra ink on the downslopes. There was a familiar seal of wax that would have dripped from a bar he must have bought at Spitalfields.

"What does he say in the letter?" she asked.

There was no talk of the secret cellar of feast days or fast days. There was just a series of oblique messages from Álvaro de Castro: "We scarce have room for any more guests in the tavern"; "the children are learning the language of their fathers"; and "Moyses Ambrosius is sent back to Italy for sodomy of all things but swears he will one day be back." He also wrote, "Zuniga is free and on his way to Charles V."

Would Zuniga be good to his word that he would help me and my sisters? Would we be safe for much longer? Must we up and move again? No, that is one thing we cannot do. We cannot wander any more.

The king became impatient with Wolsey, and London was alive with talk of the witch, Anne Boleyn. Reginald Pole and his mother, the Countess Salisbury, took over the education of the princess and isolated her further. What fire will they ignite in her soul? I wrote something down:

> Álvaro, like a brother to me,
> Whose children are my children, will ever more be so,
> Will keep the flame alive in that country called England,
> That one day will be a safe place, a haven, a spring-pad
> Into the new World, where we can hold our heads up high
> And do no harm
> And breathe in peace, a brother to a brother,
> a father to a son, a brother to a long-lost sister.

The next morning, I took the letter to the dock and walked home along the street known as Konewinkel. I passed the house of Johannes Van der Poel. A blackbird flew past and almost clipped my ear, and I swore it was singing, "Go on, be brave and enter. Go on Vives!" Would he be at home or in the workshops, spinning yarn and making money? I rapped on the door and waited.

"You have a visitor, sir," the maid called out. "He calls himself Vives."

"Show him in. Get him here at once!"

I entered and saw his smiling face and shock of blond hair.

"Señor! I am blessed! Promise me you are here to stay this time." He shuffled away some papers and said, "Who needs these when I have you here, the master of words and papers?"

I nodded.

"Master Vives, that nod means that I can send my sons to learn from you?"

"Yes, Johannes. You can send your sons, as many as you like! This will be my final resting place, though not too soon, I hope. And what of you, my brightest star, the one who brought me that leather-bound diary all those years ago?"

"Juanito, you know Master de Praet delivered sermons on health, poverty, brotherhood, and how they relate to God's message. He doesn't show it, but de Praet is quite modest actually. We are about to open a house for the poor, and we've a tariff from the burghers and merchants, so there's a new hospital with running water planned. Also, we've funds for our own college of physicians and our school for the poor."

"My goodness, it is a phenomenon, Johannes," I said and hugged him tightly with my right arm. "Tell me, what will you do for the poor in your house?" I was intrigued, for I was ever a man of theory and not so good with action.

"Get them a skill—an apprenticeship paid for by the taxes. Whatever happens—a peasant revolt or an English invasion— they'll still be able to work, feed their wives, and train their children."

The poor wouldn't be eternally trapped. I was lost for words.

"It is all because of you, señor, and your example and—"

"And what, Johannes?"

"I wronged you long ago, tried to expose you because I didn't realise the strength of words."

I shrugged my shoulders. "Things like this happen," I said.

"I have tried to imagine what it was like for you and your family and have tried very hard to make amends."

"But, Johannes," I said, "you were young, and the young don't understand the world. I'm not even sure the old do." I needed him to know that I believed him. I reached out and touched his hand. "It's all right."

"Yes, but it was words like mine that sent your father to the stake."

"I know this like I know my own hand, but the future is the country for us. That is the place we have to live in now, all of us under God's great sky, one family, one brotherhood."

We drank to the future and made plans for his poor house and sharing the taxes with Antwerp, Ghent, and Louvain. He made me see that I had indeed done great work; he made me see that I was not too damaged; he made me see that there was great work to do and that there was no better time than now.

*　　*　　*

I went back into the world. The drive to be a great man in my own right, not just a clever little fish swimming alongside the great fish, was born. The desire to shape words into action seemed to be fuelled by an incredible new strength. It was as if I was working in a mighty blast furnace, like a blacksmith from a Norse myth. Once I finished writing, I would go to Spain and get my sister, risk everything, and then it would be published, my greatest work known as *Of Concord and Discord*. What words! What heresy! Surely, we must have a League of Nations, a united body from many lands to subvert wars and build a peaceful New World. Moreover, there must be an abolition of the Holy Inquisition and a National Health Service, with trained professionals funded by a tax, not the charity of the church. What I wrote about the church—no one would believe it: "They live by the people's charity, and nevertheless they are pleased with being feared and are proud of inspiring terror and of injuring the very people who support them."

It was published and spread around Europe—even back to England—reaching farther than the plague. In horror, I realised I could become the new Luther but was unable to run if the officers of the king of Spain came after us. But he had other entanglements now: Rome, the French, and his growing empire. I had stared death in the face already and seen it so many times that it had lost its sting. I was all in the writing, hidden beneath piles of correspondence. I hardly noticed the geraniums coming into bloom or heard the children playing late in the street, my own little boy, Zeek, among them, shrieking and glowing with sweat and vigour. He'd come, eat, and then sleep comfortably, placated by his new home, the place that I prayed he would always have for sanctuary.

When I was least expecting it, the truly great thing happened.

1 October 1529

It was early autumn now: breezy and cold. But there was a kindness in the light that I couldn't quite articulate. Was it the kindness of healing? The light bounced off the windowpanes and lit up the streets, and there were the promises of the season: chestnuts, storytelling, nights snuggled together by the fireside. And there was a new smell that Henry the hound picked up before we did: the early falling of leaves, the winter kale being brought into the market, the salted fish.

I approached the door of our house by early evening, but I found myself standing there, transfixed, unable to move. Was it fear that coursed from my temples down to my feet like a lightning strike? Was it hope, that most difficult visitor, the one I found so hard to give a home? Henry looked at me as if he had the answer. I looked at him and found myself saying, "What is it, Henry?" He stood on his hind legs at the front door, as only a giant poodle can, and sniffed it, twitched his nose, and cocked his head. He wagged his tail and put his wet nose to the lock and door handle.

I turned it, and it opened. We entered and found nothing but silence. The oil lamps weren't lit. There was no smell of the tallow or of food slowly cooking or of my wife's gentle songs. Where was the sound of laughter that usually greeted me when I got home? Slowly, I walked forwards in the dim light and opened the kitchen door.

There were two figures at the table, but they were both immobile. Zeek, who played with his soldiers on the floor, didn't look up. My eyes adjusted to the poor light, and Henry crept forwards, assessing whether to attack or to welcome.

"Marguerite?" There was nothing—no movement and no response.

The skinny figure straightened at the neck and cocked its head. It was almost lizard-like in its movement, but it was a woman's figure—skinny and tattered. As she looked up, a face gradually revealed itself, worn, lined with pouches under dark eyes, skin as thin as paper. The face had something in it that I knew. She smiled, and I knew who this was.

The years fell away, and I fell to my knees, hands outstretched before me. "Oh my. How can this be?" I almost couldn't get the word out. "Beatriz?" I prayed that this was not a vision, a delusion, that my mind, after all it had been through, wasn't collapsing in on itself. But then something in her face lightened. She sighed, and I recognised the dark eyes of my mother, the lined forehead of my father.

"Yes, Juanito, it is I."

I simply stood in the moment: the culmination of all the moments, the final play of my struggle. The backdoor opened, and

Zeek and Henry came towards me. I tried to speak, but words did not come. I needed to touch her and to know that she was real.

"Don't get up, little one," I said, giving her a gentle caress. Anything more would have crushed her frail bones.

She began to shake and to tremble, fighting tears.

"My Juanito, my little one, my very own brother."

She was there at Father's death and Mother's exhumation. With a price on her head, the other two could neither shelter nor hide her. She hid in warehouses, slept under a hessian cloth, and found a church tower that had once been a minaret. From there, she watched the streets every day, certain that I would come looking for her. From her secret high place, she saw our family house taken and the ancient Arabic books ritually burnt by the priests on the street. It was then that she became the warrior Jewess. The same night the priest's family moved in, she stole through the air vent into the cellar and smeared the four pillars with goose fat. "One for my mother, one for my father, one for my brother, and one for my sisters," she said.

"But why goose fat? To remember us? We never kept geese."

"Goose fat burns, Juanito. I tied rags, laid straw, lit it, and ran. The house and the one next door that once belonged to the silversmith were gone by morning. I'm not as holy as you, brother. I'm not beyond vengeance."

"How did you get away?"

Zeek sat on the floor, knees to his chest, totally enraptured. Henry put his wet nose in her hand, as if congratulating her.

Without food or water and with an army after her, she threw herself on the order of St. Cecilia and the nuns from Navarre, a happier, more tolerant place. Beatriz, who they called Magdalena, became a repentant, fleeing her terrible family that had killed her bastard baby. It was there one night that a young nun told her, as the moon rose to its zenith, of the tale of the warrior Jewess, Beatriz Vives.

"She must be a terrible one," my sister said.

"Worse than a sorceress," the nun replied. "She cut children's necks and used the blood for Jewish rituals, then set fire to the cellar. All they found were charred bones."

One night a search party of men banged on the door of the convent, and the sisters put her in a chest, beneath linen packed so tightly that she almost suffocated. The following day, with a black mourning veil to cover her face, she climbed the wall of the convent and was gone. Across rocky mountain paths, she trekked to a village known as Almassera and a cave where we had once played as children. She thought I'd be coming for her. She trapped rabbit at sunrise and stole grain by night from a farmhouse. It was the smoke that alerted the villagers—a farm boy had been spying on her. Fearing for their lives and hoping for a handsome reward, they trapped the warrior Jewess. It was early summer by then and I had been on my way back to Bruges.

"Juanito, there were twenty with pitchforks, axes, and torches," she explained. She thought it was the end, that her darling brother would not be coming for her. The soldier at the head of the pack told her, "The Queen of England, and his Excellency, Don Zuniga de Mendoza, have spoken for you. You must come quickly."

The queen, whose words had seen Father chained to the stake, had done what she said she would do. All of my efforts were not in vain. As she'd helped the pauper apprentices, she'd helped me. And that dear man with the grey hair, with whom I was once incarcerated, had spoken the truth. The wretched Jew had succeeded.

The brotherhood, now disbanded, had succeeded. They placed six pesos in a leather purse about her neck and dragged her to the quay in front of a jeering crowd, who kicked and spat at her, a chain about the neck. The ship was soon gone and sailed through the pillars of Hercules at Gibraltar to make its way to Lisbon, where she thought she'd be safe. She slept with the homeless waifs and the rats under the arches of the great sea wall until the pepper ship arrived from Africa, bound for Antwerp. She was given scraps of bread no one else would eat, and although she would kneel and pray with them every night as she had learned to do in the convent, she was known as La Judia and was kicked around the decks like an old bucket. At Antwerp, with no language and no money, she met a family who knew a few words of Spanish. They gave her bread and cheese and pointed her to Bruges. She set out in the night, sleeping in ditches and hiding in barns. She hid in the trees, where the songs of birds urged her to keep going. On the third night from Antwerp, almost dead with fatigue, she came to a group of gypsies who gave her a woollen cape, a meal of roasted squirrel, and soup of nettles. They pointed her to Bruges, and she trudged on. Finally, she saw the city of tall buildings and shiny windows and found herself in the street, asking, "Vives, the scholar?" And so she came across our house in the Verversdijk, knocked on the door, and slumped in a heap before Marguerite opened the door.

As she told me the story, the pain of the past ten years welled up inside. I couldn't speak and just held Beatriz's sweet, frail hand.

The pain was gone. I looked up, and instead of the timber-beamed ceiling, I saw blue skies and heard the chattering of nightingales. We were in the hills around Valencia, where father took us on Sundays. We were holding hands, running into the farmer's fields, playing chase, laughing though our hair was stuck to our foreheads with sweat. Mother was singing.

Now is the time of the living.

* * *

This will be the end of the writing now that I have her here, my treasure, getting stronger and prettier day by day. Her hair is shiny now and she is able to eat. I have my wife and the boy and his best friend, Henry. You have to go, then, diaries, piss-stained writings and my ring with its Star of David. And also, the sketch of my friend, Sir Thomas More. You can go in this wooden box because I cannot bear to see your full and beautiful head as the game in England plays out. God be with you, Sir Thomas, and the queen and Meg, too. God be with the secret Jews of England, too, with your secret synagogues and Kabbalistic rituals. May you, in time, prevail and live in a better land. Yes, it's you, the hidden men of history that make the world a better place.

Where the new wall is going up, beneath the floors on the other side, I'll place the writings. I had a great teacher for hiding books: my father! He placed his Arabic books beneath the floorboards of our home in La Juderia, and they weren't found in his lifetime. No one will know that this was once a house of secret Jews until many years have passed and the persecution of the Jews is over.

Farewell.

It ought to be the duty of the public officials to take pains to see that men help one another, that no one is oppressed, no one wronged by an unjust condemnation, and that the strong come to the assistance of the weak in order that the harmony of the united body of citizens may grow in love day by day and endure forever.

—Juan Luis Vives, 1525

HISTORICAL NOTE

The dates and times of major events of Vives's life as described in the two diaries are accurate as far as can be ascertained. The dates of his arrivals and departures from England and the death of his father, as well as the dates of his incarceration in England, are known and followed faithfully. The letter he signed in support of Catherine of Aragon on the orders of Wolsey is thought to be the reason he was arrested. It is known that he was incarcerated for a time with the Spanish ambassador, Inigo Mendoza de Zuniga.

That Vives knew the More family well and stayed at their various homes is also fact. Vives's wife was Marguerite Valldaura, who came from a family of Jewish origin from Valencia and who settled in Bruges. She never came to England despite being personally invited by the queen. Her father dealt in cloth and diamonds, and her brother, Nicolas Valldaura, became a physician. Vives's friendship with Álvaro de Castro, "whom he loved like a brother" and with whom he stayed in London, is well-attested. Gasper de Castro is also recorded in state documents in London in the 1550s. Beatriz, Vives's sister, joined him in Bruges in 1531. One of Vives's brothers-in-law who remained in Valencia went before the Inquisition.

Sir Thomas More was imprisoned in the Tower of London by Henry VIII and executed on 6 July 1535, ostensibly for refusing to accept the annulment of the marriage of Henry and Catherine. His last letter from the Tower, "The Agony of Christ," was passed to his daughter Meg. In her will, she left it to Fray Pedro de Soto of Valencia, home of the Vives family. It now resides in the Corpus

Christi Museum in Valencia. At More's execution, he commented that his beard had committed no crime and thus should be spared the axe. His head was placed on a pike on London Bridge for a month after his execution, and Meg obtained it, possibly by bribery. She kept it for years under her bed, and she is thought to be buried with it in Canterbury. His hair shirt is preserved and currently on display at Syon House, formerly Syon Abbey.

The Flying Horse Inn in Houndsditch was present in the seventeenth century, and it is possible that a tavern existed there earlier as this area escaped the ravages of the Great Fire of London in 1666. Of the secret Jews of sixteenth-century London, there are tantalising glimpses. The Chancery Court records record several Londoners with Jewish surnames such as Cohen, Isaacs, and Levy. The Domus Conversorum, or house of the converts, was continually inhabited at this time. An Edward Scales left the Domus in 1527. The musician Ambrosius Moyses is attested to in the historical record as a court musician, an early violin player who sometimes was known as John Anthony.

Elements of Vives's conversation with Catherine of Aragon on the barge to Syon House are mentioned in his writings. She asked him which of the two he would choose: good fortune or adversity. She commented that she would choose an equal share, and if then she still had to choose, she would choose the latter, feeling that it would strengthen her. The reported speech at the Christmas gathering of Sir Thomas More, 1523—"Only any non-donkey of any man except Socrates and another belonging to this same man begins contingently to be black"—are the actual words of Vives, who used them to illustrate that the exclusivity of academic writing was often nonsense. He was a lifelong proponent of clarity in writing.

That Henry VIII had Jewish sympathies is generally acknowledged, and there are no records of Jewish persecutions during his reign apart from the temporary imprisonment in 1541 of the court musicians. It is thought that there may have been up to nineteen Jewish musicians in Henry's court. The imprisonment may have been an attempt to placate the Holy Roman Emperor Charles V. The king had a long association with Marco Raphael, the German rabbi mentioned in the text, and the king personally came to the defence of the wealthy financier, Diego Mendes of Antwerp, who was imprisoned on the accusation of Judaism.

The character of Johannes Van der Poel is fictitious, although Bruges became the model for secular care of the poor along the lines of *On Assistance to the Poor*. The students of Vives were instrumental in bringing this about.

Vives died on May 6, 1540, and his wife died twelve years later. Both were forty-eight years of age at death. Evidence from the history of the Jews in Spain and Portugal after the 1492 expulsion shows that many small communities of crypto-Jews lived as Catholics whilst practising Judaism in secret, sometimes for hundreds of years. An isolated community, the Belmonte Jews of Portugal, survives into the present day and finally has a synagogue in which the community may worship in peace.

Vives and his wife were both buried in the tenth-century church of St. Donatian in Bruges, which was destroyed by occupying French troops in 1799.

ACKNOWLEDGMENTS

Writing *The Secret Diaries of Juan Luis Vives* has been an absolute labour of love: an escape from a sometimes challenging world, and a leap back into another reality.

I am deeply grateful to Rafael Cordero, who indirectly gave me the reason to write the story - unbeknownst to him - and helped with the research, Spanish translation and poetry. He encouraged me at times - as well as taking an avid interest in Vives himself - when the task seemed overwhelming.

I'm eternally grateful to my feedback group - especially to Sylvia Brimson and Vicki Nicholson who read my first draft and who were kind enough to be honest with me. I am very grateful to my mother, Helen who received a rain-soaked copy of the first draft that had been thrown over the fence by a mailman, dried all the pages on radiators and commented that 'that there wasn't enough sex in it'.

Thank you to my first agent, Selwa Anthony, who did her best to get a publishing deal with one of the big four. I am very thankful to my dear friend, the late Dr Vivienne Schnieden, who listened with great patience and enthusiasm and who encouraged me in all my creative endeavours. Sincere appreciation and love go to Rabbi Jacki Ninio and the community of Emanuel Synagogue in Woollahra. Friends Wayne Hawkins and Nick Smart deserve a special mention. Thanks go to my editor Bill Hammett.

Getting to publication has taken a while, and I have to mention Regina Ramos, who told me to stop being a perfectionist and "just do it." My publisher Tellwell, have been utterly professional and patient. In particular, thank you to Rhea and Anne Marie. I want to congratulate Ferdika Permana for the cover design and photographer Colin Hutton and Trevillion Images for the cover art.

None of this would have been possible without a great story. My most profound gratitude and respect go to Señor Vives himself: an utter inspiration of strength, goodness and wily survival skills whose life story provided me with great material.

Made in the USA
Monee, IL
12 October 2020

44791826R00163